EX LIBRIS

Daisy Jones & The Six

Taylor Jenkins Reid

HUTCHINSON
LONDON

5 7 9 10 8 6 4

Hutchinson
20 Vauxhall Bridge Road
London SW1V 2SA

Hutchinson is part of the Penguin Random House group of companies whose addresses can be found at global.penguinrandomhouse.com.

First published in the USA by Random House in 2018
First published in the United Kingdom by Hutchinson in 2018

www.penguin.co.uk

A CIP catalogue record for this book is available from the British Library.

ISBN 9781786331502 (hardback)
ISBN 9781786331519 (trade paperback)

Printed and bound in Great Britain by Clays Ltd, Elcograf S.p.A.

To Bernard and Sally Hanes,
an honest love story if ever there was one

DAISY JONES & THE SIX

AUTHOR'S NOTE

This book is an attempt to piece together a clear portrait of how the renowned 1970s rock band Daisy Jones & The Six rose to fame—as well as what led to their abrupt and infamous split while on tour in Chicago on July 12, 1979.

Over the course of the last eight years, I have conducted individual interviews of current and former members of the band, as well as family, friends, and industry elite who surrounded them at the time. The following oral history is compiled and edited from those conversations, as well as relevant emails, transcripts, and lyrics. (The complete lyrics to their album *Aurora* can be found at the back of the book.)

While I have aimed for a comprehensive approach, I must acknowledge that this proved impossible. Some potential interviewees were difficult to track down, some were more forthcoming than others, and some, unfortunately, have passed on.

This book serves as the first and only time members of the band have commented on their history together. However, it should also be noted that, on matters both big and small, sometimes accounts of the same event differ.

The truth often lies, unclaimed, in the middle.

THE GROUPIE
DAISY JONES

1965–1972

Daisy Jones was born in 1951 and grew up in the Hollywood Hills of Los Angeles, California. The daughter of Frank Jones, the well-known British painter, and Jeanne LeFevre, a French model, Daisy started to make a name for herself in the late sixties as a young teenager on the Sunset Strip.

ELAINE CHANG (*biographer, author of* Daisy Jones: Wild Flower): Here is what is so captivating about Daisy Jones even before she was "Daisy Jones."

You've got a rich white girl, growing up in L.A. She's gorgeous—even as a child. She has these stunning big blue eyes—dark, cobalt blue. One of my favorite anecdotes about her is that in the eighties a colored-contact company actually created a shade called Daisy Blue. She's got copper-red hair that is thick and wavy and . . . takes up so much space. And then her cheekbones almost seem swollen, that's how defined they are. And she's got an incredible voice that she doesn't cultivate, never takes a lesson. She's born with all the money in the world, access to whatever she wants—artists, drugs, clubs—anything and everything at her disposal.

But she has no one. No siblings, no extended family in Los Angeles. Two parents who are so into their own world that they are all but indifferent to her existence. Although, they never shy away from making her pose for their artist friends. That's why there are so many paintings and photos of Daisy as a child—the artists that came into that home saw Daisy Jones, saw how gorgeous she was, and wanted to capture her. It's telling that there is no Frank Jones piece of Daisy. Her father is too busy with his male nudes to pay much attention to his daughter. And in general, Daisy spends her childhood rather alone.

But she's actually a very gregarious, outgoing kid—Daisy would often ask to get her hair cut just because she loved her hairdresser, she would ask neighbors if she could walk their dogs, there was even a family joke about the time Daisy tried to bake a birthday cake for the mailman. So this is a girl that desperately wants to connect. But there's no one in her life who is truly interested in who she is, especially not her parents. And it really breaks her. But it is also how she grows up to become an icon.

We love broken, beautiful people. And it doesn't get much more *obviously* broken and more *classically* beautiful than Daisy Jones.

So it makes sense that Daisy starts to find herself on the Sunset Strip. This glamorous, seedy place.

Daisy Jones *(singer, Daisy Jones & The Six)*: I could walk down to the Strip from my house. I was about fourteen, sick of being stuck in the house, just looking for something to do. I wasn't old enough to get into any of the bars and clubs but I went anyway.

I remember bumming a cigarette off of a roadie for the Byrds when I was pretty young. I learned quickly that people thought you were older if you didn't wear your bra. And sometimes I'd wear a bandanna headband like the cool girls had on. I wanted to fit in with the groupies on the sidewalk, with their joints and their flasks and all of that.

So I bummed a cigarette from this roadie outside the Whisky a Go Go one night—the first time I'd ever had one and I tried to pretend I did it all the time. I held the cough in my throat and what have you—and I was flirting with him the best I could. I'm embarrassed to think about it now, how clumsy I probably was.

But eventually, some guy comes up to the roadie and says, "We gotta get inside and set up the amps." And he turns to me and says,

"You coming?" And that's how I snuck into the Whisky for the first time.

I stayed out that night until three or four in the morning. I'd never done anything like that before. But suddenly it was like I *existed*. I was a part of something. I went from zero to sixty that night. I was drinking and smoking anything anybody would give me.

When I got home, I walked in through the front door, drunk and stoned, and crashed in my bed. I'm pretty sure my parents never even noticed I was gone.

I got up, went out the next night, did the same thing.

Eventually, the bouncers on the Strip recognized me and let me in wherever I was going. The Whisky, London Fog, the Riot House. No one cared how young I was.

Greg McGuinness (*former concierge, the Continental Hyatt House*): Ah, man, I don't know how long Daisy was hanging around the Hyatt House before I noticed her. But I remember the first time I saw her. I was on the phone and in walks this crazy tall, crazy skinny girl with these bangs. And the biggest, roundest blue eyes you ever saw in your life, man. She also had this smile. Huge smile. She came in on the arm of some guy. I don't remember who.

A lot of the girls around the Strip back then, I mean, they were young, but they tried to seem older. Daisy just *was*, though. Didn't seem like she was trying to be anything. Except herself.

After that, I noticed she was at the hotel a lot. She was always laughing. There was nothing jaded about her, 'least when I knew her. It was like watching Bambi learn how to walk. She was real naïve and real vulnerable but you could tell there was something about her.

I was nervous for her, tell you the truth. There were so many men in the scene that were . . . into young girls. Thirty-something rock stars sleeping with teenagers. Not saying it was okay, just saying that's how it was. How old was Lori Mattix when she was with Jimmy Page? Fourteen? And Iggy Pop and Sable Starr? He sang about it, man. He was bragging about it.

When it came to Daisy—I mean, the singers, the guitarists, the roadies—everybody was looking at her. Whenever I saw her, though, I'd try to make sure she was doing all right. I kept tabs on her here and there. I really liked her. She was just cooler than anything else happening around her.

Daisy: I learned about sex and love the hard way. That men will take what they want and feel no debt, that some people only want one piece of you.

I do think there were girls—the Plaster Casters, some of the GTOs—maybe they weren't being taken advantage of, I don't know. But it was a bad scene for me, at first.

I lost my virginity to somebody that . . . it doesn't matter who it was. He was older, he was a drummer. We were in the lobby of the Riot House and he invited me upstairs to do some lines. He said I was the girl of his dreams.

I was drawn to him mainly because he was drawn to me. I wanted someone to single me out as something special. I was just so desperate to hold someone's interest.

Before I knew it, we were on his bed. And he asked me if I knew what I was doing and I said yes even though the answer was no. But everyone always talked about free love and how sex was a good thing. If you were cool, if you were hip, you liked sex.

I stared at the ceiling the whole time, waiting for him to be done. I knew I was supposed to be moving around but I stayed perfectly still, scared to move. All you could hear in the room was the sound of our clothes rubbing up against the bedspread.

I had no idea what I was doing or why I was doing things I knew I didn't want to be doing. But I've had a lot of therapy in my life now. And I mean a lot of therapy. And I see it now. I see myself clearly now. I wanted to be around these men—these stars—because I didn't know how else to be important. And I figured I had to please them if I wanted to stay.

When he was done, he got up. And I pulled my dress down. And he said, "If you want to go back down to your friends, that's all right." I didn't really have any friends. But I knew he meant I needed to leave. So I did.

He never talked to me again.

Simone Jackson *(disco star)*: I remember seeing Daisy on the dance floor one night at the Whisky. Everybody saw her. Your eye went right to her. If the rest of the world was silver, Daisy was gold.

Daisy: Simone became my best friend.

Simone: I brought Daisy out with me everywhere. I never had a sister.

I remember . . . It was the Sunset Strip riot, when all of us went down to Pandora's and protested the curfew and the cops. Daisy and I went out, protested, met up with some actors and went over to Barney's Beanery to keep partying. After that, we went back to somebody's place. Daisy passed out on this guy's patio. We didn't go home until the next afternoon. She was maybe fifteen. I was probably nineteen. I just kept thinking, *Doesn't anybody care about this girl but me?*

And, by the way, we were all on speed back then, even Daisy as young as she was. But if you wanted to stay skinny and be up all night, you were taking something. Mostly bennies or black beauties.

Daisy: Diet pills were an easy choice. It didn't even feel like a choice. It didn't even feel like we were getting high, at first. Coke, too. If it was around, you took a bump. People didn't even consider it an addiction. It wasn't like that.

Simone: My producer bought me a place in Laurel Canyon. He wanted to sleep with me. I told him no and he bought it for me anyway. I had Daisy move in.

We ended up sharing a bed for six months. So I can tell you first-hand that that girl never slept. I'd be trying to fall asleep at four in the morning and Daisy would want the light on so she could read.

Daisy: I had pretty bad insomnia for a long time, even when I was a kid. I'd be up at eleven o'clock, saying I wasn't tired, and my parents would always yell at me to "just go to sleep." So in the middle of the night I was always looking for quiet things to do. My mom had these romance novels hanging around so I would read those. It would be two in the morning and my parents would be having a party downstairs and I'd be sitting on my bed with my lamp on, reading *Doctor Zhivago* or *Peyton Place*.

And then it just became habit. I would read anything that was around. I wasn't picky. Thrillers, detective novels, sci-fi.

Around the time I moved in with Simone, I found a box of history biographies on the side of the road one day, up in Beachwood Canyon. I tore through those in no time.

Simone: I'll tell you, she's the entire reason I started wearing a sleeping mask. *[Laughs]* But then I kept doing it because I looked chic.

Daisy: I was living with Simone for two weeks before I went home to get more clothes.

My dad said, "Did you break the coffeemaker this morning?"

I said, "Dad, I don't even live here."

Simone: I told her the one condition of living with me was that she had to go to school.

Daisy: High school was not easy for me. I knew that to get an A, you had to do what you were told. But I also knew that a lot of what we were being told was bullshit. I remember one time I was assigned an essay on how Columbus discovered America and so I wrote a paper about how Columbus did *not* discover America. Because he didn't. But then I got an F.

I said to my teacher, "But I'm *right.*"

And she said, "But you didn't follow *the assignment*."

SIMONE: She was so bright and her teachers didn't seem to really recognize that.

DAISY: People always say I didn't graduate high school but I did. When I walked across the stage to get my diploma, Simone was cheering for me. She was so proud of me. And I started to feel proud of myself, too. That night, I took the diploma out of its case and I folded it up and I used it, like a bookmark, in my copy of *Valley of the Dolls.*

SIMONE: When my first album flopped, my record label dropped me. My producer kicked us out of that place. I got a job waiting tables and moved in with my cousin in Leimert Park. Daisy had to move back in with her parents.

DAISY: I just packed up my stuff from Simone's and drove it right back to my parents' place. When I walked in the front door, my mom was on the phone, smoking a cigarette.

I said, "Hey, I'm back."

She said, "We got a new couch," and then just kept on talking on the phone.

SIMONE: Daisy got all of her beauty from her mother. Jeanne was gorgeous. I remember I met her a few times back then. Big eyes, very full lips. There was a sensuality to her. People used to always tell Daisy she looked just like her mother. They did look similar but I knew better than to tell Daisy that.

I think one time I said to Daisy, "Your mom is beautiful."

Daisy said to me, "Yeah, beautiful and nothing else."

DAISY: When we got kicked out of Simone's house, that was the first time I realized that I couldn't just float around living off other people.

I think I was seventeen, maybe. And it was the first time I wondered if I had a purpose.

Simone: Sometimes, Daisy would be over at my place, taking a shower or doing the dishes. I'd hear her sing Janis Joplin or Johnny Cash. She loved singing "Mercedes Benz." She sounded better than anybody else. Here I was trying to get another record deal—taking voice lessons all the time, really working at it—and Daisy, it was so easy for her. I wanted to hate her for it. But Daisy's not very easy to hate.

Daisy: One of my favorite memories was . . . Simone and I were driving down La Cienega together, probably in my BMW I had back then. They've got that huge shopping center there now but back then it was still the Record Plant. I don't know where we were headed, probably to Jan's to get a sandwich. But we were listening to *Tapestry*. And "You've Got a Friend" came on. Simone and I were singing so loud, along with Carole King. But I was really listening to the lyrics, too. I was really feeling it. That song always made me thankful for her, for Simone.

There's this peace that comes with knowing you have a person in the world who would do anything for you, that you would do anything for. She was the first time I ever had that. I got a little bit teary, in the car listening to that song. I turned to Simone and I opened my mouth to talk but she just nodded and said, "Me too."

Simone: It was my mission to make Daisy do something with her voice. But Daisy wasn't gonna do a single thing she didn't want to do.

She'd really come into herself by then. When I met her, she was still a bit naïve but *[laughs]* let's just say she'd gotten tougher.

Daisy: I was seeing a couple guys back then, including Wyatt Stone of the Breeze. And I didn't feel the same way about him that he felt about me.

This one night we were smoking a joint up on the roof of this apartment over on Santa Monica and Wyatt said, "I love you so much and I don't understand why you don't love me."

I said, "I love you as much as I'm willing to love anybody." Which was true. I wasn't really willing to be vulnerable with anybody at that point. I had felt too much vulnerability too young. I didn't want to do it anymore.

So that night after Wyatt goes to bed, I can't sleep. And I see this piece of paper with this song he's writing and it's clearly about me. It says something about a redhead and mentioned the hoop earrings that I was wearing all the time.

And then he had this chorus about me having a big heart but no love in it. I kept looking at the words, thinking, *This isn't right.* He didn't understand me at all. So I thought about it for a little while and got out a pen and paper. I wrote some things down.

When he woke up, I said, "Your chorus should be more like 'Big eyes, big soul/big heart, no control/but all she got to give is tiny love.'"

Wyatt grabbed a pen and paper and he said, "Say that again?"

I said, "It was just an example. Write your own goddamn song."

Simone: "Tiny Love" was the Breeze's biggest hit. And Wyatt pretended he wrote the whole thing.

Wyatt Stone *(lead singer, the Breeze)*: Why are you asking me about this? This is water under the bridge. Who even remembers?

Daisy: It was starting to be a pattern. Once, I was having breakfast at Barney's Beanery with a guy—this writer-director. Now, back then I always ordered champagne with breakfast. But I was also always tired in the morning because I wasn't sleeping enough. So I needed coffee. Of course, I couldn't order *just* coffee because I'd be too amped from the pills I was taking. And I couldn't *just* have the champagne because it would put me to sleep. You understand the problem. So I used to order champagne and coffee together. And at the places where servers knew me, I used to call it an Up and Down. Something to keep me up, something to keep me down. And this guy thought it was hilarious. He said, "I'm going to use that in something one day." And he wrote it down on a napkin and put it in his back pocket. I thought to myself, *What the hell makes you think* I'm *not going to use it in something one day?* But, of course, there it was in his next movie.

That's how it was back then. I was just supposed to be the inspiration for some man's great idea.

Well, fuck that.

That's why I started writing my own stuff.

SIMONE: I was the only one encouraging her to make something of herself with her talent. Everybody else just tried to make something of *themselves* with what she had.

DAISY: I had absolutely no interest in being somebody else's muse.

I am not a muse.

I am the somebody.

End of fucking story.

THE RISE OF THE SIX

1966–1972

The Six started out as a blues-rock band called the Dunne Brothers in the mid-sixties out of Pittsburgh, Pennsylvania. Billy and Graham Dunne were raised by single mother, Marlene Dunne, after their father, William Dunne Sr., left in 1954.

Billy Dunne *(lead singer, The Six)*: I was seven when Dad left, Graham was five. One of my first memories was when Dad told us he was moving to Georgia. I asked if I could come with him and he said no.

But he left behind this old Silvertone guitar and Graham and I would fight over who got to play it. Playing that thing was about all we did. Nobody taught us, we taught ourselves.

Then, when I got older, sometimes I'd stay late after school and mess around on the piano in the chorus room.

Eventually, when I was about fifteen or so, Mom saved up and bought Graham and I an old Strat for Christmas. Graham wanted that one so I let him have it. I kept the Silvertone.

Graham Dunne *(lead guitar, The Six)*: Once Billy and I each had a guitar, we started to write new songs together. I wanted the Silvertone but I could tell it meant more to Billy. So I took the Strat.

Billy: Everything grew from there.

Graham: Billy got really into songwriting, really into the lyrics. All he'd talk about was Bob Dylan. Me, I was more of a Roy Orbison guy.

I think we both had these stars in our eyes—wanted to be the Beatles. But everybody wanted to be the Beatles. You wanted to be the Beatles and then you wanted to be the Stones.

Billy: For me, it was Dylan and Lennon. *Freewheelin' Bob Dylan* and *Hard Day's Night*. Those just . . . I was . . . Those men were my guides.

In 1967, with the brothers in their teens, they brought on drummer Warren Rhodes, bassist Pete Loving, and rhythm guitarist Chuck Williams.

Warren Rhodes *(drummer, The Six)*: A drummer needs a band. It's not like being a singer or a guitarist—you can't just perform on your own. No girls were saying, "Oh, Warren, play me the drumbeat from 'Hey Joe.'"

And I wanted in, man. I was listening to the Who, the Kinks, the Yardbirds, stuff like that. I wanted to be Keith Moon and Ringo and Mitch Mitchell.

Billy: Warren we liked right from the start. And then Pete was an easy grab. Went to school with us, played bass for this high school band that played our prom. When they broke up, I said, "Pete, come on and join us." He was always really cool about stuff; he just wanted to rock out.

Then there was Chuck. And Chuck was a few years older than the rest of us, from a few towns over. But Pete knew him, vouched for him. Chuck was real clean-cut—square jaw and blond hair and all that. But we auditioned him and turned out he was better than me, at rhythm guitar.

I wanted to be a front man and now we had a full five-man band so I could do that.

Graham: We got a lot better, really quickly. I mean, all we were doing was practicing.

Warren: Day in and day out. I woke up, grabbed my sticks, and headed over to Billy and Graham's garage. If my thumbs were bleeding when I went to bed, it was a good day.

Graham: I mean, what else were we gonna do? None of us had girlfriends, except Billy. All the girls wanted to date Billy. And, I swear, it was like Billy was in love with a new girl every week. He'd always been like that.

In elementary school, he'd asked out his second-grade teacher. Mom always said he was born girl crazy. She used to joke it'd be the end of him.

Warren: We played house parties and a bar here and there. For maybe about six months or so, maybe a little longer. Got paid in beer. Which, when you're underage isn't so bad.

Graham: We weren't always hanging out in the, let's say *classiest* of places. There were a few times a fight would break out over something and you were worried you might get caught in the cross fire. This one time we were playing a gig at a dive bar and this guy in the front got a little too jacked up on something. He starts swinging punches at people. I'm minding my own business playing my riffs when suddenly he's coming for me!

And then it all went lightning fast. Boom. He was on the ground. Billy had taken him out.

Billy'd done the same thing when we were little kids. I was headed down to the five-and-dime and some kid tried to jump me for a couple nickels. Billy ran up to us and then just flattened him.

Warren: You knew back then not to say any shit about Graham if Billy could hear you. You know, Graham wasn't that good when we were starting out. I remember one time Pete and I were saying to Billy, "Maybe we should replace Graham," and Billy said, "Say that again and Graham and I will replace you." *[Laughs]* Honestly, I thought that was cool. I was thinking, *All right, I'm not gonna get involved then.* Never did bother me much that Billy and Graham thought of the band as theirs. I liked thinking of myself as a drummer for hire. I was just trying to have a good time playing in a good band.

GRAHAM: We started to play enough that some people around town knew who we were. And Billy was just starting to get into his lead singer thing. He had a look, you know? We all did. We stopped cutting our hair.

BILLY: I wore jeans everywhere, got really into big belt buckles.

WARREN: Graham and Pete started wearing these tight T-shirts. I'd tell them, "I can see your nipples." But they thought that was cool.

BILLY: We got hired for this wedding. It was a big deal. A wedding meant we were gonna be heard by, you know, a hundred people. I think I was nineteen.

We had auditioned for this couple with our best song. It was this slower, folkier song I'd written called "Nevermore." Just thinking about it makes me cringe. Truly. I was writing about the Catonsville Nine and things like that. I thought I was Dylan. But we got the gig.

And about halfway through our show at this wedding, I notice this fifty-something guy dancing with this twenty-something girl and I thought, *Does this guy know what a creep he looks like?*

And then I realize it's my dad.

GRAHAM: Our father was there with this young girl, about our age. I realized it before Billy, I think. Recognized him from the pictures our mom kept in the shoe box under her bed.

BILLY: I couldn't believe it. He'd been gone ten years by that point. And he was supposed to be in Georgia. That asshole was just standing right in the middle of the dance floor, no idea his sons were up onstage. It had been so long since he'd seen us, he didn't even recognize us. Not our faces or our voices, nothing.

When we finished playing, I watched him walk off the dance floor. Didn't so much as look at us. I mean, what kind of sociopath do you have to be not to notice your own sons when they are right there in front of you? How is that even possible?

In my experience, biology kicks in. You meet that kid, and you know it's yours, and you love that kid. That's just how it works.

Graham: Billy asked a few people at the wedding about him. Turns out, our father had been living a few towns over. Friends with the bride's family or something. Billy was boiling mad, saying, "He didn't even recognize us." I always thought that he probably did recognize us and just didn't know what to say.

Billy: It messes with you, when your own father doesn't care about you enough to say hello. I'm not saying it was a self-pity thing. I wasn't sitting there asking, "Why doesn't he love me?" It was more . . . *Oh, okay, this is how dark the world can be. Some fathers don't love their sons.*

It was a lesson in what not to be, I'll tell you that much.

Graham: Seemed like he was a drunk asshole anyway. So good riddance to him.

Billy: After the wedding had ended, and everyone was packing up, I had a few too many beers . . . and I saw this woman working as a cocktail waitress at the hotel bar. *[Smiles]* Gorgeous girl. Real long brown hair, down to her waist, and big brown eyes. I'm a sucker for brown eyes. I remember she was wearing a tiny little blue dress. She was short. And I liked that.

I was standing there in the hotel lobby, on my way to the van. And she was waiting on a customer over at the bar. You could tell, just watching her, that she wasn't taking shit from anybody.

Camila Dunne *(wife of Billy Dunne)*: Oh my word, was he good looking. . . . Slim but still muscular, which has always been my type. And he had these thick eyelashes. And so much confidence. And a really big smile. And when I saw him in the lobby, I remember thinking, *Why can't I meet a guy like that?*

Billy: I walked right up to her, in that bar, holding, you know, an amp in one hand and a guitar in the other. I said, "Miss? I'd like your number, please."

She was standing up at the register. She had one hand on her hip. She laughed at me and kind of looked at me sideways. I don't remember exactly what she said but it was something like "What if you're not my type?"

I leaned over the bar and said, "My name is Billy Dunne. I'm the lead singer of the Dunne Brothers. And if you give me your number I'll write a song about you."

That got her. That doesn't get every woman. But it usually gets the good ones.

Camila: I went home and told my mom I met somebody. And she said, "Nice boy?"

And I said, "I don't know about that." *[Laughs]* Nice never did much for me.

Over the summer and fall of 1969, the Dunne Brothers started to book more shows in Pittsburgh and the surrounding towns.

Graham: When Camila started coming out with us, I'll admit I didn't think she'd last much longer than the others. But I should have known she was different. I mean, first time I met her, she came to a gig of ours wearing a Tommy James shirt. She knew good music.

Warren: The rest of us were really starting to get laid, man. And Billy was taking himself off the market. We'd all be with chicks and he'd be sitting there, smoking a joint, having a beer to keep himself busy.

I came out of a girl's room one time, zipping my pants up, and Billy was sitting on the sofa, watching Dick Cavett. I said, "Man, you gotta ditch that girlfriend." I mean, we all liked Camila, she was foxy and she'd tell you your business right to your face, which I liked. But c'mon.

Billy: I'd been infatuated before, called it love. But when I met [Camila], it was something different altogether. She just . . . made the world make sense to me. She even made me like myself more.

She'd come watch us practice and listen to my new stuff and give me really good notes on it all. And there was a calmness to her that . . . nobody else had. It felt like when I was with her, I knew everything would be fine. It was like I was following the North Star.

You know, Camila was born content, I think. She wasn't born with whatever chip on her shoulder some of us are born with. I used to say I was born broken. She was born whole. That's where the lyrics to "Born Broken" came from.

Camila: When Billy met my parents for the first time, I was a little nervous. You only get one chance to make a first impression, especially with them. I picked out his outfit, down to his socks. Made him wear the only tie he had.

They loved him. Said he was charming. But my mom was also worried about me putting my trust in some guy in a band.

Billy: Pete was the only one who seemed to understand why I'd have a girlfriend. Chuck, one time, as we were packing up for a show, said, "Just tell her you aren't a one-woman guy. Girls get that." *[Laughs]* That was not gonna work on Camila.

Warren: Chuck was real cool. He would cut right to the heart of something. He sort of looked like he'd never had an interesting thought in his life. But he could surprise you. He turned me on to Status Quo. I still listen to them.

On December 1, 1969, the U.S. Selective Service System conducted a lottery to determine the draft order for 1970. Billy and Graham Dunne, both born in December, had unusually high numbers. Warren just missed the cutoff. Pete Loving fell in the middle. But Chuck Williams, born April 24, 1949, was assigned lottery number 2.

Graham: Chuck got called for the draft. I remember sitting at Chuck's kitchen table, him saying he was going to Vietnam. Billy and I kept thinking of ways he could get out of it. He said he wasn't a coward. Last time I saw him, we played a bar by Duquesne. I said, "You'll just come on back to the band when you're done."

Warren: Billy played Chuck's parts for a while but we'd heard Eddie Loving [Pete's younger brother] had gotten pretty good at the guitar. We invited him to come audition.

Billy: Nobody could be Chuck. But then we kept getting more shows and I didn't want to keep playing rhythm guitar onstage. So we invited Eddie. Figured he could pitch in for a little while.

Eddie Loving *(rhythm guitar, The Six)*: I got along well with everybody but I could tell Billy and Graham just wanted me to fit into the mold they had set for me, you know? *Play this, do that.*

Graham: Few months in, we heard from one of Chuck's old neighbors.

Billy: Chuck died in Cambodia. He wasn't even there six months, I don't think.

You do sometimes sit and wonder why it wasn't you, what makes you so special that you get to be safe. The world doesn't make much sense.

At the end of 1970, the Dunne Brothers played a show at the Pint in Baltimore where Rick Marks, lead singer for the Winters, was in attendance. Impressed with their raw sound and taking a liking to Billy, he offered them an opening spot on a few shows on their northeastern tour.

The Dunne Brothers joined the Winters and quickly became influenced by the Winters' sound and intrigued with their keyboardist, Karen Karen.

Karen Karen *(keyboardist, The Six)*: The first time I met the Dunne Brothers, Graham asked me, "What's your name?"

I said, "Karen."

And he said, "What's your last name?"

But I thought he said, "What's your name?" again, like he didn't hear me.

So I said, "Karen."

And he laughed and said, "Karen Karen?"

Everybody called me Karen Karen from then on. My last name is Sirko, for the record. But Karen Karen just stuck.

Billy: Karen added this extra layer, a lushness, to what the Winters were doing. I started thinking maybe we needed something like that.

Graham: Billy and I were starting to think . . . maybe we don't need somebody *like* Karen. Maybe we need Karen.

Karen: I left the Winters because I was sick of everyone in the band trying to sleep with me. I wanted to just be a musician.

And I liked Camila. She'd hang out after the shows sometimes, when she came up to visit Billy. I dug that Billy had her around sometimes or was always on the phone with her. It was a better vibe all around.

CAMILA: When they went on tour with the Winters, I'd drive up to any weekend shows they had, and hang out backstage. I'd have spent four hours in the car and I'd get to the venue—usually these places were pretty sketchy with gum all over everything and your shoes sticking to the floor—I'd give my name at the door and they'd show me through to the back and, there I was, a part of it all.

I'd walk in and Graham and Eddie and everybody would yell, "Camila!" And Billy would walk over and put his arm around me. Once Karen started hanging out, too . . . it just cinched it for me. I felt like, *This is where I belong.*

GRAHAM: Karen Karen was a great addition to the band. Made everything better. And she was beautiful, too. I mean, in addition to being talented. I always thought she looked a little like Ali MacGraw.

KAREN: When I said that I dug the fact that the boys in the Dunne Brothers weren't trying to get with me, that doesn't go for Graham Dunne. But I knew he liked me for my talent just as much as my looks. So it didn't faze me much. It was sweet, actually. Plus, Graham was a sexy guy. Especially in the seventies.

I never got the whole "Billy is the sex symbol" idea. I mean, he had the dark hair, dark eyes, high cheekbones thing. But I like my men a little less pretty. I like it when they look a little dangerous but are actually very gentle. That's Graham. Broad shoulders, hairy chest, dusty brown hair. He was handsome but he was still a little rough around the edges.

I will admit that Billy knew how to wear a pair of jeans though.

BILLY: Karen was just a great musician. That was all there was to it. I always say I don't care if you're a man, woman, white, black, gay, straight, or anything in between—if you play well, you play well. Music is a great equalizer in that way.

Karen: Men often think they deserve a sticker for treating women like people.

Warren: That was around the time Billy's drinking seemed like it was getting a little over the edge. He'd party like the rest of us but when we all went off with the chicks we met, he'd stay up drinking.

But he always seemed fine in the morning, and we were all kind of going crazy out there. Except for maybe Pete. He'd met this girl Jenny in Boston and was always on the phone with her.

Graham: Anything Billy does, he goes hard. He loves hard, he drinks hard. Even the way he spends money, like it's burning a hole in his pocket. It was part of the reason why, with Camila, I was telling him to take it slow.

Billy: Camila came out with us sometimes, but a lot of the time she waited at home. She was still living with her parents and I would call her every night from the road.

Camila: When he didn't have a dime to make a call, he'd call collect and when I answered he'd say, "Billy Dunne loves Camila Martinez," and then hang up before the charge kicked in. *[Laughs]* My mom always rolled her eyes but I thought it was sweet.

Karen: A few weeks after I joined the band, I said, "We need a new name." The Dunne Brothers didn't make sense anymore.

Eddie: I'd been saying we needed a new name.

Billy: We had a following with that name. I didn't want to change it.

WARREN: We couldn't decide what to call ourselves. I think somebody suggested the Dipsticks. I wanted us to go by Shaggin'.

EDDIE: Pete said, "You're never going to get six people to agree on this."

And I said, "What about The Six?"

KAREN: I got a call from a booker in Philly, where I'm from. And he said that the Winters had pulled out of a festival there, asked if we wanted to play. I said, "Right on, but we aren't called the Dunne Brothers anymore."

He said, "Well, what do I put on the flyer?"

I said, "Not sure yet but I'll get the six of us there."

And I liked how it sounded, "The Six."

WARREN: Part of the brilliance of the name was how close it was to "the Sex." But I don't think any of us ever talked about that. It was so obvious there was no need to put a finer point on it.

KAREN: I was not thinking about it sounding like anything.

BILLY: "The Sex"? No, that wasn't a part of it.

GRAHAM: It sounded like sex. That was a big part of it.

BILLY: We played that show in Philly as The Six and then we got an offer to do another show in town. Another in Harrisburg. Another in Allentown. We got asked to play New Year's Eve at this bar in Hartford.

We weren't making much money. But I'd spend my last dollar taking Camila out whenever I was home. We'd go to this pizza joint a few blocks from her parents' place or I'd borrow money from Graham or Warren to take her out somewhere nice. She always told me to cut it out. She'd say, "If I wanted to be with a rich guy, I wouldn't have given my number to the singer of a wedding band."

Camila: Billy had charisma and I fell for all that. I always did. The smoldering, the brooding. A lot of my girlfriends were looking for guys that could afford a nice ring. But I wanted somebody *fascinating*.

Graham: Around 'seventy-one, we booked a few shows in New York.

Eddie: New York was . . . it was how you knew you were somebody.

Graham: One night, we're playing a bar over in the Bowery and out on the street, smoking a cigarette, is a guy named Rod Reyes.

Rod Reyes *(manager, The Six)*: Billy Dunne was a rock star. You could just see it. He was very cocksure, knew who to play to in the crowd. There was an emotion that he brought to his stuff.

There's just a quality that some people have. If you took nine guys, plus Mick Jagger, and you put them in a lineup, someone who had never heard of the Rolling Stones before could still point to Jagger and say, "That's the rock star."

Billy had that. And the band had a good sound.

Billy: When Rod came up to us after that show at the Wreckage . . . that was the watershed moment.

Rod: When I started working with the band, I had some ideas. Some of which were well received and others . . . not so much.

Graham: Rod told me I needed to cut out half of my solos. Said they were interesting for people that loved technical guitar work but boring for everyone else.

I said, "Why would I play to people who don't care about good guitar?"

He said, "If you want to be huge, you gotta be for everybody."

Billy: Rod told me to stop writing about stuff I didn't know about. He said, "Don't reinvent the wheel. Write about your girl." Hands down, best career advice I ever got.

Karen: Rod told me to wear low-cut shirts and I said, "Dream on," and that was about the end of that.

Eddie: Rod started getting us gigs all over the East Coast. Florida to Canada.

Warren: Let me tell you the sweet spot for being in rock 'n' roll. People think it's when you're at the top but no. That's when you've got the pressure and the expectations. What's good is when everybody thinks you're headed somewhere fast, when you're all potential. Potential is pure fuckin' joy.

Graham: The longer we were out on the road, the wilder we all got. And Billy wasn't exactly . . . Look, Billy liked attention. Especially from women. But, at least at that point, that's all it was. Just attention.

Billy: It was a lot to balance. Loving somebody back home, being out on the road. Girls were coming backstage and I was the one they wanted to meet. I was . . . I didn't know what a relationship was supposed to look like.

Camila: We'd started to get into fights, Billy and I. I will admit I wanted something impractical, back then. I wanted to date a rock star but I wanted him available at all times. I'd get mad when he couldn't do exactly what I wanted. I was young. So was he.

Sometimes it would get so bad that we'd stop talking for a few days. And then one of us would call the other and apologize and things would go back the way they were. I loved him and I knew he loved me. It wasn't easy. But as my mother used to remind me, "You've never been interested in easy."

Graham: This one night, Billy and I were back home and getting in the van to head out to Tennessee or Kentucky or somewhere. Camila came to see us off. And when Rod pulled up in the van, Billy was saying goodbye.

He moved the hair out of Camila's face and put his lips on her forehead. I remember that he didn't even really kiss her. He just held his lips there. And I thought, *I've never cared about anyone like that.*

Billy: I wrote "Señora" for Camila and, let me tell you, people liked that song a lot. Pretty soon, at our best shows, people were getting up out of their seats, starting to dance, singing along.

Camila: I didn't have the heart to tell him that I was technically a "señorita." I mean, choose your battles. Besides, once I listened to it . . . "Let me carry you/on my back/the road looks long/and the night looks black/but the two of us are bold explorers/me and my gold señora."

I loved it. I loved that song.

Billy: We cut a demo of "Señora" and "When the Sun Shines on You."

Rod: My real contacts were all out in L.A. by then. I said to the band, I think it was maybe 'seventy-two . . . I said, "We gotta go out west."

Eddie: California was where the cool shit was happening, you know what I mean?

Billy: I just thought, *There's something inside me that needs to do this.*

Warren: I was ready to go. I said, "Let's get in the van."

Billy: I went to Camila's parents' house and I sat her down on the edge of her bed. I said, "Do you want to come with us?"

She said, "What would I do?"

I said, "I don't know."

She said, "You want me to just follow you around?"

I said, "I guess."

She took a moment and then she said, "No, thank you."

I asked her if we could stay together and she said, "Are you coming back?" And I told her I didn't know.

And she said, "Then, no." And she dumped me.

Camila: I got mad. That he was leaving. And I blew up at him. I didn't know how else to handle it.

Karen: Camila called me, before we left on tour. Told me she'd broken up with Billy. I said, "I thought you loved him."

And she said, "He didn't even try to fight me on it!"

I said to her, "If you love him, you should tell him."

And she said, "He's the one leaving! It's on him to fix this."

Camila: Love and pride don't mix.

Billy: What could I do? She didn't want to come with me and I . . . I couldn't stay.

Graham: We packed up and said goodbye to Mom. She'd married the mailman by then. I mean, I know his name was Dave but until the day he died, I called him the mailman because that's what he was. He delivered the mail at her office. He was the mailman.

Anyway, we left Mom with the mailman and got in the van.

Karen: We gigged everywhere along the way from Pennsylvania to California.

Billy: Camila made her choice and there was a big part of me that felt like, *All right, I'll be single then. See if she likes that.*

Graham: Billy straight up lost his mind on that trip.

Rod: It wasn't the women I was worried about, with Billy. Although there were a lot of women. But Billy would get so messed up after shows that I'd have to wake him up the next afternoon by slapping him across the face, he was that far gone.

Camila: I was sick to my stomach without him. I was . . . kicking myself. Every day. Waking up in tears. My mom kept telling me to track him down. To take it back. But it felt like it was too late. He'd gone on without me. To make his dreams come true. As he should have.

Warren: When we got to L.A., Rod hooked us up with a few rooms at the Hyatt House.

Greg McGuinness (*former concierge, the Continental Hyatt House*): Ah, man, I'd love to tell you that I remember The Six coming in and staying with us. But I don't. There was so much going on, so many bands back then. It was hard to keep track, I remember meeting Billy Dunne and Warren Rhodes later, but back then, no.

Warren: Rod called in his favors. We started playing bigger gigs.

Eddie: L.A. was a trip. Everywhere you looked, you were surrounded by people who loved playing music, who liked to party. I thought, *Why the hell didn't we come here sooner?* The girls were gorgeous. The drugs were cheap.

Billy: We played a few shows around Hollywood. At the Whisky, the Roxy, P.J.'s. I had just written a new song called "Farther from You." It was all about how much I missed Camila, how far I felt from her.

When we hit the Strip, that felt like we were really coming into our own.

Graham: All of us started to dress a bit better. You really had to step up your game in L.A. I started wearing my shirts unbuttoned halfway down my chest. I thought I was sexy as hell.

Billy: That was about when I got really into . . . what is it that people call it now? A Canadian tuxedo? I was wearing a denim shirt with my jeans, pretty much every day.

Karen: I felt like I couldn't focus on playing if I dressed in miniskirts and boots and all that. I mean, I liked that look, but I wore high-waisted jeans and turtlenecks most of the time.

Graham: Karen was so fucking sexy in those turtlenecks.

Rod: Once they were starting to get some good attention, I set up a show for them at the Troubadour.

Graham: "Farther from You" was a great song. And you could tell Billy felt it. Billy couldn't fake anything. When he was in pain or when he was joyful, you could feel it.

That show at the Troubadour that night, as we were playing, I looked over at Karen and she was in it, you know? And then I looked at Billy, and he's singing his heart out and I thought, *This is our best show yet.*

Rod: I saw Teddy Price standing in the back, listening. I hadn't met him before but I knew he was a producer with Runner Records. We had a few friends in common. After the show, he came up and found me, said, "My assistant heard you guys at P.J.'s. I told him I would come listen."

Billy: We get offstage and Rod comes up to me with this real tall, fat guy in a suit and he says, "Billy, I want you to meet Teddy Price."

First thing Teddy says is—and you have to remember he had this real thick upper-crust British accent—"You've got a hell of a talent for writing about that girl."

Karen: Watching Billy, it felt a little bit like watching a dog find a master. He wanted to please him, wanted the record deal. You could feel it dripping off him.

Warren: Teddy Price was ugly as sin. A face only a mother could love. *[Laughs]* I'm just messing around. He was ugly, though. I liked that he didn't seem to care.

Karen: That's the glory of being a man. An ugly face isn't the end of you.

Billy: I shook Teddy's hand and he asked me if I had any more songs like the ones he'd heard. I said, "Yes, sir."

He said, "Where do you see this band in five years? Ten years?"

And I said, "We'll be the biggest band in the world."

Warren: I signed my first pair of tits that night. This girl comes up to me and unbuttons her shirt and says, "Sign me." So I signed her. Let me tell you, that's a memory you have for a lifetime.

The following week, Teddy visited the band at a rehearsal space in the San Fernando Valley and listened to the seven songs they had prepared.

Shortly after, they were invited to the Runner Records offices, introduced to CEO Rich Palentino, and offered a recording and publishing deal. Teddy Price, personally, would be producing their album.

GRAHAM: We signed the deal around four in the afternoon and I remember walking out onto Sunset Boulevard, the six of us, the sun hitting us right in the eyes and just feeling like Los Angeles had opened its arms and said, "Come on in, baby."

I saw a T-shirt a few years ago that said, "I Got My Shades on Cuz My Future's So Bright," and I thought the little shit that was wearing it doesn't know what he's talking about. He never stood on Sunset Boulevard, sun blinding his eyes, with his five best friends and a record contract in his back pocket.

BILLY: That night, everybody was out partying over at the Rainbow and I walked away, walked down the street to a pay phone. Imagine achieving your wildest dream and feeling empty inside. It didn't mean anything unless I could share it with Camila. So I called her.

My heart was beating so fast as the phone rang. I put my fingers to my pulse and it was throbbing. But when Camila answered, it was like laying down in bed after a long day. I felt so much better, just hearing her voice. I said, "I miss you. I don't think I can live without you."

She said, "I miss you, too."

I said, "What are we doing this for? We're supposed to be together."

And she said, "Yeah, I know."

We were both quiet on the line and I said, "If I had a record contract, would you marry me?"

She said, "What?"

CAMILA: I was just so excited for him if it was true. He'd worked so hard for it.

Billy: I said it again. "If I had a record contract, would you marry me?"

She said, "You got a record contract?"

That's when I knew, right then. That Camila was my soul mate. She cared more about the record contract than anything else. I said, "You didn't answer my question."

She said, "Did you get a record contract, yes or no?"

I said, "Will you marry me, yes or no?"

She didn't say anything for a while, and then she said, "Yes."

And then I said, "Yes."

She started screaming, so excited. I said, "Come on out here, honey. Let's get hitched."

IT GIRL

1972–1974

Determined to make a name for herself outside of the Sunset Strip, Daisy Jones started writing her own songs. Armed only with a pen and paper—and no musical training whatsoever—Daisy created a songbook that soon grew to include rough sketches of over a hundred songs.

One night during the summer of '72, Daisy attended a Mi Vida show at the Ash Grove. She was dating Mi Vida front man Jim Blades at the time. Toward the end of the set, Jim invited Daisy onto the stage to do a cover of "Son of a Preacher Man" with the band.

SIMONE: Daisy had grown her hair out really long by then, gotten rid of her bangs. She always wore hoop earrings and she never wore shoes. She was just very cool.

That night at the Ash Grove, she and I were sitting in the back and Jim tried to get her to go up there and she kept saying no. But he kept at it most of the night and eventually, Daisy got on that stage.

DAISY: It was a surreal feeling. All of those people looking at me, expecting something to happen.

SIMONE: When she started singing with Jim, she was kind of timid about it, which surprised me. But I could feel her getting more and more into it as the song went on. And then somewhere around the second chorus she just let it rip. She was smiling. She was happy up there. And people couldn't take their eyes off of her. By the time they got toward the end, Jim had stopped singing and just let her go. She brought the house down.

Jim Blades *(lead singer of Mi Vida)*: Daisy had this incredible voice. It was gritty but never scratchy. You'd have thought she had rocks in her throat that the sound had to travel over. It made everything she sang complex and interesting and kind of unpredictable. I've never had much of a voice myself. You don't have to have a great voice to be a singer if your songs are good enough. But Daisy had the whole thing going, man.

She was always singing from deep in her belly. It takes people years to learn something like that and Daisy just did it naturally, did it singing in the car next to you, or folding the laundry. I was always trying to get her to sing with me and she always said no until that night at the Ash Grove.

I think she finally agreed to sing in public because of how bad she wanted to be a songwriter. I told her, "The biggest thing your songs have going for them is that you might sing them." Her biggest asset was that people couldn't take their eyes off her. I told her to use that.

Daisy: I felt like Jim was basically saying that nobody cared what I was singing about as long as they could get a good look at me. Jim always made me mad.

Jim: If memory serves, Daisy threw her lipstick at me. But when she calmed down, she asked me where she should try to play some gigs.

Daisy: I wanted to get my songs heard. So I started singing a bit around L.A. I'd sing a few of my songs, do some stuff with Simone.

Greg McGuinness: You know, Daisy was dating everybody.

Like, ah, man, when that fight broke out between Tick Yune and Larry Hapman outside Licorice Pizza and Tick busted Larry's eyebrow open? That was crazy stuff. I was there. I'd been buying my *Dark Side of the Moon* LP. So when was that? Late 'seventy-two?

Maybe early 'seventy-three? I looked outside and Tick's got Larry in a headlock. People said they were fighting over Daisy.

Plus, I'd heard Dick Poller and Frankie Bates had both tried to get her to record a demo and she'd turned them down.

Daisy: Suddenly, there were so many people trying to convince me to do a demo. All these guys wanted to be my manager. But I knew what that meant. L.A. is full of men just waiting for some naïve girl to believe their bullshit.

Hank Allen was the least smarmy. He was the one that I could tolerate the most.

By that point, I had moved out of my parents' house and into the Chateau Marmont. I'd rented a cottage in the back. And Hank was at my door all the time, leaving messages. He was the only one not just talking about me but also about my songs.

I said, "All right, if you want to manage me, you can manage me."

Simone: When I met Daisy, I was the older, wiser, cooler one. But by the early seventies, Daisy was it.

I remember I was in her room at the Marmont one time and I'm looking in her closet and I see all these Halston wraps and jumpsuits. I said, "When did you get all these Halstons?"

She said, "Oh, they sent them over."

I said, "Who did?"

She said, "Somebody at Halston."

This was a girl that hadn't ever released a single piece of work. No album, no single. But she was in the magazines in photos with rock stars. Everybody loved her.

I took some of those Halstons though.

Daisy: I went over to Larrabee Sound to record the demo Hank wanted me to record. I think it was a Jackson Browne song. Hank wanted me to sing the song really sweet and I wasn't feeling it. I sang it the way I wanted to. A little bit rough, a little bit breathy. Hank said, "Can we please just do one take where you sing it smooth, maybe a key higher?"

I grabbed my purse and said, "Nope." And I left.

SIMONE: She got signed to Runner Records right after that.

DAISY: I didn't care about anything but songwriting. The singing was okay but I didn't want to be some puppet up there, singing other people's words. I wanted to do my own thing. I wanted to sing my own stuff.

SIMONE: Daisy doesn't value anything that comes easy to her. Money, looks, even her voice. She wanted people to *listen* to her.

DAISY: I signed the deal with Runner Records. But I didn't read the contract.

I didn't want to read contracts and pay attention to who I was supposed to pay what money to and what was expected of me. I wanted to write songs and get high.

SIMONE: They scheduled her for a kickoff meeting and I went over to her place and we put together the perfect outfit, went through her songbook to get it just right. When she left to go over there that morning, she was walking on air.

But however many hours later, she showed up at my place and I could tell something was wrong. I said, "What's going on?" She just shook her head and walked right past me. She went into my kitchen, grabbed the bottle of champagne we'd bought to celebrate, popped it open, and walked into my bathroom. I followed her in there and she was running herself a bath. She stripped off her clothes and got in the tub. Took a swig right from the bottle.

I said, "Talk to me. What happened?"

She said, "They don't care about me." I guess, at the meeting, they had handed her a list of songs they expected her to do and it was stuff from the catalog. "Leaving on a Jet Plane" kind of stuff.

I said, "What about your own songs?"

She said, "They don't like my songs."

Daisy: They read through my entire book and couldn't find one song in there—not one song—they thought I should record.

I said, "What about this one? And this one? And this one?"

I was at that conference table with Rich Palentino and I was flipping through that book, panicked. I was thinking they must not have read them. They just kept saying the songs weren't ready yet. That I wasn't ready to be a songwriter.

Simone: She got drunk in the tub and all I could do was just make sure that when she passed out, I pulled her out and put her in bed. Which is what I did.

Daisy: I got up the next morning and went back to my own place. Tried to put it out of my mind by laying by the pool. When that didn't work, I smoked a few cigarettes, did a few lines in my cottage. Hank came over and tried to calm me down.

I said, "Get me out of this." And he kept telling me I didn't want to get out of it.

I said, "Yes, I do!"

He said, "No, you don't."

I got so mad I ran out of my own place faster than Hank could catch me. I drove right over to Runner Records. I was in the parking lot before I realized I was still in a bikini top and jeans. I went right into Rich Palentino's office and ripped up the contract. Rich just laughed and said, "Hank called and said you might do that. Honey, that's not how contracts work."

Simone: Daisy was Carole King, she was Laura Nyro. Hell, she could have been Joni Mitchell. And they wanted her to be Olivia Newton-John.

Daisy: I went back to the Marmont. I'd been crying; I had mascara running down my face. Hank was waiting for me, sitting on my stoop. He said, "Why don't you sleep it off?"

I said, "I can't sleep. I've had too much coke and too many dexies."

He said he had something for me. I thought he was going to hand me a quaalude, like that was going to do anything. But he gave me a Seconal. I was out like a light and I woke up feeling so much better. No hangover. Nothing. For the first time in my life, I was sleeping like a baby.

From then on, it was dexies to get through the day, reds to get through the night. Champagne to wash it all down.

The good life, right? Except the good life never made for a good life. But I'm getting ahead of myself.

DEBUT

1973–1975

The Six settled into life in Los Angeles, renting a house in the hills of Topanga Canyon. They prepared to begin recording their debut album. Teddy, along with a team of technicians, including lead engineer Artie Snyder, set up shop at Sound City Studios, a recording studio in Van Nuys, California.

Karen: The day we moved into that house I thought, *This place is a dump*. It was this rickety old thing with the front door off the hinges and chipped stained-glass windows. I hated it. But about a week or two later, Camila got to L.A. She drove down the long driveway through the woods and she got out of the car and she went, "Wow. This place is bitchin'." Once she said the house was cool, I started to dig it.

Camila: The house was surrounded by rosemary bushes. I loved that.

Billy: Man, it felt good to have Camila back. It felt so good to have that woman in my arms again. We were gonna get married and I was in L.A. and I was making a record with my brother and everything felt like it was gold.

Warren: Graham and Karen each had a bedroom off the kitchen. Pete and Eddie took the garage. Billy and Camila wanted the loft. So I got the only bedroom with a bathroom in it.

GRAHAM: Warren's bedroom had a toilet in it. He used to say he had his own bathroom but he didn't. His room had a toilet. Just in the corner of the room.

BILLY: Teddy was a night owl. So we would all head out to the studio in the afternoon and stay pretty late into the night, sometimes into the morning.

When we were recording, the rest of the world didn't exist to us. You're in that dark studio, thinking of nothing but the music.

Me and Teddy . . . we were knee-deep in it. Speeding up tempos and recording in different keys, trying out everything. I was playing around with new instruments. I was lost to it all at the studio. But then I'd come home and Camila would be asleep, the sheets around her. I'd be a little drunk, usually, and I'd slip into bed right next to her.

It was always the mornings that I got to spend with Camila back then. The way most couples go out to dinner at the end of a long day, Camila and I would go out to breakfast. Some of my favorite mornings were the ones where I wouldn't even bother going to sleep. Camila would wake up and the two of us would drive on down to Malibu and have breakfast along PCH.

Every morning, she'd order the same thing: an iced tea, no sugar, three lemon slices.

CAMILA: Iced tea, three lemons. Club soda, two limes. Martini with two olives and an onion. I'm particular about my drinks. *[Laughs]* I'm particular about a lot of things.

KAREN: You know, people think of Camila as following Billy everywhere, taking care of Billy all the time, but it wasn't like that. She was a force to be reckoned with. She got what she wanted. Almost all the time. She was persuasive and kind of pushy—although, you never really realized you were being pushed. But she was opinionated and knew how to get her way.

I remember this one time she and Billy came down into the living room one morning, just a bit before noon, maybe. We were all in last night's jeans, that kind of thing. We weren't going into the studio until much later. Camila said, "You all want to make a big breakfast? Pancakes, waffles, bacon, eggs, the whole nine?"

But Billy had heard that Graham and I were about to get a burger and he wanted to go with us.

So Camila said, "I'll just make you all burgers here."

And we said fine. So she sent Billy out for hamburger meat and told him to get bacon, too. And eggs for tomorrow.

Then she fired up the grill and came in to tell us the burger meat Billy got didn't look so good. So she'd just make bacon. And while she was making bacon, might as well make eggs, and if she had the eggs out, might as well make some pancakes, too.

Suddenly, it was 1:30 and we were all sitting around the table to eat a brunch and there wasn't a single burger in sight. All of it tasted great and no one even noticed what she had done except me.

That's what I loved about her. She was no wallflower. You just had to be paying attention to see it.

Eddie: The rest of us were always gone, most of the time at least, and I just assumed Camila might help around the house, might clean a bit, you know what I mean? I said one time, "Maybe while we're gone, you could tidy up or something."

Camila: I said, "All right." And then I proceeded to not clean a single thing.

Graham: It was a busy time. Billy was always writing. We were always working on some element or another. In and out of the studio, sleeping there sometimes.

So many nights Karen and I would stay up until the sun came up, working on a riff or a melody.

Warren: That was when I grew my mustache. See now, some men just can't pull off a mustache. But I can. I grew it when we were recording our first album and I have never shaved it.

Well, I shaved it one time and I looked like a skinned cat so I grew it back.

Graham: Recording an album, especially a debut, it takes a lot out of you. Billy became a little obsessive. I think that's why—when the rest of us might have done a bump in the studio—I think that's why Billy started doing lines every day. He was staying in the zone.

Billy: I was intent on making sure that album was the greatest album anyone had ever released since the dawn of time. *[Laughs]* Let's just say I wasn't known for keeping things in perspective back then.

Eddie: Billy took a lot of control over that album. And Teddy let him.

Billy would write the songs, write almost everybody's parts. He'd come in and he'd know the guitars and the keys and what he wanted on the drums. He wasn't on Pete as much, he let Pete have a little bit more leeway. But the rest of us, he dictated the sound and we all went along with it.

I kept looking at everybody else, wondering if someone was going to say something. But no one did. It seemed like I was the only one that cared. And when I'd push back, Teddy would back Billy.

Artie Snyder (*lead engineer for* The Six, SevenEightNine, *and* Aurora): Teddy thought Billy was the real talent of The Six. He never said that to me directly. But he and I spent a lot of time in the control room over the years. And we'd go out sometimes after the band went home, have a drink or two, get a burger. Teddy was a guy who could eat. You'd say, "Let's get drinks," and Teddy would say, "Let's get steaks." What I mean is, I knew him well.

And he really singled Billy out. He asked his opinion when he didn't ask anyone else's, looked at Billy when he was talking to the whole band.

Don't get me wrong, all of them were talented. I once used one of Karen's tracks as an example to another keyboardist of what he should be doing. And I once heard Teddy tell another producer that Pete and Warren were going to be the best rhythm section in rock one day. So he believed in all of them. But he homed in on Billy.

One night as we were walking to our cars Teddy said Billy was the one that had what you can't teach. And I think that's true. I still think that's true.

Graham: Billy was always wondering if we should lay it down one more time, if we should mess with the mix more. Teddy kept telling us that he wanted to leave it as raw as possible. Teddy spent some real energy trying to get Billy to just be Billy.

Billy: Teddy told me once, "What your sound is, is a feeling. That's it. And that's a world above everything else."

I remember saying, "What's the feeling?"

I was writing about love. I was singing with a little bit of a growl. We were rockin' hard on the guitars with some real blues bass lines. So I was thinking Teddy might say, you know, "taking a girl home from a bar" or "speeding with the top down," or something like that. Something fun, maybe, and a little dangerous.

But he just said, "It's ineffable. If I could define it, I wouldn't have any use for it."

That really stuck with me.

Karen: It was pretty boss, recording an album with a real studio. There were techs around to tune everything, people around getting lunch, somebody to go grab you a dime bag. Every day, there was a large spread for lunch that got changed out for dinner.

This one time, we were recording and in comes a dozen chocolate chip cookies delivered by some dude. I said, "We have enough cookies."

And the kid said, "Not this kind." They were laced. I have no idea who sent them.

Eddie: "Just One More" was written and recorded in one day when somebody sent over a batch of grass baked into cookies. The whole song, written mostly by Billy with my help, seems like it's about wanting to sleep with a girl one time before you hit the road. But it was about how we'd eaten all the grass and just wanted one more cookie.

Warren: I took three of the cookies myself and I hid one of 'em for later and as Billy is writing this song about wanting one more, I thought, *Shit! He knows I have one more!*

Graham: It was just a great time. We had a great time back then.

Billy: It did have that kind of feeling where . . . you know you're in a time of your life you'll remember forever.

Graham: The night before we finished recording, I came home from somewhere or other and found Karen sitting up on the railing of the deck, looking out into the canyon. Warren was in a patio chair, whittling what looked like a skinny Christmas tree out of a plastic spoon.

Karen turned to me and said, "It's a shame the water's up to my ankles. I wanted to go for a hike."

And so I said, "What are you guys on and is there any more?"

Karen: It was mescaline.

Warren: That night, when Graham, Karen, and I did peyote, I remember telling myself that if the album was shit, I was gonna be okay. Because I could make spoons for a living. That logic wasn't sound, obviously. But the thought did stick with me. You can't put all your eggs in one basket.

Graham: We finished recording everything in November, I think.

Eddie: We finished up around March.

Graham: Now, it was probably another month, maybe two, that Billy and Teddy were in the studio going over the mixes.

I would go in some days, listen to what they were doing. I had some thoughts and Billy and Teddy always heard me out. And then they played us the final mix and I was blown away.

Eddie: No one was allowed in the studio except Teddy and Billy. They were working on that thing for months. And then finally we were all allowed to hear it.

But it was dynamite. I said to Pete, I said, "We sound fuckin' great."

Billy: We played it for Rich Palentino in the conference room over at the Runner offices. I was tapping my foot so hard underneath that table. I was nervous. This was our shot. If Rich didn't like it, I was thinking I might explode.

Warren: To us back then, Rich was this old guy in his suit and tie. I thought, *This corporate fucker is judging me?* He looked like such an agent of the man.

Graham: I had to stop watching Rich and just close my eyes and listen. And when I did, I thought, *There's no way this guy isn't gonna dig this.*

Billy: The last note of "When the Sun Shines on You" played and I was staring at Rich. Graham and Teddy are staring, too—we're all staring at him. Rich gets this small smile on his face and he goes, "You've got a great album here."

And when Rich liked it, that was it. It was like the last bit of me that was grounded down to earth just flew off, like someone had pulled the rip cord and I was flying.

Nick Harris *(rock critic)*: Their self-titled debut was a respectable entrance into the rock scene. It was straitlaced and economical, sort of a no-frills blues-rock album from a band that knew how to write a decent love song and had really perfected the art of the drug innuendo. A little bit folky, very catchy, lots of swagger, big riffs, hard drums, and that great Billy Dunne smooth growl.

It was an auspicious start.

After an album cover shoot, industry events, an interview with Creem *magazine, and big early buzz for the album, Runner Records and Rod Reyes started planning a thirty-city tour.*

Billy: Everything was happening so fast. And I was . . . You're an underdog for so long and then one day you're not. And when you start to feel real success, when you start to live large and all that, you have to stop and ask yourself if you think you really deserve it.

Anyone that isn't a complete asshole will come up with the answer "No." Because of course you don't. When guys you grew up with are working three jobs. Or they're lost overseas like we lost Chuck. Of course you don't deserve it. You have to learn how to reconcile those two things. Having it and not deserving it. Or, you do what I did, and refuse to think about it.

That's why I was eager to get on the road, to start touring. When you're on the road, you don't really have to deal with real life. It's almost like hitting the pause button.

Eddie: We were headed out on a big tour, you know what I'm saying? Getting interviewed in cool places, getting our own bus. It felt good. It felt real good.

Billy: The night before we were getting on the bus, Camila and I, we were laying in bed, tangled up in the sheets. She had grown her hair out even longer by that point. God, I could just get lost in that hair.

Her hair and her hands always smelled kinda earthy, kind of herbal. She used to grab rosemary branches and crush them up in her hands and then run her hands through her hair. Every time I smell rosemary, even now, it's like I am instantly back there, stupid and young, living in a house in the canyon with my band and my girl.

And that night, the one before we left, I just kept smelling the rosemary in her hair. It was then, right before I was gonna leave for the tour in the morning, that she told me.

Camila: I was seven weeks pregnant.

Karen: Camila wanted kids. Me, I always knew kids weren't in the cards for me. I think it's a feeling you get. I think you have it in your heart or you don't.

And you can't put it in your heart if it's not there.

And you can't pull it out of your heart if it is.

And it was in Camila's heart.

Billy: I was happy, at first. I think. Or . . . *[pauses]* I was trying really hard to be happy about it. I think I knew . . . I *was* happy about it. I was just so scared it was all I could see.

I started focusing on whatever I could to make it make sense. I decided that we needed to get married right away. We had been planning to have a wedding sometime after the tour but I decided we needed to do it right then. I don't know why that mattered to me . . . but . . . *[pauses]* The moment I knew she was pregnant I felt like we had to make sure we were a proper family.

Camila: Karen knew an ordained minister. She got his number from a friend of hers and we called him late that night. He came right over.

Eddie: It was four in the morning.

Camila: Karen decorated the porch out back.

Karen: I strung strips of aluminum foil all through the trees. *[Laughs]* It doesn't sound great in the context of all the environmental shit now. It looked really pretty, in my defense. It swayed with the wind and it bounced the light of the moon.

Graham: Warren had some Christmas lights in his drum kit because he liked to light up his toms. I asked if we could use 'em and he gave me some guff about how he had already packed them up. I said, "Warren, get me your lights now before I tell everyone what an asshole you are."

Warren: It wasn't my problem Billy and Camila decided to get married in the middle of the night.

Karen: By the time Graham and I were done with it, it looked pretty far out. Almost like the sort of place you'd want to get married even if you had forever to plan it.

Billy: As Camila was getting dressed, I went into the bathroom and I looked at myself in the mirror. I just kept telling myself I could do it. *I can do this. I can do this.* I walked down to the patio and then Camila came down in a white T-shirt and a pair of jeans.

Karen: She had on a yellow crochet top. She looked so pretty.

Camila: I wasn't nervous at all.

Eddie: I had one piece of film left in my Polaroid so I took a photo. I accidentally cut off their heads. You can just see Camila's legs and her hair down her back. You can see Billy's chest a bit. They are holding hands in the picture, facing each other. I was so mad I missed their faces. But I was also trippin' balls.

Graham: Camila said something about loving Billy no matter what he did, something about them, with this baby, being a team. But she said it like they were a real sports team. I looked over and Pete was crying. He was trying to hide it but it was obvious. There were tears in his eyes. I think I gave him a look like, "Seriously?" And he just shrugged.

Warren: Pete cried the whole damn time. *[Laughs]* That guy cracked me up.

Billy: Camila said—I remember just how she said it—she said, "It's us, our team, forever and always. And I will always root for us." But there was this voice in my head that was telling me I shouldn't be anybody's father. I couldn't quiet it. It just . . . it kept reverberating in my head. *You're gonna fuck it all up. You're gonna fuck it all up.*

Graham: Look, as a man without a dad, you don't have the foggiest idea what you're supposed to do and you don't have anyone to ask.

I got it later, when I had my own kids. It's like being first in the line, cutting down the path with a machete. Just the word *Dad*. This word that we equated with *deadbeat, asshole, alcoholic*. Now it described Billy, too. He was supposed to find a way to make that word fit onto him. At least, when I went through it, I had Billy to look to. Back then, Billy didn't have anybody.

Billy: The voice kept saying, *If you don't have a father, how can you be a father?*

That voice . . . *[pauses]* That was the beginning of a bad time. Where I was not myself. Actually, no. I don't like putting it that way—you're never not yourself. You're always you. It's just, sometimes, who you are . . . who you are is a shitty person.

Karen: They kissed each other and I could tell Camila was tearing up. Billy picked her up into his arms. He ran her upstairs and we all laughed. I paid the minister guy because Billy and Camila forgot to.

Billy: I remember laying there in that bed with Camila—right after we got married—and I just wanted to leave. I kept waiting for it to be time to get on the bus, because I just . . . I couldn't face her. I knew she'd be able to tell what was going on inside my head if she got too good a look at my face.

I wasn't good at lying to her. I'm not sure if that's a good or a bad thing. People think lying is all bad but . . . I don't know. Lying protects people sometimes.

I laid there as the sun came up and I heard the bus pull in and I jumped out of bed, kissed her goodbye.

Camila: I didn't want him to go. But I also would never have let him stay.

Graham: When I got up in the morning, Billy was already standing there outside the bus, talking to Rod.

Billy: We were all loaded up and the bus driver pulled out of the driveway and Camila had just run down to the front stoop in her nightgown. She'd rushed down to wave goodbye. I waved back but . . . I had a hard time looking at her.

Graham: He was very hard to read. That morning, that bus ride.

Billy: That night, we pulled into Santa Rosa, we started getting ready for our show at Inn of the Beginning. But I wasn't in the right mind.

Eddie: Our first show of the tour did not go well. And there was no reason for it to go poorly except that we just weren't in sync the way we should have been, you know? Billy reversed two of the verses on "Born Broken." And then Graham came in late on a bridge.

Karen: I wasn't too worried about it. But you could tell Billy and Graham were upset about how it went.

Billy: Afterward, we went back to the hotel. Girls started pouring into the room. There was a loaded bar there for us. I had more to drink than I should have. I had a highball glass in one hand and the bottle of Cuervo in the other. Just kept pouring myself a new glass. New glass, new glass, new glass.

I remember Graham telling me to slow it down. But there was too much running through me.

I was gonna be a father and I was a husband and Camila was back in L.A. and we had just played this awful show, and our album had just come out and we didn't know how it would do.

Tequila quieted the whole thing down.

So when Graham told me to stop, I wasn't gonna listen. And you know, there's coke lying around. And I'm doing that. And somebody's got quaaludes and I grab a few of those.

Warren: We were in two adjoining rooms at this motel and I was getting into it with this girl over in the corner of the one room. Cool chick—she was wearing a scarf as a shirt—and all of a sudden she jumped up and asked where her sister was. I didn't even know she had a sister with her.

Somebody called out, "I think she's with Billy."

Billy: Sometime around three or four in the morning I think I blacked out. When I woke up I was in the hotel bathtub . . . I wasn't alone. *[Pauses]* There was a . . . blond girl, laying on top of me. I'm so embarrassed to be telling you this but it's true.

I got up and puked.

Graham: When I woke up, I saw Billy standing out in the parking lot smoking a cigarette. He was pacing back and forth, kind of talking to himself, looked a little crazy. I went out there and he said, "I fucked up. I fucked it all up."

I knew what had happened. I'd tried to stop it. But there was no stopping him. I said, "Just don't do it again, man. That's all. Just don't do it again."

He nodded and said, "Yeah."

Billy: I called Camila just to hear her voice. I knew I couldn't tell her what I'd done. I told myself that I would never do it again and that's what was important.

Camila: You're asking me if I knew he was going to be unfaithful as if that's a thing that you know or you don't know. Like it's black and white. But it's not. You suspect, then you sort of un-suspect. Then you suspect again. Then you tell yourself you're crazy. Then you ask yourself whether fidelity is really something you value above all else.

Let me put it this way: I've seen a lot of marriages where everyone is faithful and no one is happy.

Billy: At the end of the call, Camila said she had to go and I said, "All right," and then I remember she said, "Okay, honey, we love you."

And I said, "We?"

And she said, "Me and the baby."

And that just . . . I think I hung up the phone before I could even say goodbye.

Karen: Camila had become my friend. I hated Billy for putting me in a position to either tell Camila what he'd done or lie to her.

Billy: Drinking, drugging, sleeping around, it's all the same thing.

You have these lines you won't cross. But then you cross them.

And suddenly you possess the very dangerous information that you can break the rule and the world won't instantly come to an end.

You've taken a big, black, bold line and you've made it a little bit gray. And now every time you cross it again, it just gets grayer and grayer until one day you look around and you think, *There was a line here once, I think.*

Graham: It got to be a rhythm: get to town, sound check, play, party, get on the bus. And the better we started playing, the more we partied. Hotels, girls, drugs. Over and over. Hotels, girls, drugs. For all of us. But especially Billy.

Warren: We had a rule back then; we each had five matchsticks. That's how we'd invite people back to the party after. If they had a matchstick, they were in. We could give them out to any girl in the crowd we saw. Obviously, we tried to steer clear of weirdos.

Rod: Let me tell you what it means to manage a rock band. We're driving all over hell and creation, roadies and crew and the whole nine. And not one person—not one member of that band—asked themselves how we were always stocked up on gas.

End of 'seventy-three was the oil crisis, there was a gas shortage. The tour manager and I are bribing gas station attendants like our lives depend on it. I'm switching out license plates.

And no one even notices because they're all sleeping around and drunk and high.

Karen: Billy turned into someone I didn't recognize on that tour. He'd pass out in the bus with a girl under his arm, invite girls with us from one city to another.

Eddie: I mean, Billy had one of the roadies deliver tequila and quaaludes to him at all hours of the night.

Karen: The album was doing pretty well and our tour got extended. I was talking to Camila about it and she said, "Karen, should I come join you guys?"

I couldn't get the words out of my mouth fast enough. I said, "No, stay there."

Warren: Let me sum up that early tour for you: I was getting laid, Graham was getting high, Eddie was getting drunk, Karen was getting fed up, Pete was getting on the phone to his girl back home, and Billy was all five, at once.

Eddie: I was backstage after the Ottawa show, having a few beers with the Midnight Dawn guys. Graham was with me. Karen, too. Pete was waiting for his girl Jenny. She was driving up from Boston. I hadn't met her by that point. Because Pete was always really private. His high school girlfriend never met our parents! So I was excited to finally meet Jenny, see what all this fuss was about.

And then in she walks, tall as hell, long blond hair, wearing this tiny little dress and these super-tall shoes, legs up to her neck, and I thought, *No wonder Pete's obsessed with this girl.*

And then right behind her, I see Camila.

Camila: I wanted to surprise him. I missed him. I was bored. I was . . . getting nervous. I mean, I had gotten married, I was six months pregnant, and I was spending the majority of my time alone in a massive old house in Topanga Canyon. There were a lot of reasons I went.

But, yes, one of the reasons was to see if things were okay. To see what he was up to. Of course it was.

Karen: I had told her not to come. But she didn't listen to me. She came to surprise Billy.

She was just starting to show. Maybe five months pregnant?

Something like that. She had on this big maxidress. Her hair pulled back.

Graham: I spotted Camila and I thought, *Oh, no.* But I kind of strolled on out the door. Once I was out of view, I booked it. I figured Billy was either on the bus or at the hotel. I wasn't sure which but I had to take a chance. I ran the two blocks to the hotel.

I should have chosen the bus.

Karen: She found him on the bus. Part of me wished I could have stopped her and part of me was glad it was going to be all out in the open.

Eddie: I wasn't there but I heard she walked in on him getting, well . . . I don't know how else to say it . . . *oral sex,* I guess I should say. From a groupie.

Billy: It was like I'd been playing with fire but somehow I was genuinely surprised when I burnt myself.

I remember Camila's face. It was . . . she wasn't mad or hurt so much as truly shocked. She was just frozen, taking it in with no reaction. She stared at me as I scrambled to get myself presentable.

The girl I was with just ran out—like she didn't want to be in the middle of anything.

When the door of the bus shut, I looked at Camila and I said, "I'm sorry." That was the first thing I said, really the only thing I said. That's when Camila finally seemed to process exactly what had happened, what was happening.

Camila: I believe what I said was, and you know, earmuffs, but I believe what I said was "Who the fuck do you think you are, cheating on me? You think there's a woman alive who is better than what you have?"

Warren: I was outside talking to some of the crew guys and I caught the tail end of it. I could see a bit through the windshield. It looked to me like she hit him. I think she had a bag with her and I think she slugged him with the bag. And then the two of them left the bus.

Camila: I made him take a shower before I would say another word to him.

Billy: I wanted her to leave me. *[Pauses]* I've thought a lot about it and . . . that's what I'd been up to. I'd been hoping she'd cut me loose.

That night Camila and I were sitting in my hotel room after I got out of the shower. And I could feel myself sobering up and I didn't like it. I pulled out a bump and I remember Camila looked at me and she said, "What are you trying to do?"

She didn't say it in an exasperated way. She was really asking me. *What was I trying to do?* I didn't know how to answer her. I just shrugged and I remember how stupid I felt, shrugging at a time like that, with a woman like that. This woman carrying my child. And I was shrugging like a ten-year-old boy.

She stared at me, waiting for more of an answer, and I didn't have one. So she said, "If you think I'm gonna let you screw up our life, you've lost your mind." And she walked out the door.

Graham: Camila found me and said she was going home, wasn't gonna deal with his bullshit. She asked me to watch Billy all night. I was getting sick of watching Billy. But you don't say no to a woman like Camila, especially when she's pregnant. So I said okay.

And then she said, "When he wakes up give him this letter."

Billy: I wake up, sick to my stomach, terrible headache. Feel like my eyes are bleeding. Karen is standing over me with a piece of paper. She has this pissed-off look on her face. I grab the paper and

I read it. It was in Camila's handwriting. It said, *You have until November 30 and then you're going to be a good man for the rest of your life. You got it?*

The baby was due December 1.

Camila: I think I just refused to accept that he was as low as he claimed to be.

I'm not saying it wasn't real, what he did. Oh, it was very real. All of it was real. I've never been so lost and scared. I was sick over it, every day. And I couldn't have even told you what part of me felt the sickest. My heart hurt and my stomach felt like it was gonna turn inside out and my head throbbed. Oh, it was very real.

But that didn't mean I had to *accept it.*

Rod: I wasn't close with Camila but her decision to stick with Billy wasn't so hard to understand. She'd gotten mixed up with him when he was a good guy. And by the time she realized he was coming apart at the seams, she was too far in.

If she wanted her baby to have a daddy, she had to fix Billy. What's not to get?

Billy: Like an idiot, I said to myself, *Okay, I'll just take until November 30 and get all of this out of my system. Do it all now. So I don't ever have to do it again.*

Sometimes I wonder if addicts aren't all that different from anybody else, they are just better at lying to themselves. I was great at lying to myself.

Karen: He didn't stop messing around with all of it.

Rod: The tour got extended again when we picked up some shows opening for Rick Yates. It was good news. It was great exposure. The album was off to a respectable start. "Señora" was climbing up the charts.

But yeah, Billy was off the rails. Going at it double time after Camila caught him. The coke and girls and the booze and all that.

To be honest, I thought all of that was manageable. Not great, but manageable.

I figured as long as he wasn't hitting the strong downers—benzos, heroin—maybe he'd be all right.

Graham: I didn't know what to do. I didn't know how to help him or whether to trust what he was saying to me. I felt, stupid, honestly. I felt like, *I'm his brother. I should know what he needs. I should always be able to tell when he's high and lying about it.*

But I didn't know. And I felt . . . embarrassed that I didn't always catch what he was up to.

Eddie: We were all sort of counting down the days. You know, *sixty days until Billy has to get clean*. Then it was forty days. Then it was twenty days.

Billy: We were in Dallas opening up for Rick Yates. And Rick was really into snorting heroin. I thought, *I need to try heroin at least once*.

That made perfect sense to me: that it would be easier to get clean if I tried heroin. And it wasn't like I was going to use a needle. I was gonna snort it. And I'd had opium in the past. We all had. So when I was with Rick backstage at Texas Hall, and he offered me a bump . . . I rolled on up and took it.

Rod: I always tell my people to stay away from benzos and heroin. People don't die staying up, they die when they go to sleep. Look at Janis Joplin, Jimi Hendrix, Jim Morrison. Downers kill you.

Graham: It all spiraled from there. Once he and Yates started snorting H, I lived with this dread in my belly. I tried to keep an eye on him. I kept trying to get him to stop.

Rod: When I found out he was with Yates, I called Teddy. I said, "We've got a dead man walking." Teddy said he'd handle it.

Graham: No amount of advice or lectures or trying to chain somebody down ever stopped anyone who didn't want to stop in the first place.

Eddie: When it got down to ten days left, and he was forgetting the words onstage, I remember thinking he was never gonna clean up.

Billy: On November 28, Teddy shows up at our show in Hartford. He's there backstage when we're done with our set.

I say, "What are you doing here?"

He says, "You're going home," and he takes me by the arm and holds on to me until we're practically on the plane. Turns out, Camila had gone into labor.

We land and he drags me into his car and drives me to the hospital. We're double-parked in a red zone in front of the lobby. Teddy says, "Get up there, Billy."

This whole long journey and all I had left to do was walk in the double doors . . . but . . . I couldn't do it. I couldn't meet my kid like that.

Teddy got out of the car and went up there himself.

Camila: I'd just spent eighteen hours in labor with only my mom by my side. And I'm expecting my husband to walk in the door and straighten up. I understand now that you can't just fix yourself. It doesn't work like that. But I did expect it to work like that then. I didn't know.

Well, the door opened and it wasn't Billy . . . it was Teddy Price.

I was so tired and I was sweating bullets from the hormones running through me, and I was holding this tiny baby that I've just met, this girl who looks just like Billy. I decided to name her Julia.

My mom was ready to take us both back with her to Pennsylvania. And I was tempted. Right then, giving up on Billy felt easier than trying to have faith. I wanted to say, "Tell him I'll raise this baby on my own." But I had to keep trying for what I wanted for me and my kid. So I told Teddy, "Tell him he can start to be a father this second or he's going to rehab. Now."

And Teddy nodded and left.

Billy: I waited for what felt like hours, outside the lobby, fiddling with the latch on the door. Teddy came down finally and said, "You have a baby girl. She looks like you. Her name is Julia."

I wasn't sure what to say.

And then Teddy said, "Camila says you have two choices. You can get your ass up there right now and be a good husband and father or I can drive you to rehab. Those are your choices."

I put my hand on the door handle and I thought, you know, *I can just run*.

But I think Teddy knew what I was thinking because he said, "Camila didn't give any other options, Billy. There are no other options. Some people can handle their booze and their dope. You can't. So it's over for you now."

It reminded me of being a kid, maybe six or seven—I had gotten really into collecting those little Matchbox cars. I was obsessed with them. But my mom didn't have enough money to get us very many. So I'd search for them on the sidewalk, in case any kid lost one. Found a few that way. And then when I was playing with other boys in the neighborhood, sometimes I'd palm one or two of theirs. A few times, I outright stole them from the store. My mom found my stash and sat me down and said, "How come you can't just be happy playing with a few cars like everybody else?"

I never did have an answer for that.

It's just not my way.

That day at the hospital, I remember looking at the lobby door and seeing this man coming outside wheeling a lady with a baby. I looked at him and . . . he just seemed like a man I didn't know how to be.

I just kept thinking about walking into the hospital and looking at my kid and knowing that I was the shit deal she got.

[Chokes up] It wasn't that I didn't want to be with [her]. I wanted to be with [her] so bad. You have no idea how bad. I just . . . I didn't want my girl to have to meet me.

I didn't want . . . that early into her life, I didn't want my kid to have to look up and see this man, this drunken, strung-out, piece of shit and think, *This is my dad?*

That's how I felt. I was embarrassed to be seen by my baby.

So I ran away. I'm not proud of it, but that's the truth, I went to rehab to avoid meeting my own daughter.

CAMILA: My mom said, "Honey, I hope you know what you're doing." And I think I yelled at her, but inside I was thinking, *I hope I do, too.*

You know, I've thought about this for a long time. Decades. And here is what it comes down to. Here is why I did what I did.

It didn't seem right to me that his weakest self got to decide how my life was going to turn out, what my family was going to look like.

I got to decide that. And what I wanted was a life—a family, a beautiful marriage, a home—with him. With the man I knew he truly was. And I was going to get it, hell or high water.

Billy entered rehab in the winter of 1974. The Six canceled the few remaining dates on the rest of their tour.

The other band members took some time off. Warren bought a boat and docked it off the shore in Marina del Rey. Eddie, Graham, and Karen stayed in the Topanga Canyon house, while Pete temporarily moved to the East Coast, to be with his girlfriend, Jenny Manes. Camila rented a house in Eagle Rock and settled into motherhood there.

After sixty days in a rehabilitation center, Billy Dunne finally met his daughter, Julia.

Billy: I'm not sure I went to rehab for the right reasons. Shame and embarrassment and avoidance and all that. But I *stayed* for the right reasons.

I stayed because on my second day there, the group therapist told me to stop imagining my daughter ashamed of me. He said to start thinking of what I'd need to do to believe my daughter was proud of me. I'll tell ya, that stuck. I couldn't stop thinking about that one.

Slowly, it became the light that was calling to me at the end of that tunnel . . . imagining a daughter . . . *[pauses, gains composure]* Imagining myself as a man my daughter would feel lucky to have.

I kept working, every day, to get closer to being that man.

Graham: The day Billy was coming out of rehab, I picked up Camila and the baby and we drove over together.

Now, Julia was the fattest baby you ever saw. *[Laughs]* It's true! I said to Camila, "Are you feeding her milkshakes?" Biggest cheeks in the world, beer belly. Couldn't have been cuter.

There was a tiny little picnic table and an umbrella outside the facility. So Camila sat there with Julia on her lap. I went in and got Billy. He was wearing the same thing he was wearing the last time I'd seen him, in Hartford. But he had gained some weight, his face looked healthier.

I said, "Are you ready?"

He said, "Yeah," but he seemed kind of unsure.

I put my arm around him and I said what I figured he needed to hear. I said, "You're gonna be a great dad." I think I should have told him that sooner. I don't know why I didn't.

Billy: Julia was sixty-three days old when I met her. It's hard, even now, to . . . to not hate myself for that. But the second I met her, my

God. *[Smiles]* Standing there at that picnic table with them, it was like someone just took an ax to me, just shattered all the crust. I felt raw. In the way where you can feel everything, feel it deep down into your nerves.

I had . . . I'd built a family. By accident and without thinking and without so many of the qualities that you should have to deserve a family, I think, but I had built one. And here was this tiny, new person—who had my eyes, who didn't know who I used to be, who only cared who I was now.

I fell to my knees. I was just so grateful for Camila.

I . . . I couldn't believe what I put Camila through and I couldn't believe that she was still standing there, giving me another shot. I didn't deserve it. And I knew it.

I told her then that I would spend the rest of our life together trying to be twice as good as she deserved. I don't know that I've ever promised anyone anything as humbly and with as much gratitude in my heart as I promised her that day.

I know I technically married her almost a year before but I submitted myself to her then. Forever and always. My daughter, too. I dedicated myself to both of them, to raising this girl with my whole heart into it.

As we got in the car, Camila whispered, "It's us, forever and always. Don't go forgetting that again, all right?"

And I nodded and she kissed me. And Graham drove us home.

Camila: I think you have to have faith in people before they earn it. Otherwise it's not faith, right?

FIRST

1974–1975

By 1974, Daisy Jones had refused to show up to any of her recording sessions at the Record Plant in West Hollywood and was in breach of contract with Runner Records.

Meanwhile, Simone Jackson, now signed with Supersight Records, was finding international success with her R & B dance hits, which would come to be seen as classics of the protodisco genre. With her songs "The Love Drug" and "Make Me Move," Simone was topping the dance club charts in France and Germany.

As Simone set out to tour Europe the summer of '74, Daisy was growing more and more restless.

Daisy: I was spending my days getting sunburns and my nights getting high. I'd stopped writing songs because I didn't see a point to it if no one would let me record them.

Hank was checking on me every day, pretending he was doting on me but really just trying to convince me to get to the studio, like I was some sort of prize horse that wouldn't race.

Then one day, Teddy Price shows up at my door. He was put in charge of me, I guess. He was supposed to convince me to show up to the studio. Teddy was probably in his forties or fifties around then, British guy, really charming, kind of paternal.

I open the door to see him on my doorstep and he doesn't even say hello. He says, "Let's cut the crap, Daisy. You need to record this album or Runner's taking you to court."

I said, "I don't care about any of that. They can take their money back, get me kicked out of here if they want. I'll live in a cardboard box." I was very annoying. I had no idea what it meant to truly suffer.

Teddy said, "Just get in the studio, love. How hard is that?"

I told him, "I want to write my own stuff." I think I even crossed my arms in front of my chest like a child.

He said, "I've read your stuff. Some of it's really good. But you don't have a single song that's finished. You don't have anything ready to be recorded." He said I should fulfill my contract with Runner and he would help me get my songs to a point where I could release an album of my own stuff. He called it "a goal for us all to work toward."

I said, "I want to release my own stuff *now.*"

And that's when he got testy with me. He said, "Do you want to be a professional groupie? Is that what you want? Because the way it looks from here is that you have a chance to do something of your own. And you'd rather just end up pregnant by Bowie."

Let me take this opportunity to be clear about one thing: I never slept with David Bowie. At least, I'm pretty sure I didn't.

I said, "I am an *artist*. So you either let me record the album I want or I'm not showing up. Ever."

Teddy said, "Daisy, someone who insists on the perfect conditions to make art isn't an artist. They're an asshole."

I shut the door in his face.

And sometime later that day, I opened up my songbook and I started reading. I hated to admit it but I could see what he was saying. I had good lines but I didn't have anything polished from beginning to end.

The way I was working then, I'd have a loose melody in my head and I'd come up with lyrics to it and then I'd move on. I didn't work on my songs after one or two rounds.

I was sitting in the living room of my cottage, looking out the window, my songbook in my lap, realizing that if I didn't start trying—I mean being willing to squeeze out my own blood, sweat, and tears for what I wanted—I'd never be anything, never matter much to anybody.

I called Teddy a few days later, I said, "I'll record your album. I'll do it."

And he said, "It's your album." And I realized he was right. The album didn't have to be exactly my way for it to still be mine.

Simone: One day, when I was back in town, I went over to Daisy's place at the Marmont and I was in the kitchen and I saw one piece of paper, with a bunch of lyrics scribbled on it, taped to the fridge.

I said, "What's this?"

Daisy said, "It is my song that I'm working on."

I said, "Don't you normally have dozens?"

She shook her head and said, "I'm trying to get this one just right."

Daisy: It was a big lesson for me when I was young—being given things versus earning them. I was so used to being given things that I didn't know how important it is for your soul to earn them.

If I can thank Teddy Price for anything—and to be honest, I have to thank him for a lot of things—but if I had to pick one it's that he made me earn something.

And that's what I did. I showed up at the studio, I tried to stay relatively sober, and I sang the songs they told me to sing. I didn't sing them the way they wanted *all* the time, I gave a little pushback—and I do think the album is better for my having held on to a little bit of my own style. But I did what was asked of me. I played the game.

And when we were done, ten ballads in a pretty little package, Teddy said, "How do you feel?"

And I told him I felt like I'd made something that wasn't exactly what I'd envisioned, but it was maybe good in its own right. I said it felt like me but it didn't feel like me and I had no idea whether it was brilliant or awful or somewhere in between. And Teddy laughed and said I sounded like an artist. I liked that.

I asked him what we should call it and he said he didn't know. I said, "I want to call it *First*. Because I plan on making a lot more of these."

Nick Harris: Daisy Jones put out *First* at the beginning of 1975. They marketed her as a Dusty Springfield wannabe. On the cover, she's looking in a mirror placed over a pale yellow background.

It wasn't groundbreaking material, by any means. But looking back on it, you can start to see the grit and the edge under the surface.

Her first single, a version of "One Fine Day," was more complex than most other takes of the song, and her second single—she recorded a take of "My Way Down"—was warmly received.

I mean, the album is fairly middle of the road but it did what it needed to do. People knew her name. She did a spot on *American Bandstand*, she did a great spread in *Circus* with her trademark hoop earrings.

She was gorgeous and outspoken and interesting. The music wasn't there yet but . . . you knew Daisy Jones was heading somewhere. Her moment was coming.

SEVEN EIGHT NINE

1975–1976

Fresh out of rehab and at home with Camila and his new daughter, Billy Dunne started writing songs again. When he had enough material, The Six got back into the studio to record their second album. From June to December of 1975, The Six recorded the ten songs that would become SevenEightNine. *But when the band was done, Teddy told them that Rich Palentino did not feel confident they had a number one single on the album.*

BILLY: It felt like being cut off at the knees. We were ready to go. We were proud of that album.

EDDIE: To be honest with you, I was surprised Teddy had not brought this up sooner. I heard the master of the album and it felt soft to me—at least in terms of what we were making songs *about.* Everything Billy had written was about his family.

Pete said it best. "Rock 'n' roll is about getting it on with a girl for the first time. Not about making love to your wife." And that was Pete saying that! He was as whipped as Billy.

GRAHAM: I told Teddy we had a lot of songs that could be good singles. I said, "What about 'Hold Your Breath'?"

He said, "Too slow."

I said, "What about 'Give In'?"

He said, "Too hard rock."

I kept naming songs and Teddy kept saying that Rich was right.

The songs were good but we needed something with crossover appeal. He said we had to aim for number one. Our first album had done well but if we wanted to grow, we needed to aim higher.

I said, "Sure, but we aren't trying to get to number one, necessarily. That's for lowest common denominator stuff."

Teddy said, "You should be aiming to be number one because you're making the greatest fucking music out there."

It was a fair point.

Billy: I don't remember whose idea it was to do a duet. I know I wouldn't have come up with it.

Eddie: When Teddy said he thought we should make "Honeycomb" a duet, I was even more confused. He was going to take the softest song on the album, add a female vocal to it, and *that* was going to fix the problem? That just made it even more of a Top 40 thing.

I said to Pete, "I will not be in a fucking soft rock band."

Billy: "Honeycomb" is a romantic song, but it's also kind of wistful. I'd written it about the life that I promised Camila. She wanted to move to North Carolina one day, when we were old and settling down. Her mother had grown up there. She wanted to get a place close to the water. Have a big lot of land with the closest neighbor a mile away.

It was a pledge I'd made her. That I would give her that one day. A big farmhouse, lots of kids. Some peace and quiet after all the storms I'd put her through. That's what "Honeycomb" was about. It didn't make any sense to have someone else come in on it.

Teddy disagreed. He said, "Write a part for a woman in it. Write what Camila would say back to you."

Graham: I thought we should give Karen a shot at the duet. She had a great voice.

Karen: I don't have the kind of voice that can carry a lead part. I can do you a solid and back you up in the chorus but I can't hold my own.

Warren: Graham was always tripping over himself to pay Karen a compliment. I was always thinking, *It's not gonna happen for you, man. Get over it.*

Billy: Teddy had all these ideas about bringing in a woman from the dance club scene. I did not like that.

Karen: Teddy named about ten girls until Billy finally relented. I watched it happen.

Billy was going down the list Teddy had written just going, "No. No. No. Tonya Reading? No. Suzy Smith? No." And then Billy goes, "Who is Daisy Jones?"

And Teddy got all amped up, said he was hoping Billy would ask that because he thought Daisy was the one.

Graham: Now, I'd heard Daisy sing at the Golden Bear a few months back. I thought she was sexy as hell. Her voice was so raspy and cool. But I didn't think she fit on the record. She was younger, poppier. I said to Teddy, "Why can't you get us Linda Ronstadt?" Everybody had a thing for her back then. But Teddy said it should be someone from our label. He said Daisy had a more commercial vibe that we could benefit from.

I had to admit I saw where Teddy was coming from.

I said to Billy, "If Teddy is trying to bring in a different demographic, Daisy makes sense."

Billy: Teddy wasn't letting up. *Daisy Daisy Daisy.* Even Graham started in on me. I said, "Fine. If this girl Daisy wants to do it, then we'll try it."

Rod: Teddy was a good producer. He knew people in town were just starting to get excited about Daisy Jones. If this song turned out well, it could make a splash.

Daisy: I had heard of The Six, obviously, being on the same label and everything. And I'd heard their singles on the radio.

I hadn't bothered to listen to their debut album that much but when Teddy played me *SevenEightNine,* I was blown away. I loved that album. I must have listened to "Hold Your Breath" about ten times in a row.

I loved Billy's voice. There was something so plaintive about it. So vulnerable. I thought, *This is the voice of a man who's seen things.* I thought it was so evocative to sound broken the way he did. I didn't have that. I sounded like a cool new pair of jeans and Billy sounded like the pair you've had for years.

I could see the potential of how we could really complement each other. So I kept listening to their cut of "Honeycomb," and I could feel something missing. I read the lyrics and I . . . I really *got* that song.

This felt like my shot to offer something up, to add something. I was excited to get in the studio because I thought I could really be of *use.*

Billy: We were all there in the studio that day when Daisy came in and I thought everybody but me and Teddy should have gone home.

Daisy: I was going to wear one of my Halstons. And then I woke up late and lost my keys and couldn't find my pill bottle and the morning got away from me.

Karen: When she showed up, she was wearing a men's button-down shirt as a dress. That was it. I remember thinking, *Where are her pants?*

Eddie: Daisy Jones was the most gorgeous woman I ever laid eyes on. She had those big eyes. Those super-full lips. And she was as tall as I was. She looked like a gazelle.

Warren: Daisy had no ass, no tits. A carpenter's dream as they call 'em. Flat as a board, easy to nail. Well, I don't know if she was easy to nail. Probably not. The way men reacted to her, she held all the cards and she knew it. When Pete saw her, he might as well have let his tongue roll out of his mouth.

Karen: She was so pretty that I worried I was staring at her. But then I thought, *Hell, she's probably been stared at her whole life. She probably thinks looking means staring.*

Billy: I saw her and I introduced myself, and I said, "Glad to have you here. Thanks for helping us out." I asked if she wanted to talk about the song a bit, practice what she was gonna lay down.

Daisy: I'd been working on it all night. I'd been in the studio with Teddy a few days before, listening to it over and over. I had a good idea of what I wanted to do.

Billy: Daisy just said, "No, thanks." Like that. Like I had nothing of value to offer.

Rod: She went right into the booth and started warming up.

Karen: I said, "Guys, we don't all need to be here watching her." But nobody moved.

Daisy: I finally had to say, "Can I have some room to breathe, please?"

Billy: Finally everybody started funneling out except me, Teddy, and Artie.

Artie Snyder: I miked her up in one of the iso booths. We did a couple test runs and for whatever reason, the mike wasn't working.

It took me about forty-five minutes to get that mike going. She was standing there, singing into it on and off, going, "Testing, testing, one two three." Helping me out. I could feel Billy getting more and more tense. But Daisy was so calm about it. I said, "I'm sorry about this," and she said, "It takes as long as it takes and you'll get it when you get it."

Daisy always did right by me. She always made it seem like she cared about how my day was going. Not a lot of people did that.

Daisy: I had read the lyrics to the song what felt like a million times. I had my own idea of how I wanted it to go.

Billy sang it in this sort of pleading way. I thought the way he sang it made it seem like he wasn't sure he believed his own promise. And I loved that. I thought that made it so interesting. So I had this plan to sing my part like I *wanted* to believe him but maybe deep down inside I didn't. I thought that gave the song some layers.

When we got the mike working—you know, Artie's giving me the signal to start and Billy and Teddy are watching me—I got up into the mike and I sang it like I didn't believe Billy was going to buy a house near the honeycomb, that it wasn't really ever gonna happen. That was my angle on it.

During the refrain, the lyrics were originally "The life we want will wait for us/We will live to see the lights coming off the bay/And you will hold me, you will hold me, you will hold me/until that day."

I sang it straight through on the first go-around but the second time I sang it, I changed it up a bit. I said, "Will the life we want wait for us?/Will we live to see the lights coming off the bay?/Will you hold me, will you hold me, will you hold me until that day?"

I sang them as questions as opposed to statements.

Billy didn't even let me finish before he popped up and hit the talkback.

Billy: She sang the words wrong. It didn't make sense to have her keep going with the words wrong.

Artie Snyder: Billy would never have allowed someone to interrupt him like that. I was genuinely surprised when he did that.

Billy: The song was about a happy ending after turmoil. I didn't think doubt worked in that context.

Karen: Billy wrote that song trying to convince himself that this future he saw with Camila was a sure thing. But he and Camila both knew Billy could relapse at any moment.

I mean, the first month he was out of rehab, he gained ten pounds because he was eating chocolate bars in the middle of the night. And then when he stopped doing that, there was all the woodworking. You'd go over to Billy and Camila's and Billy would be obsessing over some mahogany dining room table he was trying to make and there were all these shitty dining chairs he'd nailed together.

And don't get me started on the shopping. Oh, and the running was maybe the worst of it. For about two months, Billy would run however many miles a day. He'd be wearing those little dolphin shorts and muscle tanks bobbing down the street.

Rod: Billy was trying. This was a guy who made so many things seem easy. But he was trying very hard to stay sober. And you could see the strain on him.

Karen: Billy was writing songs trying to tell himself he had got it all under control, that decades out he'll still have his sobriety and his wife and his family.

And in about two minutes of singing, Daisy pulled the tablecloth from under the dishes.

Rod: Daisy did a few more takes and it really seemed easy for her. She didn't have to work for it. She wasn't bleeding for every note.

But when Billy left the studio, I could tell he was pretty tense. I said, "Don't take work home with you." But the problem wasn't that he had brought work home with him. It was that he had brought home into work.

Karen: "Honeycomb" used to be a song about security, and it became a song about insecurity.

Billy: That night, I told Camila about how Daisy sang it, with the questions.

You know, Camila's got her hands full with Julia and I'm talking her ear off complaining about this song. She just said, "It's not real life, Billy. It's a song. Don't get bent out of shape." It was so simple for her. I should just get over it.

But I couldn't get over it. I did not like that Daisy turned those lines into questions and I didn't like that she had felt the right to do it.

Camila: When you put your life in your music, you can't be clear-headed about your music.

Graham: I think Daisy was just very unexpected for Billy.

Artie Snyder: When we cut together the version with Daisy, it was so compelling—their voices together—that Teddy wanted to strip almost everything else away. He had me soften the drums a bit, amp up the keys, cut out some of Graham's more distracting flourishes.

What we were left with was this sprawling acoustic guitar and percussive piano. Most of the attention went to the vocals. The song became, entirely, about the relationship of the voices. I mean . . . it *moved*—it was still up-tempo, it still had a rhythm—but it was eclipsed by the vocal. You were hypnotized by Billy and Daisy.

Eddie: They took a rock song and they made it a pop song! And they were so pleased with themselves about it.

Rod: Teddy was over the moon with how it turned out. I liked it, too. But you could see the way Billy bristled as he listened to it.

Billy: I liked the new mix. But I did not like Daisy's vocals. I said, "Just do the new mix without her vocals. It doesn't need to be a duet." Teddy just kept telling me I had to trust him. He said that I had written a hit song and that I had to let him do his thing.

Graham: Billy was always in charge, you know? Billy wrote the lyrics, Billy composed and arranged all of the songs. If Billy goes to rehab the tour is over. If Billy is ready to go back to the studio, we all have to report for duty. He ran the show.

So "Honeycomb" was not easy for him.

Billy: We were all a team.

Eddie: Man, Billy was in such denial of what a bulldozer he was to the rest of us. Billy got Billy's way every time and when Daisy showed up, he stopped getting his way every time.

Daisy: I did not understand what Billy had against me. I came in and I made the song just a little bit better. What was there to be upset about?

I ran into Billy at the studio a few days later, to hear the final cut, and I smiled at him. I said hello. He just nodded his head at me. Like, he was doing me a favor by acknowledging my presence. He couldn't even extend a professional courtesy.

Karen: It was a man's world. The whole world was a man's world but the recording industry . . . it wasn't easy. You had to get some guy's approval to do just about anything and it seemed like there were two ways to go about it. You either acted like one of the boys, which is the way I had found. Or you acted real girlie and flirty and batted your eyelashes. They liked that.

But Daisy, from the beginning, was sort of outside of all that. She was just sort of "Take me or leave me."

Daisy: I didn't care if I was famous or not. I didn't care if I got to sing on your record or not. All I wanted to do was make something interesting and original and cool.

Karen: When I first started, I wanted to play the electric guitar. And my dad got me piano lessons instead. He didn't mean anything by it—he just thought the keys are what girls play.

But it was stuff like that, every time I tried anything.

When I auditioned for the Winters, I had this really great minidress I'd just bought, it was pale blue with a big belt across it. It felt like a lucky dress. Well, the day I tried out, I didn't wear it. Because I knew they'd see a girl. And I wanted them to see a keyboardist. So I wore jeans and a University of Chicago T-shirt I stole from my brother.

Daisy wasn't like that. It would never have occurred to Daisy to do that.

Daisy: I wore what I wanted when I wanted. I did what I wanted with who I wanted. And if somebody didn't like it, screw 'em.

Karen: You know how every once in a while you'll meet somebody who seems to be floating through life? Daisy sort of floated through the world, oblivious to the way it really worked.

I suppose I probably should have hated her for it, but I didn't. I loved her for it. Because it meant she was less inclined to take the shit I'd been taking for years now. And with her around, I didn't have to take that shit either.

Daisy: Karen was the kind of person who had more talent in her finger than most people have in their whole body and The Six was underutilizing her. She fixed that, though. She fixed that on the next one.

Billy: When the record was about to be pressed, I said to Teddy, "You made me hate my own song."

And Teddy said to me, "You're going to need to work really hard at getting over yourself. Something tells me hitting the top of the charts is going to ease the sting a bit."

Nick Harris *(rock critic)*: On "Honeycomb," Billy and Daisy and the way they play off each other was the beginning of what worked so well about Daisy Jones & The Six.

The chemistry between their voices—his vulnerability, her fragility—it grabs you and doesn't let you go. With his voice deep and smooth, and her voice higher and raspier, they somehow still meld together effortlessly, like two voices that have been singing together for ages. They created a deeply heartfelt call and response—a story of this romantic and idealized future that may never come to pass.

The song verges on being a bit saccharine. But the end undercuts the sweetness just enough. It could have been the kind of song teens play at prom. Instead, we have a passionate testament to the fact that things don't always work out.

SevenEightNine was a good album, in some ways a great album. It was more explicitly romantic than their debut—fewer allusions to sex or drugs. It still rocked, though. It had that driving rhythm section, those piercing riffs.

But "Honeycomb" was the clear standout. "Honeycomb" showed the world that The Six could put out a first-class pop song. It was a pivot, to be sure, but it's the beginning of their rise to the top.

THE NUMBERS TOUR

1976–1977

SevenEightNine was released on June 1, 1976. "Honeycomb" debuted at number 86 but was headed up the charts at a steady clip. The band, playing an unofficial residency of sorts at the Whisky, was gearing up to headline their own national tour.*

Graham: We hung out in L.A. for a while, perfecting our set. The songs were coming together onstage. I say that but I guess I don't mean "Honeycomb." Billy did a rendition of it without Daisy. He just lifted her half of it and sang it as he originally intended on the album. It was good, but you could feel a hole in it. It was missing something. The rest of the album was playing great, though. We were playing tight, every song, every note. We had it down. We were putting together a great show.

Billy: We had the same people coming to see us two or three nights a week sometimes. And the crowds were growing the more we played.

Rod: Billy should have invited Daisy to some of those L.A. shows. I told him that. But it was in one ear out the other with him.

Simone: Daisy was frustrated they were excluding her. At least I got that impression, when we talked. Which wasn't as often anymore, with all my touring. But I still made sure I knew what was going on with her. She did the same with me.

Karen: Daisy knew everybody at the Whisky. She was more connected on the Strip than we were. So it was only a matter of time before she showed up.

Daisy: I wasn't trying to crash anything. If Billy didn't want to invite me to sing with them, that was fine. But I wasn't going to stay away just because they were playing my single without me.

Also, I'd started sleeping with Hank, which wasn't a great move on my part, but, to be blunt, I was drunk or high a lot of the time back then and it's a bit hazy. I don't even think I was attracted to Hank or even liked him all that much. He was a little short, had a square jaw, but he had a nice smile, I guess. Really, he just seemed to be *there* all the time.

Anyway, Hank and I had been out at the Rainbow and as we were walking, some of his friends were standing outside the Whisky, so we went in.

Karen: Graham nodded at me and pointed with his eyes to where she was on the floor. And then we saw Billy spot her, too.

Eddie: The whole time we were playing the Whisky back then, almost every night, Billy'd have some sort of note on how I was playing. He was such a control freak. But Daisy showing up, he couldn't control that.

And man, she looked good. She had on a tiny little dress. Girls didn't wear bras back then and it's a crying shame that ever ended.

Billy: What was I going to do? Not invite her to sing the song with me while she was standing right there? She forced my hand.

Graham: Billy said, into the mike, "Ladies and gentlemen, we have Daisy Jones here tonight. What do you all say we sing a song called 'Honeycomb' for you?"

DAISY: I walked up to the mike as Billy was facing the audience, and I thought, *Does Billy Dunne ever wear shirts that aren't denim?*

BILLY: She came on the stage barefoot and I just thought, *What is this girl doing? Put some shoes on.*

DAISY: The band all kicked in, and I stood at the mike, waiting. The first line is Billy's so I just watched the people in the crowd as he started singing. I watched the way they watched him. He was a real showman.

I don't know if he gets enough credit for that. People now talk about how good we were together but I've seen Billy when he's just on his own and that man is talented. He was born to be in front of a crowd.

BILLY: When Daisy's part came in, I turned and looked at her and watched her sing. We hadn't rehearsed it, we had never sung together. I was half-expecting it to be a disaster. But after a second or two, I just watched her.

She really did have a dynamite voice. She smiled almost the entire time she was singing. I think you can tell that, when you're listening. It comes through. That's something Daisy was great at. You could hear her smile in her words.

DAISY: I thought about changing the lyrics back, on the second reprise. I knew Billy hated the way I had changed it to the questions. But just before I was about to start singing those lines I thought, *I'm not here to make Billy like me. I'm here to do my job,* and I sang it the way it was on the track.

BILLY: I cringed as I heard her sing it.

KAREN: Daisy and Billy were standing right next to each other, singing into the same mike. And . . . the way Billy would watch her as she sang . . . The way she'd watch him . . . It was intense.

Daisy: We harmonized at the end together. It wasn't that way on the record. It just sort of happened that way.

Billy: I could tell, as we were singing it, that we had everybody. When the song finished, the crowd started screaming. I mean actually screaming.

Daisy: I just knew, at that show, that we had something special. Just knew it.

And it didn't matter how much of an asshole I thought Billy was. When you can sing like that with someone, there's a small part of you that feels connected to them. That sort of thing that gets under your skin and doesn't easily come out.

Billy was like a splinter. That's exactly what he was like.

On the heels of their thrilling performance at the Whisky, Runner announced that Daisy Jones would be the opening act on The Six's world tour, dubbed the Numbers Tour.

Billy appealed to Rod, Teddy, and Rich Palentino to change their minds and drop Daisy from the ticket, but he was finally forced to agree to the billing when Teddy showed him that ticket sales were climbing rapidly. Holdover dates were being added to the itinerary.

As the band and Daisy set out on tour, "Honeycomb" had just hit the Top 20.

BILLY: I wasn't focused on who was opening for us. I was focused on how to stay sober on the tour. It was my first time out on the road since rehab.

CAMILA: Billy was telling me how he was going to call me three times a day and keep a journal of everything he did and I explained to him that I didn't want him proving himself to me. That would just add more pressure, which was the last thing he needed. He needed to know that I believed in him. I said, "Tell me what I can do to make it easier, not harder."

BILLY: I decided to bring Camila and Julia out on the road with me. Camila was about two months pregnant with the twins by that point. We knew that, once she got further along, she wasn't going to be able to be there as much. But I wanted her there to start off on the right foot.

Daisy: I was excited to get out on the road. I'd never toured before. My album was doing all right. I was getting some good attention. And "Honeycomb" was helping my album sell a bit better, too.

Graham: We were all happy to have Daisy with us. Daisy could do the hang. Daisy was a cool chick.

We were in that period of time when you're doing radio spots and photo shoots and your song just keeps climbing higher and higher, selling better and better. I got recognized a few times. People had been recognizing Billy for a while but now they were starting to know me and Karen a bit, too. I'd be walking down the street and see somebody with a Six shirt on.

So I didn't care who they put me out on tour with as long as things kept going the way they were going.

Billy: We played our first show in Nashville at the Exit/In. And my attitude was to include Daisy as I would include anybody else that was opening for us. We were used to being the opening band and now we were the headliner. So I wanted to be as inclusive to her as other bands had been to us. Personal feelings aside.

Karen: We were all backstage before our first show, before Daisy's supposed to go out there. And Daisy's snorting a few lines. Warren's getting a massage from some groupie that somehow worked her way back with us. Eddie and Pete are doing whatever. Billy's off by himself. Graham and I are talking. I think it was that show . . . Graham had trimmed his beard and you could see how handsome he was underneath all that scruff.

And then there's a knock at the door and it's Camila and Julia. They had come to say good night to Billy.

The second Daisy sees Camila and Julia, she puts the dope in a drawer, cleans her nose, puts down her glass of brandy or whiskey or whatever she's drinking. It was the first time I saw any awareness from her. Like maybe she didn't live on another planet. She shook

Camila's hand and she waved at Julia. I remember she called her "chickadee."

And then it was time for Daisy to go on and she said, "Wish me luck!"

Everyone else was too busy doing their own thing to even pay attention but not Camila. She wished her luck and she was so sincere about it.

Camila: The first time I met Daisy Jones, I did not know what to think of her. She seemed really scattered but also very sweet. I knew Billy didn't like her, but I also didn't think his opinion meant I couldn't have my own.

But, I mean, undeniably gorgeous. Just as pretty, maybe even prettier, than in the magazines.

Daisy: I went out onstage first, opening up in Nashville, and I was nervous. I'm not normally a very nervous person but I could feel it in my body, my nerves. And I was maybe too coked up. I walked out onto that stage expecting to see all these people waiting for The Six. But a lot of the crowd was excited just to see me. They were there for me.

I was wearing a black halter dress and my gold bangles and my gold hoops.

Except for rehearsals, that was the first time I went onto a stage by myself, with just my backing band that Hank had put together. It was the first time I heard a crowd that big roar for me. All these people, coming together, looking and sounding like a living being. This booming, bellowing, living thing.

Once I felt that, I wanted to feel that all the time.

Graham: Daisy played a good show. She had a great voice, her songs weren't bad. She was somebody that could hold a crowd. And by the time we got out there, the audience was excited. They were already having a good time.

Warren: You could smell the grass in every corner of the place. Could barely see the back of the crowd through the smoke.

Karen: The moment we stepped foot onto the stage, you could tell the people that were there . . . it was a different group of people than our first tour. There were a lot more of them, for starters. The original fans were still there but now we had teenagers and parents, now we had a lot of women.

Billy: I stood there in front of that crowd, stone sober, feeling their excitement, knowing "Honeycomb" was heading for the Top 10. And I knew I had those people in the palm of my hand. I knew they *wanted* to like us. They *already* liked us. I didn't have to win them over. I stood on that stage and . . . we'd already won.

Eddie: We really pulled out the stops that night, put it all out there on the floor for 'em.

Billy: At the end of the show I said, "What do you all say I bring Daisy Jones back out here and we play 'Honeycomb' for ya?"

Daisy: The crowd went crazy. The whole place started rumbling.

Billy: I could feel my microphone vibrating as they screamed and stomped their feet and I thought, *Holy shit, we're rock stars.*

By the end of 1976, "Honeycomb" had peaked at number 3 on the Billboard Hot 100. *The band, along with Daisy, had performed the song on* Don Kirshner's Rock Concert *and* The Tonight Show Starring Johnny Carson. *They had finished up their North American tour dates and were gearing up for the short European leg of the tour. Camila Dunne, now six months pregnant, returned with Julia to Los Angeles.*

Billy: I couldn't make Camila and Julia stay out on the road with me indefinitely, I had to take control of it myself.

Camila: I knew him well enough to know when I needed to stay and when it was okay to go.

Billy: The first night without them was hard. I remember sitting on my suite balcony after the show, hearing all the chaos outside, wanting to be a part of it. There was this voice in my head saying, *You can't do this, you can't stay sober for much longer.*

I ended up calling Teddy. It was the early hours of the morning but it was only about dinnertime for him. I made up something to talk to him about. *[Laughs]* I think we ended up discussing whether he should marry Yasmine. He was worried he was too old for her. I told him to go for it anyway. And by the end of the call, I was feeling tired. I knew I could go right to sleep. Live to see another day. When we got off the phone Teddy said, "You feeling all right now, Billy?" And I said, "Yeah, I am."

After I had that first night under my belt, I felt a bit better. I stuck to my routine. I stayed away from the partying. When the show was over, I went back to my hotel room and I'd listen to some records or I'd go get a decaf coffee and read the paper at a diner. Sometimes Pete or Graham would join me. Although, most of the time, God knows Graham was just trailing after Karen somewhere.

But I just kept on like I'd been doing when Camila and Julia had been with me. Toeing the line.

Graham: It was the same when Camila was there as when she wasn't there. Billy was with the band when there was work to be done. And Daisy was with us when there was partying to be done. And never the two shall meet, or whatever it is they say.

Rod: Right before we were heading out to Sweden, I'd told Billy and Graham that Runner was considering extending their tour once the European leg was done. I asked them what they thought of tacking on a couple more weeks once they got back to the States.

It was a nonstarter. Camila was due around when we'd be getting back. Billy felt like he was cutting it close as it was.

Graham: It was a two-second conversation. Would I have liked to have continued the tour? Of course. Did it put us in a tough spot that Billy had to go home? Yeah. But he had to go home. End of discussion.

Warren: All of us wanted to do more dates but we couldn't perform without Billy. You can plug in some guitarists for a few shows, a keyboardist. But you can't replace Billy.

Daisy: We were doing sold-out shows. And a lot of that was my doing.

Meanwhile, the band's album was selling a lot more than mine. Theirs was better than mine, so it made sense, but when it came to the live show, a lot of people really were coming to see me. And even some of the ones that didn't care who I was before they got there left with a Daisy Jones T-shirt.

I had real buzz. And I'd been working on some good songs of my own. I had one—super simple melody, not very complex—but it was good. It was called "When You Fly Low." I'd written it about selling yourself short, how some people try to keep you small. "They want you humble/want to atrophy that muscle/want to stunt the hustle/get you to call uncle/to keep you flying low."

I'd been saying to Hank that it was time to talk to Teddy about a new album. And Hank kept saying that I should slow down. I got the impression that he thought I was asking too much. Like I thought I deserved more than I did.

Our relationship was not in a good place. I should never have been with a guy like that.

That's one thing they don't mention when they tell you to stay away from drugs. They don't say, "Drugs will have you sleeping with some real jerks." But they should.

And I had let Hank into every part of my life: He often stood between me and Teddy, he was the one who hired my entire band, my money was funneling through him. And he was in my bed.

Karen: When we were heading out to Stockholm, we went out on Runner's private jet.

Daisy: Hank and some of the crew had flown out the day before but I waited and hitched a ride with the band. I made it seem like I wanted to hang out with them on the plane but I just didn't want to fly over with Hank.

Eddie: It was on the flight out that I overheard Graham talking to Karen about turning down the extension. Man, that was the first I'd heard of it. No one had told me or Pete.

We had a hit song, we were selling out shows with Daisy. Lots of people making a lot of money. The band, the roadies, everybody working on our tour and at the venues—we all have to pack it in because Billy got his wife pregnant?

And it's not even put up to a vote. We have to find out about it after the decision has already been made.

KAREN: That was an interesting flight. I think that was the flight Warren got slapped by the stewardess. I only heard the slap, I didn't see it.

WARREN: I asked her if she was a natural blonde. Lesson learned. Not all women think that's funny.

KAREN: Daisy and I were in the back minding our business the majority of that flight. We had these two chairs facing each other, a couple of cocktails, looking out the window. I remember Daisy pulled out a pillbox and knocked back two pills, washed 'em down with a sip of her drink.

She'd started wearing all of those bangles by then, as many as would fit on her arms. Everything clinked when she moved. So as Daisy is putting her pillbox back in her pocket, her bangles start clanging and I made a joke about how they were built-in tambourines. And she thought that was cool. She took a pen and wrote it down on her hand.

And then when she put the pen away, she took out the pillbox again and took two pills from it and put them in her mouth.

I said, "Daisy, you just took two."

She said, "I did?"

I said, "Yeah."

She just shrugged and swallowed them.

I said, "C'mon, don't be one of those people."

DAISY: I was irritated by that. I shoved the pillbox in her hand. I said, "Take them if you're so worried about it. I don't even need them."

Karen: She threw the pills at me.

Daisy: But the moment I handed the pillbox over to her and I saw her put it in her back pocket, I started panicking. The dexies were one thing. That was fine. I could snort coke if I needed to.

But I could not sleep without the Seconals.

Karen: It surprised me how easy it was for her. To just hand it all over and stop.

Daisy: When we got to the hotel, Hank was already in my room. I said, "I ran out of reds." He just nodded and picked up the phone. By the time I wanted to go to sleep, I had another bottle in my hand. It depressed me, how easy it was. Don't get me wrong, I wanted the pills. I needed the pills. But it was just so boring, so repetitive. Having any narcotic I needed at any time, nobody really stopping me.

As I fell asleep that night—I think I was still holding a brandy glass—I heard myself say, "Hank, I don't want to be with you anymore." At first I thought there was another woman in the room, saying those words, but then I realized I was saying them. Hank told me to go to sleep. And I didn't so much fall asleep as feel like I was disappearing.

When I woke up in the morning, I remembered what had happened. I felt embarrassed but also sort of relieved, to have actually verbalized it. I said to Hank, "We should talk about what I said last night."

And he said, "You didn't say anything last night."

I said, "I told you I didn't want to be with you."

He just shrugged and said, "Yeah, but you say that all the time when you're falling asleep."

I'd had no idea.

Graham: It was pretty clear to everybody that Daisy needed to drop Hank.

Rod: There are a lot of slimy managers out there and they make the rest of us look bad. Hank was taking advantage of Daisy, clear as day. Somebody needed to be looking out for her.

I said, "Daisy, if you need help, I'm here."

Graham: I think Daisy saw what Rod was doing for us—the way he made sure everything was taken care of. Rod was the first guy to tell anybody that we were going to rule the world. He wasn't telling us to be happy with what we had and to keep our mouth shut. And, not to be a jerk but . . . he wasn't sleeping with us and keeping us high as fuck so we didn't know heads from tails.

I told Daisy, "Leave Hank and team up with Rod. He's got you covered."

Rod: I was already doing so much for Daisy anyway. I'd hooked up *Rolling Stone* to see the show. They were sending Jonah Berg out to come watch the set and then hang out afterward. It was a potential cover. I'd made a point of including Daisy in that. I didn't have to. I could have pushed for it to be just a story on the band but I figured what's good for the goose is good for the gander.

Karen: The day that Jonah Berg was coming, we were in Glasgow.

Daisy: I was stupid. I picked a fight with Hank right after sound check that day.

Karen: Graham had come over to my room that afternoon to bring me one of my suitcases. Somehow my things had ended up with his stuff. He was standing in the hotel hallway, at my door, holding a duffel bag of my bras and underwear. He said, "I believe this is yours."

I grabbed it from him and rolled my eyes at him. I said, "Oh, I bet you just love having your hands on my panties." I was just joking around.

But he shook his head and he said, "If I get my hands on those panties, I want to have earned it the old-fashioned way."

I laughed and said, "Get out of here."

And he said, "Yes, ma'am."

And he walked back to his room. But when I shut the door, I . . . I don't know.

Daisy: I broke it to Hank when it was just the two of us in my hotel room. He was putting his arms around me and I was done with it. I kept snapping at him and he asked me what my problem was and I said, "I think it's time we part ways." Hank tried to ignore me a few times, kept telling me I didn't know what I was saying. So I said it really clear. "Hank, you're fired. You should leave." Well, he heard it that time.

Graham: Billy and I were planning on going out to grab a bite—I'd bet him he wouldn't eat haggis.

Daisy: Hank got in my face. He was so angry and he was standing so close to me that as he spoke, his spit landed on my shoulder. He said, "You'd still just be screwing rock stars if I hadn't found you."

When I didn't say anything back to him, Hank cornered me, up against the wall. I didn't know what he was going to do. I'm not sure *he* knew what he was going to do.

When you're in a situation like that, when you have a man looming over you, it's as if every decision you made to lead to that moment—alone with a man you don't trust—flashes before your eyes.

Something tells me men don't do that same thing. When they are standing there, threatening a woman, I doubt they count every wrong step they made to become the asshole they are. But they should.

My body was stick straight—I felt sort of shockingly sober—and I put my arms out in front of me, holding on to whatever space I could try to defend. Hank was staring right into my eyes. I don't know if I was even breathing. And then Hank punched the wall and walked out of the room, slamming the door on his way out.

After he left, I triple-locked the door behind him. He yelled something in the hall but I couldn't make it out. I just sat on the bed. He never came back.

Billy: I was walking out of my room to go meet Graham when I saw Hank Allen coming out of Daisy's room muttering, "That fucking bitch." But he seemed to be calming down so I was thinking I should let it go. Then I saw him stop and turn, like he was going to go back into Daisy's room. I could tell he was trouble right then. You can see it in somebody's gait, you know? Hands balled up into fists and jaw tight and all that. I caught his eye and he saw me. We looked at each other for a moment. I shook my head, to say, *That would be the wrong move*. He kept looking at me. And then he looked down at the ground and walked out.

When he was gone, I knocked on Daisy's door. I said, "It's Billy."

It took a moment but she opened the door. She was wearing a navy dress—that kind where the sleeves are off the shoulders. I knew people always talked about how blue Daisy's eyes were but that day was the first time I really noticed them. They were so blue. You know what they looked like? They looked like the middle of the ocean. Not the shoreline, not that light blue. They looked like the dark blue of the middle of the ocean. Like deep water.

I said, "Are you okay?"

She looked sad, which I'd never really seen before. And she said, "Yeah, thank you."

I said, "If you need to talk . . ." I wasn't sure how I could really help but I figured I should offer all the same.

She said, "No, that's all right."

Daisy: I didn't realize just how much of a wall Billy put up around himself when he was near me until that moment, when suddenly there was no wall. Like how you don't register you're hearing the hum of a car engine until it's turned off.

But I looked him in the eye then and I saw the real Billy.

I realized I'd been looking at this guarded, cold version of him the whole time up until then. I thought, *It might be nice to know this Billy.* But then it was over. Just one second of realness from him and then, poof, gone the way it came.

GRAHAM: I was waiting for Billy when my phone rang.

KAREN: I don't know why it was that day that I decided to do it.

GRAHAM: I said, "Hi."

And Karen just said, "Hi."

KAREN: We were sort of quiet on the phone for a second. And then I said, "How come you've never made a move on me?"

I could hear him drinking a beer. I could hear him take a sip. He said, "I don't take shots I know I'll miss."

It was out of my mouth before I'd decided to say it. I said, "I don't think you'll miss, Dunne."

And then as soon as I said it, there was a dial tone.

GRAHAM: I have never run anywhere faster than down that hall to her room.

KAREN: Three seconds later—that's not an exaggeration—there's a knock on my door. I opened it and Graham was out of breath. A tiny run down the hall and he was out of breath.

GRAHAM: I looked right at her. She was so gorgeous. Those thick eyebrows. I'm a sucker for a girl with thick eyebrows. I said, "What are you saying to me?"

Karen: I said, "Just go for it, Graham."

Graham: I stepped right into her room, I shut the door behind me, and I grabbed that woman and kissed her good.

You don't usually wake up in the morning and think, *This is going to be one of the most exciting days of my life.* But that day was. That day with Karen . . . that was one of them.

Warren: Here's something I've never told anyone. No, this is good. You're gonna like this.

When we were doing our show in Glasgow, sometime after sound check, I'm taking one of my beer naps—which is what I would call having a beer and taking a nap—and I wake up because Karen is having sex with somebody in the next room! I can't even sleep it's so loud.

I never found out who it was but I did see her being a little flirty with our lighting tech so, anyway, I think Karen had a thing with Bones.

Billy: After I left Daisy, I tried to find Graham for lunch but he wasn't anywhere.

Graham: When it was time to leave to get down to the venue, Karen made me sneak out her door, go to my room, change, and then meet her at the elevators.

Karen: I didn't want anyone to know anything.

Billy: By the time we all got backstage, everybody was running around like chickens with their heads cut off because Daisy's band was nowhere to be found.

Eddie: Apparently, Hank went down to the Apollo on his way out of town and took all five of Daisy's band members out with him. They just up and left.

Karen: It was such a low blow.

Graham: Nothing was supposed to come before the music. Our job was to go out there and play for the audience. No matter what personal shit was going on.

Daisy: My band had walked out. Just walked out. I didn't know what to do.

Hank Allen *(former manager, Daisy Jones)*: All I care to say is that Daisy Jones and I had a strictly professional relationship from 1974 to 1977, which was mutually terminated due to differences of opinion regarding the trajectory of her career. I continue to wish her the best.

Billy: I find Rod and he's already in damage control mode. I said to him, "Is it really that bad if Daisy doesn't play one night?"

And then I realized, as I said that, that he was probably her manager now. And so, you know, to him . . . yeah, it was.

Rod: Jonah Berg was in the audience. From *Rolling Stone*.

Karen: Everybody was trying to figure out what to do. But Graham is trying to catch my eye every second no one's looking. I was laughing to myself thinking, *We are supposed to be trying to solve a problem here.*

Graham: I couldn't stop looking at Karen.

Karen: Graham was always the guy I would talk to about stuff. And that night I found myself wanting to tell him about this great afternoon I'd had. It was like I wanted to talk to him about him.

Daisy: I said to Rod, "Maybe I should go out there on my own." I didn't want to give up. I wanted to do *something*.

Eddie: Rod had suggested that Graham go out there with Daisy and the two of them do a few acoustic versions of some of the songs from her album. But Graham wasn't really paying attention. I said, "I can do it."

Rod: I sent Daisy and Eddie out there with no idea what was going to happen and the whole time I'm watching them walk out to the mike like a cat on hot bricks.

Daisy: Eddie and I did a few songs. Really pared down. Just his guitar and me singing. I think we did "One Fine Day" and "Until You're Home." It was fine but we did not blow anybody away. And I knew *Rolling Stone* was out there and I needed to make a good impression. So on the last song, I decided to go off script.

Eddie: Daisy leaned over to me and she gave me this vague beat and a key and told me to come up with something. That was it. Just "Come up with something." I did my best, you know what I mean? You can't exactly make up a song on the fly like that.

Daisy: I was trying to get Eddie to play something I could sing my new song to. I wanted to sing "When You Fly Low." He started and I sang a few bars, tried to get into a rhythm with him, but it wasn't working. I finally said, "Okay, forget that." I said it right in the mike. The audience was laughing with me. They were rooting for me. I could feel it. So I started singing it a cappella. Just me and my voice, singing this song I'd written.

I'd worked hard on it, I'd polished it up from beginning to end. There wasn't a stray word in the whole thing. And it was just me and my tambourine with the stomp of my feet.

Eddie: I was there behind her, tapping a beat out on the body of the guitar for her, helping her out. The crowd was into it. They were watching our every move.

Daisy: It was such a rush, singing like that. Singing a song that I felt in my heart. Words that I had written that were all mine.

I watched the people at the front of the crowd listening to me, hearing me. These people from a different country, people I'd never met in my life, I felt connected to them in a way that I hadn't felt connected to anyone before.

It is what I have always loved about music. Not the sounds or the crowds or the good times as much as the words—the emotions, and the stories, the truth—that you can let flow right out of your mouth.

Music can *dig,* you know? It can take a shovel to your chest and just start digging until it hits something. That night, singing that, just reaffirmed that I wanted to put out an album of my own songs.

Billy: I was standing backstage watching Daisy and Eddie when she started singing "When You Fly Low." She was good. Better than . . . Better than I'd realized.

Karen: Billy was staring at her.

Daisy: When I was done, the audience was hooting and hollering and I felt like I'd gone out there and done the very best with what I had. I felt like I'd really turned it around and put on a good show for them.

Billy: After she finished the song, I heard her saying goodbye to the audience and I thought, *We could do "Honeycomb" now. Just me and her.*

Graham: I was surprised to see Billy going out there.

Daisy: I used my usual line, "That's it for me tonight! It's time for The Six! Everybody get your hands together." But in the middle of me talking, Billy walked out onto the stage.

Billy really shined onstage. Some people, you bathe them in

those lights and they disappear. But some people, they glow. Billy was like that. I mean, offstage, no. Offstage, he was sullen and sober and he barely had any sense of humor that I could see. At that point, I thought he was sort of a bore, to be honest with you.

But onstage he looked like there was no place he'd rather be than standing right there with you.

Eddie: I was sitting there with the guitar and Billy comes up to me. I said, "What do you want me to play?"

But instead, Billy put his hand out, asking for my guitar. I'm the fucking guitarist. And he's trying to take my guitar.

He said, "Can I borrow it, man?"

I wanted to say, "No, you cannot borrow it." But what could I do? I'm standing up in front of thousands of people. I handed it over and Billy took it and walked right up to the mike with Daisy. I'm standing there with my dick in my hand, no reason to be on the stage. I had to slink off.

Billy: I waved to the crowd and said, "How about this Daisy Jones, everybody?" And the audience cheered. "Do you all mind if I ask Daisy a question?" I put my hand on the mike and I said, "How about 'Honeycomb' now? Just me and you?"

Daisy: I said, "All right, let's do it." There was only one mike out there. So Billy stood right next to me. He smelled like Old Spice and his breath smelled like cigarettes and Binaca.

Billy: I started playing it acoustic.

Daisy: It was a bit slower than we normally played the song. It gave it a tender feel. And then he started singing, "One day things will quiet down/we'll pick it all up and move town/we'll walk through the switchgrass down to the rocks/and the kids will come around."

Billy: And Daisy sang, "Oh, honey, I can wait/to call that home/ I can wait for the blooms and the honeycomb."

Karen: You know how sometimes people will describe other people and say they make you feel like you're the only one in the room? Billy and Daisy could both do that. But they somehow did it with each other. They each seemed like they thought the other one was the only person in the room. Like we were watching two people who didn't realize thousands of people were watching them.

Daisy: Billy was a great guitar player. There was an intricacy, a delicateness when he played.

Billy: At that slower tempo, the song started to seem even more intimate. It was gentler, softer. And I was sort of taken aback, in that moment, that Daisy could so easily go where I was taking us. If I played slower, she could bring a warmth to it. If I played faster, she'd bring the energy. She was so *easy* to be good with.

Daisy: When we finished, he put the guitar in one hand and he grabbed my hand with the other. All the skin on the soft side of his fingers was callused. Just by touching you, he'd scrape you.

Billy: Daisy and I waved to the audience and they cheered and whooped and hollered.

Daisy: And then Billy said, "All right, ladies and gentlemen, we are The Six!" And the rest of the band came out onstage and went right into "Hold Your Breath."

Eddie: I came back out onto that stage and my guitar is sitting on the side there and I have to go and pick it up. And that chapped my ass. It's not enough he tells me how to do my job, he controls when we can go on tour, now he's taking my goddamn instrument from me and taking my place onstage. And he can't even bother to hand it back to me when I get back up there? Do you understand where I'm coming from?

Daisy: As they were all walking out, I whispered into Billy's ear. "Should I leave?" And he shook his head no. So I joined in, started harmonizing when I could, banging my tambourine. It was such a fun show being up there with them the whole time.

Billy: I don't remember why Daisy stayed that night. I think I assumed she'd leave but when she didn't, I thought, *All right, then. I guess she's staying*. I mean, the whole night was a fly-by-the-seat-of-your-pants kind of deal.

Warren: I swear to you, Karen had this "I just got laid" vibe to her all night. And I was convinced Bones was lighting her special.

Billy: I leaned over to Eddie, between one of the songs, and I was going to thank him for earlier but he wouldn't even look at me. I couldn't get his eye.

Eddie: I was so over Billy's nice-guy routine. He was an asshole. A complete and utter selfish prick. Sorry to say it but that's how I saw it. To be honest, I still see it that way now.

Billy: I finally tapped Eddie on the shoulder, right before the finale, I said, "Thanks, man. I just wanted to really give 'em a good show since *Rolling Stone* is out there."

Eddie: He said he'd normally let me play but since it was *Rolling Stone,* he wanted to really do it right.

Graham: Pete gave me a look between sets and I was trying to figure out what the problem was. He finally nodded toward Eddie.

Look, I got it. With Billy, it was easy to feel like a second-class citizen. But how we all feel about it doesn't change the fact that people were paying money to see Billy. People liked his songs, the way he wrote them. They liked watching him up there. Billy was right to go out onto that stage and take Eddie's guitar. It wasn't respectful, necessarily. It certainly wasn't flattering or nice. But it made for a better show.

The band was a meritocracy for the most part. Even though it functioned like a dictatorship. Billy wasn't in charge because he was a jerk, he was in charge because he had the most talent.

I had told Eddie before. . . . It's a losing battle if you're going to try to compete with Billy. That's why I don't. Eddie didn't get that.

Karen: We ended the show by playing "Around to You" with Daisy harmonizing with Billy for the whole song. We hadn't done a pure vocal harmony song before. It sounded good.

It seemed like Daisy and Billy had a sort of unspoken language, they could pick up stuff quick with each other.

Billy: When we ended that song, I thought that was the best show we'd ever played. I turned back to the band and I said, "Great job, everybody."

Warren: Eddie got really heated and he snapped. "So happy to please you, boss."

Billy: I should have read the situation and just backed away. But I didn't. I don't know what I said but clearly, whatever it was, I shouldn't have said it.

Eddie: Billy got up close to me and said, "Don't be a dick to me just because you're having a bad night." And that was it for me. You know why? Because I'd had a *great* night. I played *great* that night.

So fuck him. And that's what I said, I said, "Fuck you, man."

And Billy said, "Take it down a notch, all right?"

BILLY: I probably told him to calm down or something.

EDDIE: Just because something doesn't matter to Billy, doesn't mean it doesn't matter to me. And I was real sick and tired of people expecting me to feel exactly Billy's way about something.

BILLY: I looked out to the crowd, thinking nothing was going on. And I said, "Thanks, everybody! We're The Six!"

KAREN: Right before the lights went out, I looked over at Eddie and I saw him lift the guitar off his shoulders and I could just tell.

DAISY: Eddie took his guitar and lifted it into the air.

GRAHAM: It just came smashing down.

EDDIE: I smashed my guitar and walked off. I instantly regretted it. It was a 'sixty-eight Les Paul.

WARREN: The neck broke off of it and Eddie just swung it and let it land on the ground and he walked off. I thought about kicking my snare just to join the fun but it was a Ludwig. You don't go kicking a Ludwig.

ROD: When they came off the stage, I was of two minds. On the one hand, they had just put on a crack fire show. On the other hand, I was afraid Eddie might slug Billy if given the chance. And Jonah Berg was about to come backstage.

So when I saw Eddie, I pulled him aside and gave him a glass of water and told him to take five.

EDDIE: Rod tried to get me to back off. I said, "You get Billy to back off."

ROD: You know, some days, you're just trying to get your job done. And musicians can make that a lot of fun or a real drag.

Billy came off the stage as everybody else trickled down. I said to him, "Don't start, all right? Just put it behind you. Jonah Berg's coming back here any second and you need to keep the good show going."

Daisy: It was a great show. A great show. I felt like dynamite after that show.

Jonah Berg (*rock journalist,* Rolling Stone, *1971–1983*): When I first came back and met the band after the Glasgow show, I was surprised at the level of camaraderie. They were out there, rocking out, smashing guitars. But backstage, everything seemed really calm. They seemed completely normal. Which is weird for rock stars.

But The Six was never what you expect.

Karen: It was so much pretending.

Billy and Daisy are pretending they normally hang out after shows, which they had never done. Eddie's pretending he doesn't hate Billy's guts. I mean, obviously, we were *all* preoccupied with other things that night and we all just had to put it aside to show Jonah Berg a good time.

Billy: Jonah was a cool guy. Kind of a shaggy look to him. We were hanging out for a few minutes backstage and I offered him a beer. I had a Coke.

He said, "You're not drinking?"

I said, "Not tonight."

I didn't want my personal life to be any journalist's business. I was very protective of that. Of what I'd put my family through. No need to air any of that type of dirty laundry.

Warren: Somehow we all ended up at a piano bar a few blocks away. It was the first time that all of us went out together. The six of us and Daisy, too.

Daisy was wearing this coat over her shorts and shirt. The coat was longer than her shorts and it had real deep pockets. And when we got into the bar, she pulled a few pills out of those deep pockets and threw 'em back with the beer.

I said, "What you got there?"

Jonah was up at the bar, ordering drinks.

Daisy said, "Don't tell anybody. I don't wanna hear about it from Karen. She thinks I quit."

I said, "I'm not asking so I can rat on you. I'm asking so I can have one."

Daisy smiled and handed me another one from her pocket. She put it in my hand and it had lint on it. They were just loose pills in her pockets. She had pills in all her pockets back then.

Billy: I'm sitting down with Jonah and he's asking me questions about how we got started and what's next for us and all that.

Jonah Berg: When you're interviewing a band, you're interested in talking to everybody. Because a good story can come from anyone. But you're also keenly aware that it's people like Billy and Daisy—maybe Graham, Karen—that the readership is interested in.

Eddie: Of course, Billy corners Jonah. Hogs his attention. Pete kept telling me to light a doobie and chill out.

Karen: When everybody else was over talking to the guy at the piano, I pulled Graham into the ladies' bathroom.

Graham: I'm not about to go telling who did what where in public.

Billy: I was surprised to find myself having a good time. I mean, I knew Eddie hated my guts but the rest of us were getting along well and it was fun, being out again. And we'd just played this great show.

Daisy: Some of my best nights back then were the nights I hit the dope just right. Perfect amount of coke, perfect timing on the pills, with just enough champagne to keep me bubbly.

Karen: After Graham and I rejoined the party, I sat down with Daisy and split a bottle of wine. Or maybe it was that we each had our own bottle?

Billy: One thing led to another.

Jonah Berg: I think it was me who suggested they play something.

Daisy: I ended up on top of the piano belting out "Mustang Sally."

Graham: You have not seen anything until you've seen Daisy Jones dancing on a piano in a fur coat with no shoes on singing "Mustang Sally."

Billy: I don't remember how I ended up on the piano.

Warren: Daisy pulled Billy onto the piano.

Billy: The next thing I know, I'm singing with her.

Karen: Would Billy have agreed to get on top of a piano with Daisy Jones if Jonah Berg wasn't there? *[Shrugs]*

Eddie: This was not a cool bar. Most places by that point, if you sang a few bars of "Honeycomb," you'd get a "Oh man! That's you?" These guys had no idea.

Karen: When the song was over, Billy went to get down off the piano and Daisy grabbed his hand, held him up there. I said to the piano player, "Do you know 'Jackie Wilson Said'?" When he shook his head, I said, "May I?"

He got up and let me sit down and I started playing.

Graham: Daisy and Billy just nailed it. The whole place was excited, dancing and singing along. Even the guy Karen had kicked off the piano was singing the chorus with them. "Dang a lang a lang," you know that whole thing.

Jonah Berg: They were magnetic. That's the only word for it. *Magnetic.*

Billy: When the bar started to close, Daisy and I got down off the piano and this guy said to us, "You know, you two should take your thing on the road."

Daisy and I looked at each other and laughed. I said, "That's a great idea. I'll think on it."

Karen: We all walked back to the hotel together.

Daisy: I was behind the rest of the group, putting my shoes on. And I thought I was alone until I saw that Billy hung back for me. He was standing there with his hands in his pockets, shoulders hunched, looking at me as I put my sandals on. He said, "I want to give the other guys time to talk to Jonah."

The two of us walked a bit slower behind the rest of them, talking about how much we both loved Van Morrison.

Billy: We got to the hotel lobby and said goodbye to Jonah.

Jonah Berg: I excused myself and went back to my hotel. I knew what I wanted to write about and I was eager to get started.

Karen: I told everybody I was going to bed.

Graham: I got off the elevator and acted like I was going to my room and then I went straight to Karen's.

Daisy: Billy and I walked back to our rooms, still talking.

Karen: I'd left the door open a crack for Graham.

Eddie: I was so glad to be rid of Jonah and not have to pretend I could stand Billy anymore. I smoked a bowl with Pete and went to bed.

Daisy: Billy and I were walking down the hall and as we got to my door I said, "Do you want to come in?"

I was just enjoying the conversation we were having. We were finally getting to know each other. But when I said it, Billy looked down at the floor and said, "I don't think that's a good idea."

When I shut the door behind me, alone in my room, I felt so stupid. It was so obvious that he thought I was hitting on him and that made me so sad.

Billy: When she took her key out of her pocket, she also took out a bag of coke. She was going into her room, and she was gonna, at the very least, have a bump. I . . . I didn't want to be around it.

I couldn't go into that room.

Daisy: I had thought for a moment that he and I could be friends, that Billy could see me as an equal. Instead, I was a woman he shouldn't be alone with.

Billy: I knew myself. And it just wasn't an option. So it all had to stop right there.

Daisy and I had just put on this great show together. And we'd had a great night together. She was a knockout. She really was. There was no denying it. Her eyes were big and her voice was gorgeous. Her legs were long. Her smile was . . . it was infectious. You'd see her smile and then you'd watch smiles open up on the faces of the people around her like a virus passing through.

She was fun to be around.

But she was . . . *[pauses]*

Look, Daisy was barefoot when it was cold, wearing jackets when it was hot, sweating no matter the temperature. She never thought before she spoke. She seemed sort of manic and half-delusional sometimes.

She was a drug addict. The type of addict that thinks that other people don't know she's using, which is maybe the worst type of addict of all.

There was no way—no matter what was happening, even if I wanted to—that I could let myself be around Daisy Jones.

Daisy: I didn't know why he insisted on rejecting me time and again.

Billy: When someone's presence gives you energy, when it riles up something in you—the way Daisy did for me—you can turn that energy into lust or love or hate.

I felt most comfortable hating her. It was my only choice.

Jonah Berg: From my vantage point, the biggest part of what made that band original and first-rate was the combination of Daisy and Billy. Daisy's solo album was nothing compared to what The Six was doing. And The Six without Daisy wasn't anything *near* what they were with her.

Daisy was an integral, necessary, inescapable part of The Six. She belonged in the band.

So that's what I wrote.

DAISY: Rod brought us the article before it came out and when I saw the headline I was so excited. I loved it.

JONAH BERG: I knew the headline before I even finished writing it. "The Six That Should Be Seven."

ROD: It was a great cover. A clear shot of all of them onstage together, Billy and Daisy singing into the same mike, Graham and Karen looking at each other. Everybody else really rocking out. In the foreground were about four or five people holding up lighters in the audience. And then there was the headline.

WARREN: We were on the cover of *Rolling Stone*. *Rolling* Goddamn *Stone*. I mean, you get jaded about a lot of things when you're ascending. But not that.

BILLY: I grabbed the paper from Rod.

GRAHAM: I don't think Billy was happy about it.

BILLY: "The Six That Should Be Seven."

ROD: I believe Billy's exact words were "Are you fucking kidding me?"

BILLY: I mean, *are you fucking kidding me?*

Daisy: I knew not to say a single thing about that article. None of us acknowledged it except Rod and I when no one else was around. Rod told me that if I wanted to officially join The Six, I should just hang tight and the opportunity might present itself.

Rod: Billy started to calm down after a few days. By the time we all got back on the plane to head to L.A., he was downright reasonable.

Billy: I wasn't trying to be . . . ignorant. I was aware of the fact that our biggest hit had been with Daisy. And Teddy had been floating the idea of another song or two with Daisy in the future. I knew that we were more mainstream, more marketable, with Daisy—obviously I was aware enough to see that. But I was taken by surprise at the idea of having her formally join the band. . . . And also that the suggestion was made so publicly.

Graham: The article was about how good we were with Daisy. Sure, it was *with Daisy* but I really felt like the takeaway was how *good we were*.

Eddie: By the time the article came out, the tour was over. The seven of us, Rod, the engineers, the roadies . . . we were all headed home.

Warren: We had to take a commercial flight, back to the States. I felt like a pauper.

Billy: I got out of my seat pretty soon after we took off. I walked over to Graham and Karen. I said, "What would it look like, do you think? Letting Daisy join the band?"

Karen: I thought the article was right. She was an honorary part of the group. Why not make it official? Why not have her on all our songs?

Graham: I told Billy to let her join.

Billy: They were no help.

Warren: At one point in the flight, Billy was sitting next to me making a list of pros and cons, you know, whether Daisy should join the band or not. And I see Karen coming out of the bathroom looking like somebody's balled her. All flushed and her hair messed up. So I turn around and who's mysteriously gone from his seat? Bones.

Eddie: I'm sitting in the back of the plane and I could see Graham getting up, Karen's walking around, Billy's talking to them. I'm watching, trying to figure out what the hell's going on. I turn to Daisy and I say, "What do you think they're doing up there?"

But she's got her nose in some book and she goes, "Shut up, I'm reading."

Warren: I looked over when Billy was writing his little list about whether Daisy should join the band, and he didn't have that many cons and it seemed like he was really searching his brain for some.

I said, "Make sure you write 'Gives you a hard-on you'd rather not have' in the cons section."

He told me I didn't know what I was talking about. I said, "All right, you don't want my opinion."

He said, "Yes, I do." And I looked at him and he said, "Fine, I don't."

So I sat back, sipped my Bloody Mary, and went back to reading the instructions on the barf bag.

Karen: Billy came back to where Graham and I were with this list. He'd slowly come to the conclusion that he wanted more hits and Daisy would bring us more hits.

I said, "You know, she might turn us down." That thought never occurred to Billy or Graham. But Daisy had more hype than even we did.

Graham: We decided we'd do one album with Daisy. See how it went.

Billy: I was making a decision that affected a lot of people. What is good for me might not necessarily be good for everybody else. I had to weigh that. Warren, Graham, Karen, Rod. They all wanted to get bigger, to top the charts. We all did. I had to take that into account.

No matter how much I may have preferred to keep a healthy distance from her personally.

Warren: I wasn't sure why Billy was stressing about it so much. He was just going to do whatever Teddy told him to do anyway.

Karen: People have said Billy didn't want Daisy to join the band because he didn't want to share the spotlight but I don't think that was the case. Billy wasn't really an insecure guy in that way. That was sort of the problem with him, really. Was that he *wasn't* intimidated by anyone else's talent.

I think she just . . . unsettled him. However you want to interpret that.

Billy: By the time we landed at LAX, I decided that it was a good idea to at least float the idea by Teddy. If he thought we should do an album with Daisy, then I'd ask her.

Rod: When we landed, I caught up to Billy and checked in, asked him what he was thinking. He said he wanted to talk to Teddy about whether Daisy should join the band. So I pulled Billy over to a pay phone and I called Teddy and I said, "Teddy, tell Billy what you told me this morning."

Graham: Of course Teddy was on board with Daisy joining the band!

Billy: Teddy reminded me that when we first met, I'd told him I wanted to be the biggest band in the world. He said, "You two singing together is how you do that."

Eddie: When we landed, Pete and I caught up with Warren and Graham and Karen and they said, "We're gonna ask Daisy to join the band," and I couldn't believe it.

Once again, No. One. Fucking. Asked. Me.

Daisy: They were all whispering and huddled up and I caught Rod's eye and he winked at me and I knew.

Billy: I got off the phone with Teddy and I said to Rod, "All right, tell her she's in." And then I got in a cab and went straight home to my girls.

Karen: When we all left the airport that day, we all headed in our own directions. It was like school was out for the summer.

Billy: The moment I walked in the door of my home, it was like Daisy and my band and the music and the gear and the tour . . . none of it existed. I was ready to get Camila strawberry ice cream at any hour of the night and to play any tea parties Julia wanted. My family was all that mattered.

Camila: Billy came home and he needed a day or two, to decompress. But then there he was. With us when he was with us. And happy. And I thought, *Wow. Okay. We're figuring this out. We're doing this right.*

Rod: I gave it a few days. I let the dust settle a little bit, made sure Billy wasn't going to change his mind. And then I called Daisy.

Daisy: I'd checked back in to my favorite cottage at the Marmont.

Simone: When Daisy got back from the road, I was back, too. And I think it is important to mention that after that tour, Daisy was jacked up. I mean, she was higher than all get-out, all the time. I thought, *What happened to you out there?* She could barely handle being alone. Always calling people to come over, always begging me not to get off the phone. She didn't like being home by herself. She didn't like things being calm.

Daisy: I was having a few people over when Rod called. It was the day I'd shot my *Cosmo* cover. I'd done an interview while we were in Europe and that afternoon I'd done the photo shoot.

Some of the girls from the shoot came over to my place afterward and we were drinking pink champagne and about to go for a swim when the phone rang. I picked it up and I said, "Lola La Cava speaking."

Rod: Daisy's pseudonym was always Lola La Cava. She had too many men trying to corner her. We had to start deflecting about where she was at any given time.

Daisy: I remember the phone call exactly. I had the bottle of champagne in my hand and there were two girls on the couch and another one doing a line off my vanity. I remember being irritated because she was getting coke in the spine of my journal.

But then Rod said, "It's official."

Rod: I said, "The band wants you to do a full album with them."

Daisy: I was through the roof.

Rod: I could hear Daisy doing a bump as I talked to her. I always struggled with that when it came to my musicians—and it never got easier. Should I monitor their drug use or not? Was it any of my business? If I knew they were using, was it my place to determine how much was too much? If it *was* my place, then how much *was* too much?

I never came up with an answer.

Daisy: When we got off the phone, I screamed into the room and one of the girls asked what I was so excited about and I said, "I'm joining The Six!"

None of them cared very much. In general, when you have drugs to spare and a nice cottage to do them in, you're probably not attracting people that care about *you*.

But I was so happy that night. I danced around the room for a bit. I opened another bottle of champagne. I had more people over. And then, around three in the morning, when the party died down, I was too amped to go to bed. I called Simone and I told her the news.

Simone: I did worry. I wasn't sure being on tour with a rock band was turning out to be good for her.

Daisy: I told Simone I was going to go pick her up and we were going to celebrate.

Simone: It was the middle of the night. I'd been sleeping. I had my hair wrapped, my sleep mask on. I wasn't going anywhere.

Daisy: She told me that she would come meet me in the morning for breakfast but I kept insisting. She finally told me I didn't sound safe to drive. I got mad and got off the phone.

Simone: I thought she was going to bed.

Daisy: I had too much energy running through me. I tried to call Karen but she didn't answer. I finally decided I had to tell my parents. For some reason, I thought they would be proud of me. Not sure why. After all, I had the number 3 song in the country just a few months prior and they hadn't so much as tracked me down to send a note. They didn't even know I was back in town.

Suffice it to say, heading to their house at 4:00 A.M. was not the smartest idea. But you don't get high for smart ideas.

Their place wasn't far—a mile down the road, a world away—so I decided to walk. I started up Sunset Boulevard and into the hills. I got to my parents' about an hour later.

So there I was, standing in front of my childhood home, and somehow I decided that my old room looked lonely. So I climbed over the fence and up the gutter pipe, smashed the window of my bedroom, and got in my own bed.

I woke up to see the cops standing over me.

Rod: I do wonder what I should have done differently with Daisy.

Daisy: My parents didn't even know it was me in the bed. They heard somebody and called the police. Once it was straightened out, they weren't going to press charges. But by that point, the bag of coke in my bra, the joints in my change purse—it didn't look good.

Simone: I got a call that morning from Daisy from jail. I bailed her out and I said, "Daisy, you gotta stop all this." And she just let it go in one ear and out the other.

Daisy: I wasn't in jail long.

Rod: I saw her a few days later and she had this cut on her right hand, from the outside edge of her pinkie all the way down past her wrist. I said, "What happened here?"

She looked at it like it was the first time she'd seen it. She said, "I have no idea." She started talking about something else. And then out of nowhere, about ten minutes later, she goes, "Oh! I bet it's from when I smashed the window to break into my parents' house."

I said, "Daisy, are you okay?"

She said, "Yeah, why?"

Billy: A few weeks after the tour ended, I woke up at four in the morning to Camila shaking my shoulders and telling me she was in labor. I grabbed Julia out of bed and raced Camila to the hospital.

When she was lying in that bed, sweating and screaming, I held her hand and I put a cold cloth on her head and I kissed her cheeks and I held her legs. Then we found out she had to have a C-section, and I stood right there—as close as they'd let me—and I held her hand as she went in and I told her she didn't need to be scared, that everything was going to be okay.

And then there they were. My twin girls. Susana and Maria. Squooshed little faces, heads full of hair. But I could instantly tell them apart.

I realized, looking at them . . . *[pauses]* I realized that I'd never seen a newborn. I'd never seen Julia as a brand-new baby girl.

I handed Maria over to Camila's mom for a moment and I went into the bathroom and I shut the door and I broke down. I . . . I needed some time to deal with my own shame.

But I did deal with it. I didn't try to bury it in something else. I went into that bathroom and I looked at myself in the mirror and I faced it.

Graham: Billy was a good father. Yes, he'd been a drug addict who missed the first few months of his daughter's life. And yeah, that's shameful. But he was fixing himself. For his kids. He was making it right and doing better every single day. It was a hell of a lot more than any man in our family had ever done.

He was sober, he put his kids first, he would and did do anything for his family. He was a good man.

I guess I'm saying . . . if you redeem yourself, then believe in your own redemption.

Billy: I had this moment there in the hospital, when it was just me, and Camila, and my three girls, and I thought, *What am I doing out on the road?*

I went on this long epic speech to Camila, I said, "I'm giving it all up, honey. I don't want anything but this family. The five of us. That's all I want or need." I really meant it. I probably went on for ten minutes. I said, "I don't need rock 'n' roll. I just need you."

And Camila—keep in mind she's just had a C-section—I will never forget it, she goes, "Oh, shut the hell up, Billy. I married a musician. You'll be a musician. If I wanted to drive a station wagon and have a meatloaf ready at six o'clock, I would have married my father."

Camila: Billy would sometimes make these grand proclamations. And they sounded good, because he's an artist. He knows how to paint a picture. But he was almost always on some flight of fancy. I'm the one that often had to say, "Yoo-hoo, hi, hello, come back down to the earth now, please."

Karen: Camila knew who Billy was better than he did. A lot of women would have said, "You've had your fun, but we've got three kids now." Camila loved Billy exactly as he was. I dug that about her so much.

And I really think Billy loved her the same way she loved him. I really do. When they were in the same place at the same time, you could tell he was just so taken with her. He'd stay quiet and let her be the one to talk. And I always noticed that he used to squeeze the lime into her drink before he handed it to her whenever we were all out somewhere. He'd take his own lime and squeeze it into her glass, too. He'd squeeze the two wedges in and then throw them in with the ice. It seemed like a beautiful thing to have, somebody giving you their lime wedge. I mean, I hate lime, actually. But you get the point.

Graham: Karen hated all citrus because she said it felt sticky on her teeth. That's why she hated soda, too.

Billy: Teddy came and visited us in the hospital. He brought this big bouquet for Camila and stuffed animals for the girls. As he was leaving, I walked him down to the elevators and he told me he was proud of me. He said I'd really turned it all around. I said, "I did it all for Camila."

And Teddy said, "I believe that."

Camila: When the twins were just a few weeks old, my mom had taken them for a walk one afternoon and Billy asked me to sit down. He said he'd written another song for me.

Billy: It was called "Aurora." Because Camila . . . she was my aurora. She was my new dawn, my daybreak, my sun peeking over the horizon. She was all of it.

It was just a piano melody at that point, but I had all the lyrics. So I sat down at the piano and played it for her.

Camila: The first time I heard it, I cried. I mean, you know the song. It would have been impossible for me to not feel bowled over by those words. He had written me others but . . . this one . . . I loved it and I felt loved listening to it.

And it was pretty, too. I would have loved that song even if it wasn't about me. It was that good.

Billy: She got teary and then she said, "You need Daisy on it. You know that."

And you know what? I did know that. Even as I was writing it, I had known it. I wrote it to be a piano and vocal harmony. Before we even got back into the studio, I was writing for Daisy.

Graham: That period of time when Billy was with his girls and Daisy was coming on board . . . well, it was a great opportunity for me to step up and take more of a center role in things. I was coordinating getting us all back together to start talking about a new album. I was discussing time lines with Rod and Teddy. It was fun.

Actually, it wasn't that fun, it was just that I was happy. Everything seems fun when you're happy.

Karen: The money was rolling in. I wanted to make smart decisions with it so I went out with a realtor for one day, and found a pad in Laurel Canyon and bought it.

Pretty soon, Graham unofficially moved in. We spent that spring and summer just the two of us together. We'd grill on the patio for dinner and go see shows every night and sleep late in the mornings.

Graham: Karen and I spent whole weekends high as shit, rich as hell, playing songs together, and not telling anybody where we were or what we were up to. It was our little secret. I didn't even tell Billy.

People say that life keeps moving, but they don't mention that it does stop sometimes, just for you. Just for you and your girl. The world stops spinning and just lets you two lie there. Feels like it, anyway. Sometimes. If you're lucky. Call me a romantic if you have to. Worse things to be.

Billy: I trusted Graham to handle everything with the band. I knew it was in good hands and my head was elsewhere.

Daisy: Simone left to make the rounds on another tour.

Simone: I was hitting the road for the *Superstar* album. And in between shows, I was going to be based more in New York than L.A. The disco scene was really about doing the Hustle at Studio 54. So that's where I was going.

Daisy: She seemed worried about me. I told her, "Go on. I'll see you soon." I was excited about everything I had in front of me. I was joining a band.

Graham: I had everything straightened out. I'd talked to Rod and Teddy. Billy said he was ready to get started. And I had come up with a date to reasonably deliver an album. So I called a meeting.

Warren: I was starting to live large from the money coming in. I'd bought my boat by then. I had a one-bedroom Gibson that I docked in Marina del Rey. Lots of cool chicks hanging out around there. Kept my drums at the house in Topanga and wasted away my nights and weekends drinking beers on the water.

Eddie: Pete had spent our downtime with Jenny back in Boston. They were getting really serious.

Me, I didn't like being home. I liked being on the road, you know what I mean? So I was ready to get back to work. I didn't even mind the idea of dealing with Billy that much. Now, that's saying something.

When Graham called to say it was time for us all to get together, I couldn't get there fast enough. I called up Pete and said, "You got to get on the first flight back out here. Vacation's over."

Daisy: We all met up at the Rainbow—the band, me, Rod, Teddy—and everybody was catching up. Warren was talking about his boat and Pete was talking about Jenny Manes and Billy was showing Rod pictures of his twins. Everyone was really getting along. I mean, even Eddie and Billy seemed like they were doing all right. And Rod got up and he had his beer in his hand and he gave a toast about me joining the band.

Rod: I think I said, "The seven of you are only headed higher and higher," or something like that.

Billy: I thought, *Boy, seven people in a band sounds like a lot.*

Daisy: Everyone was clapping and Karen hugged me and I felt really welcomed, I really did. So I stood up as everyone was talking and I picked up my brandy and I held it out for a toast and I said, "I am so glad you all invited me to join you on this album."

Graham: Daisy starts doing this little speech and at first I think it's nothing major.

Daisy: It was tough to get a read on Billy. He hadn't called me since I'd been offered a spot in the band. I hadn't heard much from anyone about how this was all going to go or how he was feeling about it. I just wanted to make sure everything was clear. I said, "I'm coming on board officially because I want to be a member of this team. An important member. I hope you all see this album as mine just as much as it's anybody's. Graham's or Warren's or Pete's and Eddie's or Karen's . . ."

Karen: "Or Billy's," she goes. I looked right to Billy to see his reaction. He was sipping a soda out of a beer stein.

Billy: I thought, *Why does she need to start trouble already?*

Daisy: I said, "You all brought me on because when we work together, we make better music than what we do apart. So I want a say in what music we're putting out. I want to write this album with you, Billy."

Teddy had told me I could write my second album and this felt like that chance. And I wanted to be clear out of the gate, that's what I was chasing. I wanted to stand up in front of a crowd, like I had that night singing "When You Fly Low" a cappella. I wanted to sing songs from my heart right to the people in front of me.

If The Six didn't want me for that, I didn't want whatever second prize they were offering.

GRAHAM: Daisy didn't want Billy throwing a temper tantrum every time she tried to contribute something of her own. She was laying down the law early. Probably the way the rest of us should have from the beginning. If we wanted any sort of meaningful say.

Certainly if Eddie had half of Daisy's balls, he would have solved his issues with Billy like that years ago.

BILLY: I said, "That's fine, Daisy. We're all in this together."

WARREN: I didn't bother getting riled up about it because what was the point? But Billy was acting like this was one big hippie commune where everyone had a say. And that was a lie.

KAREN: Billy did have a way of making you think you were crazy for even *thinking* things were unfair when, in fact, they were completely unfair. He wasn't even aware of the way everyone revolved around him.

ROD: The Chosen ones never know they are chosen. They think everyone gets a gold carpet rolled out for them.

GRAHAM: Pete chimed in at one point and said, "While this is all out on the table, I'm taking full control over my own bass lines from here on out."

Billy: I told Pete I was fine with him writing his bass lines. He'd been writing most of his bass lines for a while.

Karen: I said, "I'd like to step it up a bit. I think we can use me more often to round out songs. Maybe even do a song just keys and vocals."

Eddie: I wanted a say in what I was playing. Everyone's chiming in like Billy's trying to control them—and he did. But he was really controlling me. I said, "I write my own riffs from here on out."

Billy: I just kept thinking, *Of course Eddie's throwing a fit.* I started to say something and Teddy put his hand out, kind of gave me a look like *Don't talk right now. Just hear them out.*

Teddy and I both knew that some people needed to feel heard whether or not you actually listened to them.

Eddie: Look, I really liked Daisy. And I liked Karen, I wanted her to be able to contribute more. But a female vocalist on the whole album and *more* keys? Karen's keys were softening us too much as it was, if you asked me.

I said, "I want to make sure we're still a rock band."

Graham said, "What do you mean?"

I said, "I don't want to be in a pop band. This isn't Sonny & Cher over here." Billy bristled at that.

Billy: I was just getting shit on all night. I'm thinking, *What did I ever do to you people except take us this far?*

Graham: I thought Eddie's point was well made. How was our music going to change with Daisy coming in? Especially if she was writing. But, of course, Billy felt like it was just people attacking him.

When you have everything, someone else getting a little something feels like they're stealing from you.

Karen: Everything that was happening, it was all really undefined. Was Daisy a *permanent* part of The Six? I didn't know. I know Daisy didn't know. I don't even think Billy knew.

Daisy: I had been mulling this over for a while, of how the billing would work and what I felt I deserved.

I said, "If you all will commit to this and you want me to join as a member of The Six, then I'll be a member of The Six. My name doesn't need to be featured. But if it's temporary, then we need to discuss some other type of billing."

Graham: You could just tell that Daisy was expecting us to say she was a member of The Six.

Karen: Billy said, "How about The Six featuring Daisy Jones?"

Rod: That's how "Honeycomb" was billed. So I understood what Billy was trying to do.

Daisy: I thought, *Wow, okay, he didn't even give it a second thought.*

Billy: She gave me two options. If she didn't want me to have two options, she shouldn't have given two options.

Warren: I just thought, *Let the girl join the band, man.*

Rod: Teddy could see that things were headed in a tense direction. He had tried to keep quiet most of the discussion but he finally piped in and said, "You'll be Daisy Jones & The Six." And no one was happy but everyone was kind of equally dissatisfied.

Daisy: I think Teddy wanted to make sure my name was prominent. I brought attention to the band. My name needed to be front and center.

Billy: Teddy was trying to protect the sanctity of The Six. We didn't want to promise anything to Daisy.

Daisy: I don't think Billy actually resented anything I asked for. All of it was reasonable. He was just pissed because I knew how much power I had and he would have preferred I either not know it or not use it. I am sorry but that is not my style. I mean, it shouldn't be anybody's, really.

Billy had been riding a bit too comfortable on the fact that everybody let him do what he wanted. And I was the first person to say, "You're only in charge of me as much as I'm in charge of you." And that opened the floodgates for Pete and Eddie and, well, everybody.

Rod: Teddy told the band that Runner wanted the album toward the top of 'seventy-eight. It was already August. Creative differences and ego checks and all of that aside, it was back to the salt mines.

Karen: After we walked out of there that night, I thought, *Holy shit.* Daisy had just joined our band with top billing and fundamentally changed the dynamics of the group in a way that none of us had done before.

Billy: Everyone always acted like I was such a difficult guy. But Daisy asked for an equal say and billing and I gave her both. What more did she want?

I mean, I wasn't even sure it was the right thing to do. But I did it to keep her happy, to keep everybody happy.

Graham: We became a democracy instead of an autocracy. And democracy sounds like a great idea, but bands aren't countries.

Billy: To be honest, I thought Daisy'd get tired of trying to write an album pretty quickly. I underestimated her.

Let me tell you this. Don't ever doubt Daisy Jones.

AURORA

1977–1978

In August 1977, the seven members of the band entered Wally Heider's Studio 3 to begin the process of recording their third album.

Graham: Karen and I left her place that morning, heading over to Heider. I said to her, just as we walked out of the door, "Can't we just drive over together?"

She said she didn't want people thinking we were sleeping together.

I said, "But we are sleeping together."

She still made us take two cars.

Karen: You know how easy it is to screw up your entire life by sleeping with somebody in your own band?

Eddie: Pete and I drove over that morning. By that point, I think he and I were the only two still staying at the place in Topanga Canyon. Before he'd gotten back from the East Coast, I'd had the place all to myself.

I said to Pete on the way there, I said, "This should be interesting."

And he told me to not take it all so seriously. He said, "It's just rock 'n' roll. None of this really matters."

Daisy: When we all met up at the studio that first day, I brought this basket of cakes that someone had sent over to my place at the Marmont and my notebook full of songs. I was ready.

Eddie: Daisy showed up in a thin tank top and these tiny cutoff shorts. Barely covered anything.

Daisy: I run hot and I always have. I am not going to sit around sweating my ass off just so men can feel more comfortable. It's not my responsibility to not turn them on. It's their responsibility to not be an asshole.

Billy: I had written about ten or twelve songs so far. All of them in great shape. But I knew I couldn't go in there and tell them that I'd written the album already. Like I did with the other two albums. I couldn't say that.

Graham: It was kind of funny, to be honest. Watching Billy put on this act like he gave a shit what anyone else wanted on the album. God bless him. You could see the effort he was putting in. Talking all slow, thinking about his words.

Daisy: We were sitting around and I handed over my notebook. I said, "I've got a lot of good stuff in here to start from." I thought maybe everyone could read it all and we could discuss it from there.

Billy: Here I am, holding back my twelve great songs, so that no one thinks I'm trying to control things, and Daisy's just walking into a band she's brand new to, expecting everyone to read a whole journal of ideas.

Daisy: He didn't even flip through it.

Billy: If Daisy and I were going to write an album together, it needed to be just the two of us. You can't give seven people a say in the words. Somebody had to take charge and control the process.

So I said, "Look, I wrote this song 'Aurora.' It's the one I really believe in out of everything I'm working on for this album. The rest is up to us all. Daisy and I will write some songs and everyone will take a crack at the arrangements and once we've got a slate of great songs that we all love, we'll narrow it down to the best of the best."

Karen: Maybe it's revisionist history, but I think when Billy played "Aurora" it felt clear that we could build an album around it.

Graham: We were all on board with "Aurora" as a great place to start—it was a great frickin' song. After that, Daisy started talking about ideas for the album as a whole.

Warren: I wanted no part in writing. That morning felt like a waste of my time. Everyone's sitting around, talking about shit I don't care about. I finally just said, "Don't you all think that Daisy and Billy should go write the songs and come to us when they have them?"

Karen: Teddy was really decisive about it. He handed Billy the keys to his guesthouse and said, "You two pop on over to my place, set up in my guesthouse, and get to writing. Everyone else is going to get to work on this new one."

Eddie: Billy didn't want us composing anything for that song without him. But he also didn't want Daisy writing songs without him. So he had to choose whether he went with Daisy and got started writing or stayed with us and worked on the arrangement for his new song.

And he chose Daisy.

Billy: I got to Teddy's pool house first and so I got settled. Made myself a cup of coffee, sat down, looked through my notes trying to decide what to show Daisy.

Daisy: By the time I opened the door, Billy's already there, he's got his notebook out to show me. Not so much as a hello. Just "Here, read my stuff."

Billy: I told her the truth, I said, "I've got a lot of the album written already. Do you want to take a look at it and see where we can make adjustments together? See if maybe there's some gaps that we can fill in with some new stuff or the stuff you've written already?"

Daisy: I shouldn't have been surprised. It was never gonna be easy with him, was it? I think I grabbed one of the bottles of wine I saw on Teddy's counter and I opened it up and flopped myself down on the sofa and just started drinking it. I said, "Billy, that's great that you've written a bunch of songs already. I have, too. But we're writing this album together."

Billy: The woman is drinking warm white wine before it's even noon and trying to lecture me on how things should go. She hadn't even read my songs yet. I handed my work over to her and I said, "Read it first before you go telling me I should throw it away."

Daisy: I said, "Ditto then." And I shoved my notebook in his face. I could tell he didn't want to read it. But he knew he had to.

Billy: I read her stuff, and it wasn't bad, but I thought it wasn't The Six. She used so many biblical metaphors. So when she asked me what I thought, I told her that. I said, "We should start with my stuff as the backbone. We can refine it together."

Daisy was sitting on the sofa with her feet up on the coffee table, which irked me. And then she said, "I'm not singing an entire album about your wife, Billy."

Daisy: I really liked Camila. But "Señora" was about her. "Honeycomb" was about her. "Aurora" was about her. It was boring.

Billy: I said, "You're writing the same song, too. We both know every song in this book is about the same thing." Well, that got her upset. She put her hands on her hips and said, "What is that supposed to mean?"

And I said, "Every single one of these songs is about the pills in your pockets."

Daisy: Billy got this smug look on his face—Billy had this face that he would make when he thought he was smarter than everyone in the room. I swear, I have nightmares still about that goddamn face. I said to him, "You just think everybody's writing about dope 'cause you can't have any."

And he said, "You just go ahead and keep popping pills and writing songs about it. See where that gets you."

I tossed his pages at him. I said, "Sorry we all can't be sober and writing songs as interesting as wallpaper paste. Oh, here's a song about how much I love my wife. And another! And another!"

He tried to tell me I was wrong but I said, "This whole pack of songs is about Camila. You can't keep writing apology songs to your wife and making the band play them."

Billy: So out of line.

Daisy: I said, "Good for you for finding some other shit to be addicted to. But it's not my problem and it's not the band's problem and nobody wants to listen to it." You could see it on his face. That he knew I was right.

Billy: She thought she was brilliant because she'd realized that I'd replaced my addictions. Like I didn't already know that I clung to my love for my family to keep me sober. That just made me even more mad, that she thought she knew more about me than me.

I said, "You want to know your problem? You think you're a poet but other than talking about getting high, you don't have anything to say."

Daisy: Billy's one of those people who has a sharp tongue. He can build you up and he can take you down, too.

Billy: She said, "I don't need this shit." And she left.

Daisy: I started heading out to my car—getting more rip-roaring angry with every step I took. I had a cherry red Benz back then. I loved that car. Until I crashed it by accident by leaving it in neutral on a hill.

Anyway, that day with Billy, I was headed out to that Benz and I had my keys in my hand and I'm ready to get as far away from him as I can and I realize that if I leave, Billy would just write the album himself. And I turned right back around and I said, "Oh, no you don't, asshole."

Billy: I was really surprised that she came back.

Daisy: I walked right into the pool house and I sat down on the couch and I said, "I'm not giving up my chance to write a great album just because of you. So here's how it's gonna go. You hate my stuff, I hate your stuff. So we'll scrap it all, start from nothing."

Billy said, "I'm not letting go of 'Aurora.' It's going on the album."

I said, "Fine." And then I picked up one of his songs lying around where I'd thrown them and I shook it at him and I said, "But this shit isn't."

Billy: I think that was the first time I realized that there's . . . There is no one more passionate about the work than Daisy. Daisy cared more than anybody. She was ready to put her whole soul into it. Regardless of how difficult I tried to make it.

And I kept thinking about Teddy telling me she was how we were going to sell out stadiums. So I put out my hand and I said, "Fine." And we shook on it.

Daisy: Simone used to say that drugs make a person look old, but when I was shaking Billy's hand—his eyes were already wrinkling at the corners, his skin was freckled, he looked weathered, and he couldn't have been more than twenty-nine or thirty. I thought, *It's not drugs that make you look old, it's sobering up.*

Billy: It wasn't very easy, thinking about writing together when we'd said what we'd said to each other.

Daisy: I told Billy I wanted to get lunch before we did much of anything. I wasn't going to deal with the headache of trying to write with him before I had a burger. I told him I'd drive us to the Apple Pan.

Billy: I grabbed her keys just as she was about to get in her car and I told her I wasn't letting her drive anywhere. She was half in the bag already.

Daisy: I grabbed my keys back and told him if he wanted to drive, we could take his car.

Billy: We got into my Firebird and I said, "Let's go to El Carmen. It's closer."

And she said, "I'm going to the Apple Pan. You can go to El Carmen by yourself."

I just could not believe she was being so goddamn difficult.

Daisy: I used to care when men called me difficult. I really did. Then I stopped. This way is better.

Billy: On the way there, I turned on the radio. Immediately, Daisy changed the station. I changed it back. She changed it again. I said, "It's my car, for crying out loud."

She said, "Well, they're my ears."

I finally put in an 8-track of the Breeze. I put on their song "Tiny Love." Daisy started laughing.

I said, "What's so funny?"

She said, "You like this song?"

Why would I put on a song I didn't like?

Daisy: I said, "You don't know anything about this song!"

He said, "What are you talking about?" He knew it was Wyatt Stone that wrote it, obviously. But he didn't know the rest of it.

I said, "I dated Wyatt Stone. This is my song."

Billy: I said, "You're Tiny Love?" And Daisy started telling me this story about her and Wyatt and how she came up with those lines about "Big eyes, big soul/big heart, no control/but all she got to give is tiny love." I loved the chorus of that song. I had always loved it.

Daisy: Billy listened to me. The whole way to the restaurant, as he drove, he was listening. For what felt like the first time since I met him.

Billy: If I had a great line like that, and someone else pretended it was theirs, I'd be pretty angry.

She made more sense to me after that. And, to be honest, it was harder to tell myself she had no talent. Because she clearly did. It was a real reality check. That voice that whispers in the back of your head, *You have been acting like an asshole.*

Daisy: It made me laugh. That to Billy I needed a reason to want an equal say in the art I created. I said, "Cool, man. Now that you dig it, maybe you can stop being such a dickhead."

Billy: Daisy could really give you the grief you deserved. And if you took it in the spirit it was intended . . . she wasn't so bad.

Daisy: We sat down at the counter and I ordered for both of us and then put the menus away. I just wanted to put Billy in his place a little bit. I wanted him to have to deal with me being in charge.

But of course, he couldn't let it go, he said, "I was going to order the hickory burger, anyway." I think I've rolled my eyes about five thousand more times in my life just on account of Billy Dunne.

Billy: After we both ordered, I decided to try a little game. I said, "How about I ask you a question, you ask me a question? No one can dodge the answers."

Daisy: I told him I was an open book.

Billy: I said, "How many pills do you take a day?"

She looked around and fiddled with her straw. And then she turned to me and said, "No one can dodge the answer?"

And I said, "We have to be able to tell the truth to each other, to really be honest about ourselves. Otherwise, how can we ever write anything?"

Daisy: He was open to writing with me. That's what I took from that.

Billy: I asked the question again. "How many pills do you take a day?"

She looked down and then back up at me and she said, "I don't know."

I was skeptical but she put her hands up and said, "No, really. That's the truth. I don't know. I don't keep track."

I said, "Don't you think that's a problem?"

She said, "It's my turn, isn't it?"

Daisy: I said, "What makes Camila so great that you can't write anything that isn't about her?"

He was quiet for a really long time.

I said, "C'mon, now, you made me answer. You can't weasel out of it."

He said, "Would you wait a minute? I'm not trying to weasel out of anything. I'm trying to think about my answer."

After another minute or two, he said, "I don't think I am the person Camila believes I am. But I want to be that person so bad. And if I just stick with her, if I work every day to be the guy she sees, I've got the best chance at coming close to it."

Billy: Daisy looked at me and said, "Oh, for fuck's sake."

And I said, "What did I do to make you mad this time?"

And she said, "There's just as much to hate about you as there is to like about you. And that's annoying."

Daisy: Then he said, "It's my turn."

I said, "Out with it then."

Billy: "When are you going to quit the pills?"

Daisy: I said, "Why are you so obsessed with the goddamn pills?"

Billy: I told her the truth. I said, "My father was a drunk who was never there for Graham and me. I never wanted to be that way. And then the first thing I do, my first act as a father, was to get all messed up in all the shit you're messed up in—even heroin, too, I'm afraid—and I let my daughter down. Even missed her birth. I turned out to be exactly what I've always hated. If it wasn't for Camila, I think I'd still be that way. I think I would have made all my own nightmares come true. That's the kind of guy I am."

Daisy: I said, "It's like some of us are chasing after our nightmares the way other people chase dreams."

He said, "That's a song, right there."

Billy: It wasn't behind me. My addiction. I kept hoping it would feel like it was. Like I didn't need to keep looking over my shoulder all the time. But that doesn't really exist. At least not for me. It's a fight you keep fighting, some times are easier than others. Daisy made it harder. She just did.

Daisy: I was paying the price for the parts of himself that he didn't like.

Billy: She said, "If I was a teetotaler you'd like me more, huh?"

And I said, "I'd like to be around you more. Yeah, probably."

And Daisy said, "Well, you can just forget that. I don't change for anybody."

Daisy: I finished my burger and threw down some money and I got up to go. Billy said, "What are you doing?"

And I said, "We're going back to Teddy's. We're gonna write that song about chasing our nightmares."

Billy: I grabbed my keys and walked out after her.

Daisy: On the way back to Teddy's, Billy was singing me this melody he'd had in his head. We were at a red light and he was tapping the steering wheel and humming along.

Billy: I had a Bo Diddley beat I was thinking of. Something I wanted to try.

Daisy: He said, "Can you work with that?"

I said I could work with anything. So when we got back to the pool house, I started sketching some ideas out. And he did, too. After about a half hour, I had stuff to show him but he said he needed more time. I kept hanging around, waiting for him to be done.

Billy: She was pacing around me. She wanted to show me what she was writing. I finally had to say, "Will you get the fuck out of here?"

And I . . . on account of how rude I'd been to her in the past I realized I needed to be clear that I just meant it the same way I'd say it to Graham or Karen, you know? I said, "Please, will you get the fuck out of here? Go get a donut or something."

She said, "I ate a burger already." That's when I realized Daisy only ate one meal a day.

Daisy: I picked the lock to Teddy's house, borrowed his girlfriend Yasmine's bathing suit and a towel, and went for a swim. I was in there long enough to prune. And then I went back in, put the bathing suit in the wash, took a shower, and went back into the pool house and Billy was still sitting there, writing.

Billy: She told me what she did and I said, "That's weird, Daisy. That you borrowed Yasmine's bathing suit." And Daisy just shrugged.

She said, "Would you have rather I skinny-dipped?"

Daisy: I took his pages from him and I gave him mine.

Billy: She had a lot of imagery of darkness, running into darkness, chasing darkness.

Daisy: When it came to the structure of the verses, his were better than mine. But he didn't have a really fun chorus yet and I thought that I did. I showed him the part I'd written I liked the most and I sang it to him with his melody he'd given me. I could tell on his face, he knew it sounded good.

Billy: We went back and forth a lot on that song. Just hours of talking it out, playing with the melodies on the guitar.

Daisy: I don't think any of our original lines made it into the final version.

Billy: But when we sang it—when we worked out the lyrics and who should sing what, and refined the melody of the vocal and that interplay between those two things—we started singing it together and fine-tuning it. You know what? I'll tell you, it was a great little song.

Daisy: Teddy came in the door and he said, "What the hell are you two still doing here? It's almost midnight."

Billy: I did not realize how late it was.

Daisy: Teddy said, "Also, did you break into my house and use Yasmine's bathing suit?"

I said, "Yeah."

He said, "I'd love it if you didn't do that again."

Billy: I was going to leave then but I thought, *You know what, let's show Teddy what we've come up with.* So Teddy sat down on the couch and we sat across from him.

I was saying, "This isn't the final" and "We just came up with this." And all that.

Daisy: I said, "Stop, Billy. It's a good song. No disclaimers."

Billy: We played it for Teddy and when we were done, he said, "This is what you two come up with when you're on the same team?"

And we looked at each other and I said, "Uh, yeah?"

And he said, "Well, then, I'm a genius." He sat there laughing, real proud of himself.

Daisy: It was like we all agreed not to discuss that Billy needed Teddy's approval like a son needs his father's.

Billy: I left Teddy's that night and I rushed home because it was late and I was feeling guilty about it. I walked in the door and the kids were asleep and Camila was sitting in the rocking chair watching the

TV on low volume and she looked up at me. I started apologizing and she said, "You're sober, right?"

And I said, "Yeah, of course. I was just writing and I lost track of time."

And that was it. Camila didn't care that I hadn't called her. She just cared that I hadn't relapsed. That was all.

CAMILA: It's hard to explain, because I really do think it defies reason. But I knew him well enough to know that he could be trusted. And I knew that no matter what mistakes he made—no matter what mistakes I might make, too—that we would be fine.

I don't know if I would have believed in that type of security before I had it. Before I chose to give it to Billy. And by giving it to Billy, I gave it to myself, too. But saying to someone, "No matter what you do, we're not over . . ." I don't know. Something about that relaxed me.

BILLY: All those weeks that Daisy and I worked on songs together, I'd work as late as I needed. I'd stay out with Daisy as long as we needed. And every night when I came home, Camila was in that chair. She'd get up when I got home and I'd sit down and then she'd sit in my lap and put her head on my chest and say, "How was your day?"

I'd tell her the highlights and I'd hear about her day and I'd hear about the girls. And I'd rock us back and forth until we went to sleep.

One night, I picked her up out of the rocking chair and I put her in bed and I said, "You don't always have to wait up for me."

She was half-asleep but she said, "I want to. I like to."

And you know . . . no crowd cheering, no magazine cover ever made me feel even remotely as important as Camila. And I think the same goes for her. I really do. She liked having a man who wrote songs about her and carried her to bed.

GRAHAM: When Billy was off writing with Daisy, it was the first time that the rest of us could be composing on our own.

KAREN: "Aurora" was a great song with a great spine to it and we all had a lot of fun building it out.

Billy tended to want a more spartan keyboard. But I wanted to get into more atmospheric, lush sounds. So when we started working on "Aurora," I came in with those sustained roots and fifths. I kept some of the melodic chords broken up a bit, to keep it moving. But I was pedaling a lot of the bass notes. Shifted from staccato to legato.

And because the keys shifted, that meant Pete shifted the bass a bit. Now it's his bass that is keeping your foot tapping, the rhythm guitar is keeping you going.

EDDIE: I wanted to do something a little faster, a little more propulsive. I was really into the Kinks' new album. I wanted to move more in that direction. I thought Warren should hit harder on the drums, really using the drum and bass as counter-rhythms. Plus, I had this idea of a simple drumbeat for the intro.

We had it sounding really good.

GRAHAM: When Billy checked in at the studio whatever day it was, he said he wanted to hear what we had so far on "Aurora."

EDDIE: We played it for him. I mean, we weren't set up in the studio yet. Hadn't recorded anything. But we got in there and played it out for him.

Billy: I never would have come up with what they came up with in a million years. I could barely even keep a neutral face as I was listening. It felt odd and wrong and uncomfortable. Like putting on someone else's shoes.

Every bone in my body was saying, *This is not me. This is not right. I need to fix this now.*

Graham: I could tell he hated it.

Karen: Oh, he hated it. *[Laughs]* He definitely hated it.

Rod: Teddy took him aside and they went for a drive.

Billy: Teddy made me get in his car and we drove to get lunch or maybe it was dinner. And I was lost in thought, just hearing my own song being ruined over and over in my head.

I started talking the minute we sat down and Teddy put his hand up to stop me. He insisted on ordering first. He ordered basically everything fried on the menu. If it was battered, Teddy would eat it.

Once the waitress left, he said, "Okay, go ahead."

I said, "Do you think it sounds good?"

And he said, "Yes, I do."

I said, "You don't think it should be a bit less . . . congested?"

And Teddy said, "They are talented musicians. Just like you. Let them show you what you can't see in your own stuff. Let them lay down all the tracks. And then you and I will go in and pull back where we need to and sweeten and all that. If we have to have everybody come in one at a time and overdub, then we do that. We can change the whole song piece by piece if we have to. But as the spine of the song, yes, I think they are doing a great job."

I thought about it. And I could feel my chest was tight. But I said, "All right. I trust you."

And he said, "That's good. But trust them, too."

Rod: When Billy came back in, he had very simple notes. All good stuff.

Karen: Billy changed an octave, wanted me to jump from a one-five repetition to a one-four-five. But in general, he was very supportive.

Graham: The early take of that song is one we never would have come to if it had all gone Billy's way. By having us all involved, we were evolving.

Billy: I decided, with every song on that album, to give only the feedback that felt really necessary. Because I'd go back with Teddy when we were mixing it and that's when I could really refine.

Daisy: I went into the studio to hear everybody play "Aurora" for the first time and I was blown away by it. I was really excited. Billy and I played with the vocals a bit and found a great balance for it all.

Artie Snyder: We miked everything. We must have messed with the setup a thousand times to get it just right. We had Karen and Graham on the side, Pete and Warren in the back, Eddie was toward the front, and then Billy and Daisy were in iso booths but they could still see everybody.

I had Teddy in the control room next to me. He kept smoking cigarettes, letting the ash get on my boards. I kept wiping it away and he just kept dropping it.

When everything was perfectly in place, I said, "All right, 'Aurora,' take one. Somebody count it off."

Daisy: We played it the whole way through. All of us together. We just played it over and over. As a band. A real band.

I looked at Billy at one point and we smiled at each other and I thought, *This is happening*. I was in a band. I was one of them. The seven of us, playing music.

Billy: As Daisy and I were singing it, I had to do a few takes in a row to really warm up but Daisy hit it right out of the gate. She really . . . Daisy was a natural. And if you're going up against somebody like Daisy, then yeah, that's annoying. But if she's on your team . . . wow. Powerhouse.

Artie Snyder: I was still getting a feel for how the album would sound and my team was still tinkering with the setup. The early takes sounded a little tinny, and that's what I was focused on. When you start off on an album, with new people and different sounds, in a new studio and all of that . . . you really have to get your levels right, your mikes right. I was obsessive about that stuff. Until it was coming through clean on the cans, I could not focus on anything else.

But, even knowing that about myself, looking back on it . . . I can't believe I had no idea. We were making a massive hit record. And I had no idea.

Daisy: I knew it was gonna be huge. I really think, even then, I knew.

Daisy: A few days later, I'm going through my journal, back at my place. I think maybe it was a weekend. And I find one of Billy's songs in there. One that he wrote for the album. "Midnights." I think maybe at the time it was called "Memories." I must have packed it up with my things by mistake when we were back at Teddy's. So I started rereading it. I probably read it ten times in a row, sitting there.

It was pretty sickeningly sweet. All about how Billy has these happy memories with Camila. But there were a few good lines in there. So I started scribbling on top of it. Playing with it.

Billy: The next time we met up at Teddy's, Daisy handed me "Midnights." I'd written it over the summer. It was pretty straightforward when I wrote it. But she handed it back to me, pen marks all over the place and I could barely read any of the words. I held the page in my hand and I said, "What did you do to my song?"

Daisy: I told him it was actually a great song. I said, "Turns out, it just needed a little bit of darkness to it."

Billy: I said, "I understand what you're saying but I can't read what you wrote." She got mad and snatched the paper out of my hand.

Daisy: I was going to have to read it to him. I started reading the first verse but then I realized that was dumb. I said, "Play the song as you wrote it."

Billy: I got my guitar and I started playing and singing the words as I originally wrote them.

Daisy: I cut him off once I got the gist of it.

Billy: She put her hand on the neck of the guitar to shut me up. She said, "I get where you're going. Start from the beginning. Give this a listen."

Daisy: I sang him his song back, this time with my changes.

Billy: It went from a song about your best memories to a song about what you can and can't remember. I had to admit it was more subtle, more complicated. Much more open to interpretation.

It was very similar to what I had envisioned when I wrote it, but just . . . *[laughs]* better than what I got on the page, frankly.

Daisy: I didn't change a lot of his song, really. I just added in this element of what you don't remember to highlight what you do remember. And then I restructured it, to include a second voice.

Billy: By the time she was done, I was really excited about it.

Daisy: Billy immediately went into writing mode. He took the paper from me, grabbed a pen, started reordering a little bit. That's how I knew he liked it.

By the end, we'd taken this song that Billy had about Camila and we made it about so much more than that.

Billy: We played it for everybody down at the studio. Just her and me and the guitar, over in the lounge.

Graham: I dug the song. Billy and I started talking about a solo during the bridge. We were on the same page.

Eddie: I said to Billy, "This is good, let me get started on my piece on it."

And Billy said, "Well, your part is written already. Just go with the guitar as I played it."

I said, "Let me tinker with it."

He said, "Nothing to tinker with. Daisy and I have been reworking this one back and forth. I'm telling you, play it like I played it."

I said, "I don't want to play it like you played it."

He just patted me on the back and said, "It's cool. Just play it like I played it."

Billy: The rhythm guitar part was already done. But I said, "All right, man. Go ahead and try to see what you can come up with." By the time we recorded it, he'd come back around to exactly what I played for him.

Eddie: I changed it up. He didn't have it exactly right. There wasn't only one way to play that song. I changed it up. And it was better. I knew how to play my own riffs. I knew what worked. We were all supposed to be taking our own shots. So I took my own shot.

Billy: It is very frustrating, when you know how something should be done but you have to pretend someone else has a good idea, when you know you're just going to end up using your own. But that's the price of doing business with somebody like Eddie Loving. He's got to believe everything is his idea or he won't do it.

And, look, it's my fault. I told everybody it was an equal opportunity band. And I shouldn't have done that. Because that is just not a sustainable system. Look at Springsteen. Springsteen knew how to do it. But me? I had to sit there and pretend people like Eddie Loving knew better than me how to play guitar on the songs I wrote on my guitar.

Karen: I didn't see any of the tense stuff between Billy and Eddie on that song. I heard about it later from both of them but at the time I was . . . preoccupied.

Graham: You know what's a good time? Giving your girl a roll in the closet at the studio while everybody else is recording and the two of you have to be so quiet you could hear a pin drop.

That was making love, man. It felt like love. It felt like we were the only two people in the entire world who mattered. Me and Karen. It felt like I could show her how much I loved her, right there in that tight space, not saying anything at all.

Warren: When we were messing around on that song, on "Midnights," Daisy came up to me and suggested that I hold the drums on the bridge and I thought for a moment and I said, "Yeah, that's a great idea." Daisy and I always got along really well in that regard. We were about the only two people who could manage not to have too much ego with each other.

I once told her I thought she sang "Turn It Off" like she was in heat and she said, "I see what you mean. I think I'll pull back on the chorus." Just like that.

Some people just don't threaten each other. And other people threaten everything about each other. Just the way it is.

Rod: I started to do some calculations. Could we replace Eddie if we needed to? Would Pete leave with him? What would that mean for us? I'm not gonna lie. I started putting feelers out for other guitarists. Started planning out whether Billy could just take over Eddie's parts. I saw the writing on the wall.

Turns out I wasn't reading exactly right. But I saw the writing on the wall.

Warren: Being proud that you predicted Eddie would leave the band is like saying, "I predicted the sun would come out today," the day before a nuclear disaster. Yeah, man. Great guess. But you didn't exactly notice the world was ending?

Daisy: At the end of that day, when Billy was going home, he said, "Thank you for what you did with this song."

And I said something like "Yeah, of course."

But then Billy stopped in place. He put his hand on my arm. He made a real point of it. He said, "I'm serious. You made the song better."

I . . . That meant a lot. That meant a lot. Maybe meant too much.

Billy: I was starting to see, as Teddy had pushed me to, that sometimes you get to more complex places, artistically, when you have more people contributing. That's not always true. But with Daisy and me . . . it was true.

I had to recognize that. With her, then, it was true.

Daisy: I really felt like I understood him. And I think he understood me. You know, things like that, that kind of connection with a person, it is sort of like playing with fire. Because it feels good, to be understood. You feel in sync with a person, you feel like you're on a level that no one else is.

Karen: I think people that are too similar . . . they don't mix well. I used to think soul mates were two of the same. I used to think I was supposed to look for somebody that was just like me.

I don't believe in soul mates anymore and I'm not looking for anything. But if I did believe in them, I'd believe your soul mate was somebody who had all the things you didn't, that needed all the things you had. Not somebody who's suffering from the same stuff you are.

Rod: The band was recording "Chasing the Night." They had worked on it earlier in the day and it got toward the afternoon and Daisy wasn't needed anymore so she went home.

Daisy: I decided to have some people over to my cottage. Some actress friends and a couple guys from the Strip. We were just going to hang out by the pool, a bit.

Rod: I had told Daisy to come back later. Because we were going to record her and Billy's vocals on it a few times that night. I should have done a better job setting boundaries of when everyone was working or not working. We didn't have set hours, really. It was just sort of a free-for-all.

But she was supposed to be at Heider at nine.

Billy: Graham and I were working on some licks. Laying down a few and going back over them, seeing what we liked better.

Artie Snyder: Billy and Graham were fun to work with when it was just the two of them together. They had a language all to themselves, sometimes. But I felt like I understood what they were going for. I did wonder, back then, though . . . I didn't know how they could stand it. If I had to work with my brother I'd lose my mind.

Billy: I always felt really lucky that Graham was as good as he was. So talented, always had good ideas. He made it easy. People would often say, "I don't know how you can work with your brother." But I never knew how to do it any other way.

Daisy: It got later into the night and somehow Mick Riva shows up. He'd been staying at the Marmont, too. He was in his forties by then, I think. Married however many times, had like five kids. But partied like he was nineteen. He was topping the charts even then. Everybody still loved him.

I'd partied with him a few times. He was always decent to me. But he was a real . . . There were always a lot of groupies with Mick. He could really get a party out of control.

Rod: Billy and Graham finished up and Graham left around eight or so. So Billy and I decided to go get some dinner. But we got back a few minutes after nine and Daisy wasn't there.

Daisy: Suddenly, the whole place is packed. Mick's invited everyone he knows, basically. He's ordered bottles of liquor from the bar at the hotel, paid for it all.

I lost track of time. Forgot what I was doing. God only knows what I was on. I just remember champagne and cocaine. It was that kind of party. Those are the best parties. Champagne and coke and bikinis around the pool before we realized the drugs were killing us and the sex was coming for us, too.

Billy: We waited an hour before thinking anything of it. I mean, you know, it's Daisy, and showing up on time is something she does by accident.

Simone: I was in town to do *American Bandstand.* Daisy and I had plans to meet up. I got to Daisy's around maybe ten. And it was packed. Mick Riva was there, making out with two girls that couldn't have been more than sixteen. Daisy's laying out on a pool chair in a white bikini like she's tanning, wearing a pair of sunglasses, when it's pitch black out.

Daisy: I don't remember anything that happened after Simone showed up.

Rod: Teddy and Artie were going to go home. They weren't too worried about it. But I felt responsible for her. It didn't seem like her. To ditch a session.

Simone: I said, "Daisy, I think it's time to call it a night." But she barely even heard me. She sat up real fast and looked at me and said, "Have I shown you the caftan Thea Porter's people sent me?"

And I said, "No."

And she got up and ran into her cottage. It's full of people doing God-knows-what. They were barely paying attention to her. We walk into her bedroom and there are two men making out on her bed. It was like her house wasn't even her own. She walks right past them and opens her closet and pulls out this dress, this caftan. It's gold and pink and teal and gray. It was so beautiful. I mean, your heart broke looking at it, it was just so beautiful. Velvet and brocade and chiffon and silk.

I said, "That is stunning."

And she takes off her bathing suit, right there in front of everyone.

And I say, "What are you doing?"

And then she steps into it and twirls around and says, "I feel like a sprite in it. Like I'm a sea nymph."

And then . . . I don't know what to tell you. One minute she was in my sight and the next minute, she's way out past me, running back out to the pool, and then stepping into the water, one step at a time, in that gorgeous caftan. I could have killed her. That dress was art.

By the time I got to her, she was floating on her back, in the pool alone, all these people watching her. I don't know who snapped the photo. But it is my favorite picture of her ever, I think. She just looks so much like herself. The way she's floating, with her arms out to her sides, the dress floating with her. It's so dark out but the pool is lit so the dress and her body are bright. And then there's that look on her face, that way she's smiling right at the camera. Gets me every time.

Rod: I called her at the Marmont about ten times and she wasn't answering and I said to Billy, "I'm gonna head over there. Just to make sure she's okay."

Billy: Daisy loved the work of recording an album. I knew she loved it. I'd seen it. The only way Daisy would pass up an opportunity to record her own song is if she was doped up beyond all recognition.

It hurts to care about someone more than they care about themselves. I can tell that story from both sides.

So Rod and I went over there. We got to her cottage at the Marmont in about fifteen minutes, it wasn't far. And we started asking where Lola La Cava is—she's got an alias because of course she does. Finally someone says check the pool.

And when we get there, Daisy is in a pink dress, sitting on the edge of a diving board, surrounded by people, and she's soaking wet. Her hair was slicked back and this dress was sticking to her.

Rod walked up to her and I didn't know what he was saying but the moment she saw him, I saw this recognition in her eyes. She had forgotten where she was supposed to be until she saw him. It was exactly what we thought. Blotto. I mean, the only thing that was gonna come before her music was her dope.

As she's talking to Rod, I see Rod point to me and Daisy's eye follows his hand in my direction and she was . . . She looked sad. To see me there. Looking at her.

There was a guy next to me, some guy I would have told you was an old geezer except he was probably only forty. I could smell the whiskey in his glass, that smoky, antiseptic scent. It's always been the smell for me. The smell of tequila, the smell of beer. Even coke.

The smell of any of it. It takes me right back. To those moments when the night is just starting, when you know you're about to get into trouble. It feels so good, the beginning.

There was that voice again, inside my head, that was telling me I was never going to be able to stay sober for the rest of my life. *What is the point of getting sober at all if I know I'll never kick it forever? I'll fail one day anyway. Shouldn't I pack it all in? Quit on myself? Quit on everybody? Spare Camila and my girls the heartbreak later and admit who I really am.*

I looked over at Daisy, she was coming up off the diving board. She had a glass in her hand and she dropped it right there on the side of the pool. I watched her step onto the broken glass, not realizing it was under her feet.

Rod: Daisy's feet started bleeding.

Simone: There was blood mixing with the pool water on the concrete. And Daisy didn't even notice. She just kept walking, talking to somebody else.

Daisy: I couldn't feel the cuts on my feet. I couldn't feel much of anything, I don't think.

Simone: In that moment, I thought, *She's going to be the girl bleeding in a beautiful dress until it kills her.*

I felt . . . lost, sad, depressed, sick. I felt really hopeless but also like I didn't have the luxury of giving up. Like I was going to have to fight for her—fight for her against her—until I lost. Because there was no winning. I didn't see how I could win the war.

Billy: I couldn't stay. I couldn't stay because when I looked at Daisy, wet and bleeding and out of it and half-near falling down, I did not think, *Thank God I stopped using.*

I thought, *She knows how to have fun.*

Rod: I was getting Daisy a towel to dry off when I saw Billy turn and leave. I'd driven us there so I wasn't quite sure where he was going. I tried to catch his eye but he didn't see me until the last moment, when he went around the corner. He just gave me a nod. And I understood. I was thankful he'd come up with me in the first place.

He knew how to take care of himself and that's what he was doing.

Billy: I told Rod I was leaving and made sure he was all right to take a cab home because I'd driven us over. He was really supportive. He understood why I needed to leave.

When I got home, I got in bed right next to Camila, so thankful to be there. But I couldn't sleep. I kept wondering what I'd be doing that very moment if I'd taken the whiskey out of that man's hand. If I'd poured it down my throat.

Would I be laughing and playing a song for everybody? Would I be skinny-dipping with a whole bunch of strangers? Would I be puking my guts out watching somebody strap up and shoot heroin?

Instead, I was laying in the darkest quiet, listening to my wife snore.

The thing is, I'm a person who survives despite his instincts. My instincts said to run toward the chaos. And my better brain sent me home to my woman.

Daisy: I don't remember seeing Billy there. I don't remember seeing Rod. I don't know how I made it to my bed.

Billy: I knew I wasn't going to fall asleep that night. So I got up out of bed and I wrote a song.

Rod: Billy comes into the studio the next day. Everybody else is there, ready to get to recording. I've even got Daisy there, relatively sober, drinking a coffee.

Daisy: I felt bad. I did not mean to blow off the recording session, obviously.

Why did I hurt myself like that? I can't explain it. I wish I could. I hated it about myself. I hated it about myself and I kept doing it and then I hated myself more. There are no good answers about this.

Rod: Billy comes in and he shows us all a song he wrote. "Impossible Woman."

I said, "You wrote this last night?"

He said, "Yeah."

Billy: Daisy reads it and goes, "Cool."

Graham: It was clear, from the feeling in the room, that none of us, not even Daisy and Billy, were going to acknowledge it was about Daisy.

Billy: It's not about Daisy. It's about when you're sober, there are things you can't touch, things you can't have.

Karen: After Graham and I heard Billy play it for the first time, I said to Graham, "That song is . . ."

And Graham just goes, "Yup."

Daisy: It was a great damn song.

Warren: Didn't care then, barely care now.

Karen: "Dancing barefoot in the snow/cold can't touch her, high or low." That's Daisy Jones.

Billy: I decided to write a song about a woman that felt like sand through your fingers, like you could never really catch her. As an allegory for the things I couldn't have, couldn't do.

Daisy: I said, "This song is for us to sing?"

Billy said, "No, I think you should give it a shot on your own. I wrote it for your register."

I said, "It seems more obvious that a man would be singing this about a woman."

Billy said, "It's more interesting if a woman is singing it. It gives it a haunting kind of quality."

I said, "All right, I'll take a stab at it."

I took some time with it while everybody was lining out their parts. A few days later, I went in. I listened as everybody laid their tracks down. Just trying to find a way into it.

When it was my turn to get in there, I gave it my best. I tried to make it feel a little sad, maybe. Like I missed this woman. I was thinking, *Maybe this woman is my mother, maybe this woman is my lost sister, maybe there is something I need from this woman.* You know?

I thought, *It's wistful, it's ethereal.* That kind of a thing. But I was doing take after take and I could tell it wasn't working.

And I kept looking to everybody, thinking, *Somebody get me out of this mess. I'm flailing over here.* And I didn't know what to do. And I started getting angry.

Karen: Daisy has absolutely no formal training. She does not know the names of chords, she does not know various vocal techniques. If what Daisy does naturally doesn't work, then you have to take Daisy off the song.

Daisy: I'm just hoping somebody saves me from myself. I say I want to take five. Teddy suggests I go for a walk, clear my head. I walk around the block. But I'm only making it worse because I just keep thinking *I can't do it* and *Of course I can't do it* and all that. And I finally just give up. I get in my car and I drive away. I couldn't deal with it, so I left.

Billy: I wrote the song for her. I mean I wrote it for her to sing. So that made me mad. Her giving up like that.

Obviously, I understood why she was frustrated. I mean, Daisy is shockingly talented. Like it will shock you, to be near it. Her talent. But she didn't know how to control it. She couldn't call on it, you know? She just had to hope it would be there.

But giving up wasn't cool. Especially not after trying for, you know, a couple of hours, tops. That's the problem with people who don't have to work for things. They don't know how to work for things.

Daisy: That night, somebody knocks on my door. I was with Simone making dinner. I open the door and there's Billy Dunne.

Billy: I went there with the express purpose of getting her to sing the damn song. Did I want to go back to the Chateau Marmont? No, I did not. But that's what I had to do, so I did it.

Daisy: He sits me down and Simone is in the kitchen making Harvey Wallbangers and she offers Billy one.

Billy: And immediately Daisy blocks me and says, "No!" As if I was going to take the drink from Simone's hand.

Daisy: I was embarrassed that Simone had offered it to him because I knew he already felt like I was a scummy boozehound drug addict. And if Billy thought I was going to knock him off the wagon, I was going to do everything in my power to make sure that wasn't true.

Billy: It . . . surprised me. She had actually been listening to me.

Daisy: Billy said to me, "You have to sing this song." I told him that I just didn't have the right voice for it. We talked back and forth for a while, about what the song meant and whether there was a way into it for me and finally Billy just said that it was about me. That he had written it about me. That I'm the impossible woman. "She's blues dressed up like rock 'n' roll/untouchable, she'll never fold." That was me. And something kind of clicked in my head.

Billy: I absolutely never told Daisy the song was about her. I wouldn't have done that because the song wasn't about her.

Daisy: That felt like a breaking point into it. But I still said to him that I wasn't sure I was the right sound.

Billy: I told her that the song needed a raw energy. It needed to feel like it crackled under the needle. It needed to feel electric. Like she was singing to save her life.

Daisy: That's not my voice.

Billy: I said, "You need to go into the studio tomorrow and try again. Promise me that you will try again." And she agreed.

Daisy: So I go in there the next morning and they had cleared out the place. The rest of the band wasn't there. It was just Billy, Teddy, Rod, and Artie at the board. I walked in and I just . . . I knew this was going to be different.

Rod: I went out to smoke a cigarette as Billy pulled Daisy into the booth and started giving her a pep talk.

Billy: I knew how the song was supposed to sound and I just kept trying to think of how to explain it to her. What I realized, eventually, was that Daisy's all about effortlessness. And this had to be a song that sounded like it hurt to sing, like it was taking all the effort in her body. I wanted Daisy to feel, after she was done singing it, that she had run a marathon.

Daisy: There is a grit to my voice but it's not a deep-in-your-gut kind of grit. And that's what Billy wanted.

Billy: I said something like "Sing it so hard, so loud, that you can't control where your voice goes. Let your voice crack. Lose control of it."

I gave her permission to sound bad. Think of how you sing when you're singing to the radio at full volume. When you can't hear yourself, you're not afraid to really belt it out because you won't have to cringe when your voice breaks or you veer off-key. Daisy needed that kind of freedom. That takes a crapload of confidence. And Daisy didn't actually have confidence. She was always *good*. Confidence is being okay being bad, not being okay being good.

I said, "If you sing this song in a way where you sound good the entire time, you've lost."

Daisy: He said, "This song isn't meant to be pretty. Don't sing it like it is."

Rod: I came back in and Billy's got Daisy in the booth with the lights dimmed, a Vicks inhaler, a steaming mug of tea next to her, a pile of lozenges and some tissues, a huge pitcher of water, I don't know, you name it, it was in there with her.

And then Daisy sat down in a chair and Billy got right back up, jumped out of the control room, went into the booth with her again. He took the chair away, raised the mike. He said, "You need to stand up and sing so hard your knees buckle."

Daisy looked terrified.

Daisy: He wanted me to shed every inhibition I had. Billy was saying that he wanted me to be willing to fail spectacularly in front of him—and Teddy and Artie. But I knew there was no moving past my own ego stone sober.

I said, "Can we get some wine in here?"

Billy said, "You don't need it."

I said, "No, *you* don't need it."

Billy: Rod goes right in there with a bottle of brandy.

Rod: I'm not about to take away the easy stuff and have her running that much faster for the hard stuff.

Daisy: I took a few swigs and I looked at Billy through the window and I said, into the mike, "All right, you want it to sound a little ugly, right?" He nodded. And I said, "And no one's gonna judge me if I end up sounding like a screeching cat?"

And I'll never forget, Billy leaned onto the button, and said, "If you were a cat, your screech would bring every cat running to you." And I liked that. The idea that just by being me, I was doing all right.

So I opened up my mouth and I breathed in deep and then I went for it.

Billy: None of us told Daisy this and I . . . I hesitate in even saying it now but . . . her first two takes were god-awful. I mean, wow. I was starting to regret what I'd told her. But we just kept encouraging her.

When someone is out on a ledge like that, especially when you're the one that coaxed them out there in the first place, you don't dare do anything to unbalance them.

So I said, "Great, great." And then eventually after, I think, the third take, I said, "Go one octave deeper."

Rod: It was either Daisy's fourth or fifth take. I think maybe fifth. And it was fucking magic. I mean, magic. I don't use that word lightly. But it felt like you were witnessing something that only happened a few times in a lifetime. She just wailed. The record that you hear, that was Daisy's fifth take, start to finish.

Billy: She started so assured in the first verse, not quiet, necessarily, but even. Leveled. "Impossible woman/let her hold you/let her ease your soul."

And she let that simmer a little bit, grew in intensity in this really subtle way through the next, you know, "Sand through fingers/wild horse, but she's just a colt." And on "colt" is where you really felt her start to amp up.

She went through another verse and then the first time she sang the chorus, I could see it in her eyes, she was looking right at me, and you could feel it building in her chest, "She'll have you running/in the wrong direction/have you coming/for the wrong obsessions/oh, she's gunning/ for your redemption/have you headed/back to confession." And it was when she repeated "confession," then she really just let it fly.

Her voice breaks, in the middle of the word, it cracks just a little. And then she goes through most of the verses again. When she gets to the chorus a second time, she just unleashes her voice on it. It's rocky and gritty and breathy and there's so much emotion in it. It's like she's pleading.

And then she closes in on the end. "Walk away from the impossible/you'll never touch her/never ease your soul." Then she added a couplet. And it was great. It was perfect. She sang, "You're one more impossible man/running from her/clutching what you stole."

She sang the entire song with such a heartbreaking lament. She made that song so much more than what I'd given her.

Daisy: I opened my eyes after that take and I barely remembered doing it. I just remember thinking, *I did it.*

I remember realizing I had even more power in me than I had originally thought. That I had more to give, more depth and range, than even I knew about myself.

Rod: She was looking right at Billy the whole time she sang. And he was staring at her, nodding along with her. When she finished the song, Teddy started clapping. And the look on her face, the delight she felt, it was like watching a kid on Christmas. Truly. She was so proud of herself.

She pulled the headphones off and threw them down and ran out of the booth and—I kid you not—ran directly into Billy's arms. He picked her up, just off the floor, and kind of swung her back and forth for a moment. And I could have sworn to you he smelled her hair before he put her back down.

Daisy: We were all in the studio recording one afternoon when Camila came in with the girls.

Graham: I had said to Camila, "Why don't you bring everybody here more often?" Because Camila would stop by occasionally but it was always for a minute to drop off something to Billy. She never came and hung out. But we had so many people hanging out back then.

Of course, the time she comes in to hang out for a little while, one of the twins starts crying for what seemed like no reason. Wouldn't stop. I don't remember if it was Susana or Maria but Billy took her and held her and tried to shush her and she would not calm down. I took her, Karen took her. It didn't matter what we all did.

Camila ended up taking both of the twins outside.

Camila: Babies and rock 'n' roll don't really go hand in hand.

Karen: I went for a walk with Camila and the girls one day at the studio. I said, "How are things going?"

And she just . . . opened up. Talking and talking like the words were tumbling out of her. The twins weren't sleeping and Julia was going through a jealous period and Billy was never home. And then she stopped in place, as she was pushing the girls along with the stroller, and she said, "Why am I complaining? I love my life."

Camila: What is it they say? The days are long but the years are short? Whoever said that was a mom with three kids under the age of three. Tired and cranky on an hourly basis, bursting with joy when you put your head on the pillow. Raising kids is hard work. It was work I was happy to do, though.

Everybody is good at something. I was good at motherhood.

Karen: Camila had said to me that day, something like "I'm living the life I want to live." And there was an ease about her, as she said it.

Graham: While Camila and the twins were outside, Billy set Julia up in the control booth. She was there hanging out with Artie and Teddy and everybody while we all laid something down.

She had such a fun time in there. She was so cute with the cans on her ears and her tiny little dress. Her hair was still blond then. Her legs were so short, they didn't even bend at the knee when she sat, just stuck straight out.

Karen: I decided to tell Camila about Graham. I needed her help figuring out what to do.

I had . . . I never told him this, but I saw a letter from his mom on his nightstand one morning. And I hadn't meant to pry but it was right there and a few lines stood out. His mom was telling him that if he really loved this girl he was with then he should make it official. And that freaked me out.

Graham: I wanted a family. Not right then. But sure, I wanted what my brother had.

Karen: I said to Camila, "What would you think if I was sleeping with Graham?"

She took off her sunglasses and looked me right in the eye. She said, "*If* you were sleeping with Graham?"

I said, "Yeah, *if*."

Camila: He'd been in love with her since God only knows how long.

KAREN: We kept talking in hypotheticals. Camila said I would have to be taking into account the fact that Graham had had feelings for me for quite a while. Which . . . I knew but I didn't know, I guess.

CAMILA: I told her that if she was sleeping with Graham and wasn't feeling about him the way I knew he felt about her . . . well, I think I told her to stop.

KAREN: I believe she said, "Don't hurt Graham or I'll kill you."

I said, "Aren't you worried about Graham hurting me?"

And she said, "If Graham broke your heart, I'd kill him, too. You know that. But we both know Graham's not going to break your heart. We both know which way this is going to go."

I got a little defensive but Camila never really backed down from too much. She was very good at knowing what everybody else should do and she had no problem telling you. It was really annoying. How right she always was. And she would tell you "I told you so." You'd do something she told you not to do and it wouldn't work out and you'd find yourself bristling around her, just waiting for that "I told you so" to come. And she'd always land it right when your defenses were down.

CAMILA: If you come to me and ask me for advice, and then you don't take my advice, and it blows up in your face exactly like I told you it would, what do you expect me to say?

KAREN: I told her, "Graham's an adult. He can handle whatever he gets himself into. It's not my job to make his decisions."

Camila said, "Yes, it is."

And I said, "No, it's not."

CAMILA: I told her, "Yes, it is."

KAREN: And we just kept going on like that until I gave up.

Daisy: We were recording and Julia was in the booth. They had all come to visit Billy that day. And there was something wrong with my mike so I was sitting it out while everyone tried to fix it.

I went into the control booth and asked Julia if she wanted to get a cookie. She took her headphones off her head and said, "Does my dad say it's okay?" It was so sweet.

Teddy leaned on the talkback button and said, "Julia would like to know if she may have a cookie."

Billy leaned in and said, "Yes, she may." And then he added, "Just make sure it's a . . . normal one."

I took Julia by the hand and we went to the kitchen and we split a peanut butter cookie. She told me she liked pineapples. I remember that because I love pineapples and I told her that. She got really excited, that we had that in common. I told her we should split a pineapple sometime. And then Karen came into the kitchen and Camila was calling out for Julia and I brought her to her. Julia waved goodbye to me and Camila thanked me for watching her.

Camila: The whole way home, [Julia was] saying, "Can Daisy Jones be my best friend?"

Daisy: As soon as they left, Eddie called me and Karen back into the booth. And somebody, I don't remember who, said I was good with kids. And then Eddie said, "I bet you'd make a great aunt."

You don't think to tell someone they will be a good aunt if you think they will be a good mom. But I knew as well as anybody, I wouldn't be a good mom. I had no place thinking of being anybody's mom.

I wrote "A Hope Like You" soon after that.

Billy: When Daisy showed me "A Hope Like You," I thought, *This could work as a piano ballad.* It was such a sad love song. About wanting somebody you can't have and knowing you're going to want them anyway.

I said, "How do you hear it?"

She sang a tiny little bit of it and I just . . . I heard it. I heard what it should be.

Daisy: Billy said, "This is your song. It should be just you and the piano on the track, that's it."

Karen: That was a great song to record. I was really proud of it. Just Daisy singing and me on the keys. That's it. Just two bitches playing rock 'n' roll.

Billy: Daisy and I wrote a lot of good stuff after that. We'd be working in the lounge at the studio or back at Teddy's pool house if we needed some peace and quiet.

I would come in with something I was working on and Daisy would help me refine it. Or vice versa. We'd work on one of Daisy's ideas.

Rod: It seemed like there was a period of time where Daisy and Billy were coming in with new stuff every day.

Graham: It's really exciting, when you're constantly creating. We'd be working on tracks for "Midnights" or adding some layers to "Impossible Woman" and then Daisy and Billy would come in with a new one we were all excited about.

Karen: It felt a little manic, that period of time. So many people in the studio. So many songs coming in and out. Recording and recording and recording. Playing things a thousand times, always trying to improve upon the last one.

There was so much to do, so much to keep us busy. But we were all coming into the studio in the morning, still hungover from the night before. It was like zombies at 10:00 A.M. Until the coffee and the coke kicked in.

Rod: The early tracks were sounding great.

Artie Snyder: When the songs started coming together, we were realizing we had something really special on our hands.

Billy and Teddy would always stay late and listen to what we had. Listen to it over and over again. There was an energy to the control booth those nights. Super quiet in the rest of the studio, real dark outside. Just the three of us listening to rock getting made.

I was going through a divorce back then so I was happy to stay as late as they wanted. We'd be up in the studio at three in the morning sometimes. Me and Teddy slept there if we wanted to. Billy always went home. Even if it was just for two hours until he came back.

Rod: It was really starting to sound out of this world. I wanted to make sure Runner was prepared to back these guys up with some real money. This album deserved to make a big splash.

I was lobbying Teddy for a huge number at the first pressing. I wanted a clear hit single. I wanted rock and pop airplay. I wanted a massive tour lined up. I was getting very ambitious. I wanted big momentum out of the gate.

Everybody knew Daisy and Billy on tour promoting this album was going to sell out venues and it was going to sell records. You could feel it. And Teddy made sure everybody was on board. Even at Runner Records, you could feel the excitement.

Daisy: Billy and I did about four songs in a mad rush of writing over about a week or two. I mean, we actually did seven songs. But only four of them made it onto the album.

Rod: They turned in "Please," "Young Stars," "Turn It Off," and "This Could Get Ugly" all within about a week.

Billy: The concept for the album took shape naturally. We—I mean, me and Daisy—we could see that we were writing about the push and pull between the lure of temptation and staying on the right path. It was about drugs and sex and love and denial and a whole mess of stuff.

That's where "Turn It Off" came from. The two of us writing about how every time you think you've got something licked, it keeps rearing its head.

Daisy: "Turn It Off" was me and Billy at the pool house, him on the guitar, me pitching the line "I keep trying to turn it off/but, baby, you keep turning me on," and then it all just snowballed from there.

I'd say a line, he'd say a line. We'd be scribbling each other's stuff out, writing over it. All just trying to get to the best version of the song.

Billy: Daisy and I got to a point where we could really tinker with something for a while. We had enough faith to keep working on something even if it didn't come easy. "Young Stars" ended up developing like that.

Daisy: We worked on "Young Stars" in fits and starts. We'd have it and then lose it and pick it up days later. I think it was Billy who suggested the line "We only look like young stars/because you can't see old scars." That worked for me. We finally built around that.

Billy: We were using a lot of words that made you think of physical pain. *Ache* and *knots* and *break* and *punch* and all that. It started to fit in well with the rest of the album—how it hurts to be fighting your own instincts.

Daisy: "I'd tell you the truth just to watch you blush/but you can't handle the hit so I'll hold the punch." That song ended up cutting so close to the heart, in a lot of ways. Maybe too close. "I believe you can break me/but I'm saved for the one who saved me."

Billy: I mean, it's hard to say what a song is about sometimes. Sometimes even you don't know why you wrote that line, or how it came into your head, or even what it means.

Daisy: The songs that we were writing together . . . *[pauses]* I started feeling like a lot of what Billy was writing about was how he was actually feeling. It seemed clear to me that there were things unsaid that were being said in our work together.

Billy: They're songs. You pull them out of wherever you can. You change the meanings to fit the moments sometimes. Some songs came more from my heart than others, I suppose.

Daisy: It's so strange, how someone's silence, someone's insistence that something isn't happening can be so suffocating. But it can be. And *suffocating* is exactly the word, too. You feel like you can't breathe.

Karen: I think Daisy showed me "Please" before she showed it to anyone else. And I thought it was a cool song. And I said, "What's Billy think?"

And she said, "I haven't shown him yet. I wanted to show you first."

I thought that was weird.

Billy: Daisy handed me the song, and I could tell she was feeling sort of nervous about it but I immediately liked it. I added a few lines myself, removed a few.

Daisy: It's very vulnerable, being an artist, telling the truth like that, like we're doing now. When you're living your life, you're so inside your head, you're swirling around in your own pain, that it's hard to see how obvious it is to the people around you. These songs I was writing felt coded and secret, but I suspect they weren't coded and secret at all.

Billy: "This Could Get Ugly." . . . That was one, we had the song before we had the lyrics done. Graham and I had come up with a guitar riff we liked and that song spiraled out of that. I actually went to Daisy and said, "Got anything for this?"

Daisy: I had this idea in my head. Of "ugly" being a good thing. I wanted to write a song about feeling like you knew you had somebody's number, even if they didn't know it.

Billy: Daisy and I met up at Teddy's place one morning and I played it for her again and she threw some stuff out. She was talking about some guy she was seeing, I don't remember who. And she had a few lines that really spoke to me. I really liked "Write a list of things you'll regret/I'd be on top smoking a cigarette." I loved that line.

I said to her, "What's this guy putting you through to write a song like this?"

Daisy: Even then, I wasn't sure if Billy and I were having the same conversation.

Billy: She was great at wordplay. She was great at flipping the meaning of things, of undercutting sentiment. I loved that about what she was doing and I told her that.

Daisy: The harder I worked as a songwriter, the longer I worked at it, the better I got. Not in any linear way, really. More like zigzags. But I was getting better, getting really good. And I knew that. I knew that when I showed the song to him. But knowing you're good can only take you so far. At some point, you need someone else to see it, too. Appreciation from people you admire changes how you see yourself. And Billy saw me the way I wanted to be seen. There is nothing more powerful than that. I really believe that.

Everybody wants somebody to hold up the right mirror.

Billy: "This Could Get Ugly" was her idea, her execution and it was . . . excellent.

She had written something that felt like I could have written it, except I knew I couldn't have. I wouldn't have come up with something like that. Which is what we all want from art, isn't it? When someone pins down something that feels like it lives inside us? Takes a piece of your heart out and shows it to you? It's like they are introducing you to a part of yourself. And that's what Daisy did, with that song. At least for me.

I could do nothing but praise her for it. I didn't change a single word.

Eddie: When they came into the studio with "This Could Get Ugly," I thought, *Great, another song that has got no room for me to try my own thing on.*

I didn't like who this was all turning me into. I'm not a bitter person. In almost every other situation in my life, I'm not this guy, you know what I'm saying? But I was getting so sick of it. Going into work every day feeling like a second-class citizen. That stuff messes with you. I don't care who you are. It messes with you.

I said to Pete, I said, "Second-class citizen. First-class resort."

Karen: It definitely became a club that we weren't in. Daisy and Billy. Even the word down from Runner Records was keep Daisy and Billy happy. Keep Daisy and Billy stable.

Warren: Daisy was always skipping out on stuff she didn't want to do. She was always coming in sauced. But everybody was acting like she was the goose that laid the golden egg.

Daisy: I honestly thought I was balancing all of it fine. I wasn't. But I really thought I was.

Karen: I had thought she had the pills under control and I realized at some point while we were recording that album that she'd just learned to hide it better.

Rod: Billy and Daisy would seem like they were getting along like a house on fire and then Daisy would be late for something or she'd be outside with somebody and nobody could find her and Billy would get pissed.

Eddie: Daisy and Billy would be outside on the sidewalk, thinking we can't hear them, and they'd be screaming at each other about something or other.

Karen: Billy got very angry when Daisy slacked off.

Billy: I don't think Daisy and I fought very much back then. Maybe normal stuff. Just as much as I'd fight with Graham or Warren.

Daisy: Billy thought he knew better than me what I should be doing. And he wasn't necessarily wrong. But I still wasn't about to have anybody telling me my business.

I was caught in a whirl of my own ego. I had this validation I'd been looking for for such a long time. But on the other hand, I was so unsatisfied in so many ways.

Back then, I had an oversize sense of self-importance and absolutely no self-worth. It didn't matter how gorgeous I was or how great my voice was or what magazine I was on the cover of. I mean, there were a lot of teenage girls that wanted to grow up and *be* me in the late seventies. I was keenly aware of that. But the only reason people thought I had everything is because I had all the things you can see.

I had none of the things you can't.

And a lot of good dope can make it so you can't tell whether you're happy or not. It can make you think having people around is the same thing as having friends.

I knew getting high wasn't a long-term solution. But God, it's so easy. It's just so easy.

But of course, it's not easy at all, either. Because one minute you're just trying to nurse a wound. And the next, you're desperately trying to hide the fact that you're now a jury-rigged, taped-up, shortcutted mess of a person and the wound you were nursing has become an abscess.

But I was skinny and pretty so who cared, right?

Rod: Teddy was always trying to keep Billy and Daisy calm. They were . . . Billy and Daisy together was like tending a little fire. Good if controlled. Just keep the kerosene away from it and we'll all be fine.

Eddie: It takes a lot of work, keeping Billy sober, keeping Daisy level. I doubt Teddy Price would have been tripping over himself to make sure I didn't step in a bar.

Graham: We started calling them the Chosen ones. I don't know if they ever knew that. But . . . I mean, that's what they were.

Rod: We were working to record the backlog of songs that Daisy and Billy had written. I think they had almost the entire album by that point. We were already talking about what could fit on the record and what couldn't.

People don't think about it anymore because the technology is so different but we had such a tight running time back then. You could fit twenty-two minutes on one side of a record most of the time.

Karen: Graham wrote a song called "The Canyon."

Graham: I had written this song, the only lyrics I'd ever written that I really liked. Now, I wasn't a songwriter. That was always Billy's thing. But I'd scratched some stuff down from time to time. And I'd finally written a song I was proud of.

The song was about how, even though Karen and I were both living large by that point, I'd be happy living in a crappy house as long as I was with her. I based it on our old house we all lived in in Topanga Canyon. Where Pete and Eddie still lived.

You know, the heat barely worked and there was rarely hot water and one of the windows was busted and all that. But that didn't matter if we were together. "There's no water in the sink/and the bathtub leaks/but I'll hold your warm body in a cold shower/stand there with you and waste the hours."

Karen: I was a little skittish about it. I never promised Graham any future for us. And I was worried he was seeing one. But unfortunately, back then at least, I tended to just avoid problems I didn't want to deal with.

Warren: Graham wrote a song and asked Billy to consider it for the album and Billy blew him off.

Billy: By the time Graham came in with this song he wanted us to record, Daisy and I had the album almost done. And the songs were complicated and nuanced and a little dark.

Daisy and I had talked about wanting to write one or two more songs and we wanted at least one of them to be a little harder, less romantic.

What Graham showed me . . . Graham wrote a love song. Just a simple little love song. It didn't have the complexity that Daisy and I were chasing.

Graham: It was the first song I really wrote and I wrote it for the woman I loved. And Billy was so involved in his own shit he didn't even know who I wrote it about and he didn't ask. He read my song in about thirty seconds and said, "Maybe on the next album, man. We got this one now."

I'd always had Billy's back. I'd always been there for him. Supported him through anything and everything.

Billy: We said, with this album, I wouldn't tell anybody how to do their jobs. So I wasn't going to listen to anybody telling me and Daisy what to sing. If we're staying in our lanes, let's stay in our lanes.

Karen: Graham sold it to the Stun Boys and they had a big hit off of it. I was happy about that. Happy how it all ended. I wouldn't have wanted to have to play that song night after night.

I never understood people putting their real emotions into something they know they have to play on tour over and over and over again.

Rod: That was around the time that Daisy and Billy started recording their vocals together. On most of the tracks, they were in the booth at the same time, singing into the same mike, harmonizing in real time together.

Eddie: Billy and Daisy on the same mike in one of those small booths . . . I mean, we'd all kill to be stuck up that close to Daisy.

Artie Snyder: It would have been a lot easier for me to have them in two different booths so I could isolate their vocals. Them singing into the same mike made my job about ten times harder.

If Daisy had an area where she was soft, I couldn't overdub it without losing Billy's. It made cutting back and forth between takes almost impossible.

We'd have to record over and over and over again to get a take where they both sounded good at the same time. The band would go home for the night and Daisy and Billy and Teddy and I would still be there, burning the midnight oil. It really limited how polished I could make the tracks. I actually was pretty pissed off. But Teddy wasn't backing me up.

Rod: I thought Teddy made the right call. Because it showed on the track. You could feel they were breathing the same air as they sang. It was . . . I mean, there's no other word for it. It was intimate.

Billy: You know, when you have music that has all the knots sanded down and the scratches buffed out . . . where's the emotion in that?

Rod: I heard this secondhand, from Teddy. So I can't vouch for how true it is. But there was a night when Billy and Daisy pulled an all-nighter doing overdubs on "This Could Get Ugly."

Teddy said during one of the takes, late at night, Billy didn't take his eyes off Daisy for the whole take. And they finished and Billy caught Teddy watching. And Billy immediately stopped—tried to pretend he hadn't been looking at all.

Daisy: Just how honest do we have to get here? I know I told you I'd tell you everything but how much "everything" do you really want to know?

Billy: We were at Teddy's pool house. Daisy was wearing a black dress with the thin straps. What are those called?

We were working on a song called "For You." We didn't have much at first but it was about me getting sober for Camila. I mean, I never expressly stated that, because I knew Daisy would give me a hard time that I was writing about Camila. So I said it was about being willing to give up something for someone else.

Daisy had reminded me we had wanted to write something a bit harder and I had said we could do that later. Because I really liked this idea. I might have said, "This one has really been on my mind."

Daisy: It was only about eleven in the morning but I was buzzed already. Billy was playing a song on the keyboard and I sat next to him. He was showing me the notes, I was playing a few with him. We were trying to figure out the right key. The few lines Billy had written already . . . I remember them exactly. "Nothing I wouldn't do/to go back to the past and wait for you." He sang that, sitting right next to me.

Billy: Daisy put her hand on mine, to stop me from playing. I looked at her and she said, "I like writing with you."

And I said, "I like writing with you, too."

And then I said something I shouldn't have said.

Daisy: He said, "I like a lot about you."

Billy: Daisy smiled when I said it, she lit up. This wide smile and this girlish laugh and I could see her eyes started to water just the littlest bit. Or maybe I was imagining it. I don't know. It . . . it feels good to make Daisy smile. It's . . . *[pauses]* I don't know. I don't know what I'm saying.

Daisy: *I like a lot about you.*

Billy: She was dangerous. And I knew that. But I don't think I could recognize that the safer she felt to me, the more dangerous she was.

Daisy: Before I even really knew what I was doing, I leaned in to kiss him. I was so close to him I could feel his breath. And when I opened my eyes, his were closed. And I thought, *This makes sense.* It made sense in this deeply gratifying way.

Billy: I lost myself, I think. For a moment, at least.

Daisy: My lips barely grazed his. I could feel them only in the sense that I was aware of having *almost* felt them. But then he pulled back.

Billy looked at me. And his eyes were so kind when he said it.

He said, "I can't."

My heart dropped in my chest. I don't mean that figuratively. I could actually feel it sinking in my chest.

Billy: I shudder thinking about it. About that time. How I could have made one small mistake that would have thrown my whole life away.

Daisy: After he turned me down, he sort of looked back at the keys, and I could tell he was trying to pretend that what had just happened hadn't just happened. Probably for my sake. Although, I think a lot for his sake, too. It was excruciating. This lie he was trying to tell us both. I'd much prefer someone screaming at me than tensing up and staying still.

Billy: When Graham and I were kids, our mom used to take us to this community pool during the summer. And this one time, Graham was sitting on the edge of the pool, toward the deep end. And this was before he could swim.

And I stood there next to him, and my brain went, *I could push him in*. And that terrified the hell out of me. I didn't want to push him in. I would never push him in but . . . it scared me that the only thing between this moment of calm and the biggest tragedy of my life was me choosing not to do it. That really tripped me out, that everyone's life was that precarious. That there wasn't some all-knowing mechanism in place that stopped things that *shouldn't* happen from happening.

That's something that had always scared me.

And that's how it felt being around Daisy Jones.

Daisy: I said to him, "I should go."

And he said, "Daisy, it's okay."

Billy: We both just wanted to pretend it hadn't happened. I desperately hoped that one of us would stand up and walk away.

Daisy: I grabbed my coat and I grabbed my keys and I said, "I'm really sorry." And I left.

Billy: Finally, I had to be the one to go. I told Daisy we'd pick it back up later in the week and I got in my car and I drove home to Camila.

She said, "You're home early."

And I said, "I wanted to be with you."

Daisy: I drove to the beach. I don't know why. I just had to drive somewhere, so I drove until the road ended. I drove until I hit the sand.

I parked my car and I was feeling so ashamed and so embarrassed and so stupid and so alone and lonely and pathetic and dirty and awful. And then, I got really mad.

I got mad at everything about him. That he'd pulled away, that he'd made me embarrassed, that he didn't feel the way I wanted him to feel. Or, maybe it was that I suspected he did feel that way and he wasn't admitting it. But any way you wanted to spin it, I was angry. It wasn't rational. I mean, what ever really is? But as irrational as it was, I was livid. I was furious. There was rage in my chest.

We are talking about probably the first man in my life who really saw me, who ever really understood me, who had so much in common with me . . . and he still didn't love me.

When you find that rare person who really knows who you are and they still don't love you . . .

I was burning.

BILLY: It was early enough in the day, I looked at Camila and I said, "What if we get in the car and drive somewhere?"

Camila said, "Where?"

I turned to Julia and I said, "If you could do anything right now, what would you do?"

And she didn't hesitate. She screamed, "Disneyland!" So we packed up the car and drove the kids to Disneyland.

DAISY: My car was parked along the PCH and I heard this line in my head. *Regret me.*

All I had in my car to use as paper was the back of my registration and a gas station napkin. And I searched high and low for something to write with. There was nothing in the door compartment. Nothing in the glove box. I got out of the car and I searched under the seats and under the passenger's seat was a stick of eyeliner.

I started writing. Lightning fast, maybe ten minutes. Beginning to end I had a song.

Billy: I was watching Julia in the teacups with Camila and I'm watching them go around and around. And the twins are asleep in the stroller. And I'm trying to put the morning out of my head. But I'm losing my mind because . . . well, it was complicated, obviously.

And then, you know what I realized? It wasn't very important. How I felt about Daisy. History is what you did, not what you almost did, not what you thought about doing. And I was proud of what I did.

Daisy: Did Billy's actions really warrant the song? Probably not. I mean, no. They didn't. But that's the thing. Art doesn't owe anything to anyone.

Songs are about how it felt, not the facts. Self-expression is about what it feels to live, not whether you had the right to claim any emotion at any time. Did I have a right to be mad at him? Did he do anything wrong? Who cares! Who cares? I hurt. So I wrote about it.

Billy: We left Disneyland really late. I mean, they were shutting down the park.

Julia fell asleep on the way home. The twins had been asleep for a while. As we were driving back up the 405, I put KRLA on low volume and Camila put her feet up on the dashboard and her head on my shoulder. It felt so good, her head on my shoulder. I held my back straight and didn't move an inch, just so she'd keep it there.

There was this unspoken thing between Camila and I back then.

I mean, she knew Daisy was . . . She knew that things were . . . *[pauses]* I guess what I'm saying is that in some marriages you don't need to say everything that you feel.

I think saying everything that you think and feel . . . well, some people are like that. Camila and I weren't. With Camila and I, it was much more . . . we both trusted each other to handle the details.

I'm trying to think of how to explain it. Because when I say it now, it seems crazy, that Camila and I never discussed the fact that

I . . . It seems crazy that Camila and I didn't have this open conversation about Daisy. Because clearly, she was a big factor in our lives.

I know it might seem like maybe it was a lack of trust. That either I didn't trust her to know just what was going on with Daisy or that she didn't trust me enough to have been able to handle that. But it's really the opposite.

Right around this same time—give or take a few years, I can't remember—Camila got a call from this guy from her high school. Some guy that was on the baseball team and took her to the prom and all that. I think his name was Greg Egan or Gary Egan? Something like that.

She said to me, "I'm gonna go get lunch with Gary Egan." And I said, "Okay." And she went and got lunch with him and she was gone for four hours. No one eats lunch for four hours.

When she got back, she gave me a kiss and she, you know, started doing the laundry or something and I said, "How was your lunch with Greg Egan?" And she said, "Fine." And that's all she said.

In that moment, I knew that what happened between her and Gary Egan—whether she still felt anything for him, how he felt about her, anything that might have taken place—all of that wasn't my business. It wasn't anything she wanted to share. That was a singular moment for her and it had nothing to do with me.

I'm not saying that I didn't care. I cared a lot. I'm saying that when you really love someone, sometimes the things they need may hurt you, and some people are worth hurting for.

I had hurt Camila. God knows I had. But loving somebody isn't perfection and good times and laughing and making love. Love is forgiveness and patience and faith and every once in a while, it's a gut punch. That's why it's a dangerous thing, when you go loving the wrong person. When you love somebody who doesn't deserve it. You have to be with someone that deserves your faith and you have to be deserving of someone else's. It's sacred.

I have no tolerance for people that waste other people's faith in them. None at all.

Camila and I promised to put our marriage first. To put our family first. And we promised to trust each other in how best to do that. Do you know what you do with that level of trust? When someone says, "I trust you so much I can tolerate you having secrets"?

You cherish it. You remind yourself how lucky you are to have been given that trust every day. And when you have moments when you think, *I want to do something that would break that trust,* whatever that is—loving a woman you shouldn't be loving, drinking a beer you shouldn't be drinking—do you know what you do?

You get your ass up onto your two feet, and you take your kids to Disneyland with their mother.

Camila: If I've given the impression that trust is easy—with your spouse, with your kids, with anybody you care about—if I've made it seem like it's easy to do . . . then I've misspoken. It's the hardest thing I've ever had to do.

But you have nothing without it. Nothing meaningful at all. That's why I chose to do it. Over and over and over. Even when it bit me in the ass. And I will keep choosing it until the day I die.

Daisy: I called Simone that night, when I got back to my place. She was in New York. I hadn't seen her in a month or so, maybe more, by that point.

And it was one of the first nights in a really long time that I spent alone, not hanging out with anybody, not partying with somebody somewhere. It was just me in my cottage. It was so quiet it hurt my ears.

I called her and I said, "I'm all alone."

Simone: I could hear this deep sadness in her voice. Which is rare with Daisy if only because she's usually hopped up on something. Do you realize how sad you have to be to be sad on coke and dexies? I knew, if she knew how often I was thinking about her, she wouldn't feel lonely.

Daisy: Simone said, "Do me a favor. Picture a map of the world."

I was not in the mood. She said, "Just picture it." So I did.

And she said, "And you're in L.A. You're a blinking light, you with me so far?"

And I said, "Sure."

"And you know you blink brighter than anybody. You get that, don't you?"

And I said, "Sure." Just humoring her.

And then she said, "And then in New York today, and London on Thursday and Barcelona next week, there's another blinking light."

"And that's you?" I said.

She said, "That's me. And no matter where we are, no matter what time of day it is, the world is dark and we are two blinking lights. Flashing at the same time. Neither one of us flashing alone."

Graham: Billy called me at three in the morning one night. Karen was with me. I only answered the phone because I thought somebody must have died if I'm getting a call at three in the morning. Billy didn't even say hello, he just said, "I don't think this is gonna work."

And I said, "What are you talking about?"

And he said, "Daisy's gotta go."

And I said, "No. Daisy is not gonna go."

But Billy said, "I'm asking you, please."

And I said, "No, Billy. C'mon, man. We're almost done with the album."

And he hung up the phone and that was the end of it.

Camila: In the middle of the night one night, I heard Billy get up and pick up the phone. I was pretty sure he was talking to Teddy. I wasn't sure.

I heard him say, "Daisy's gotta go."

And I knew. I mean, of course I knew.

Graham: I just thought he was freaking out because he wasn't the star of the album anymore. I mean, I knew things between Billy and Daisy were dicey. But back then I thought music was just about music.

But music is never about music. If it was, we'd be writing songs about guitars. But we don't. We write songs about women.

Women will crush you, you know? I suppose everybody hurts everybody, but women always seem to get back up, you ever notice that? Women are always still standing.

Rod: Daisy wasn't scheduled to be in that day.

Karen: We were sweetening "Young Stars." I was in the lounge when I saw Daisy come in. You could tell she was whacked out.

Daisy: I was drunk. In my defense, it was five o'clock. Or close to it. Isn't that the international drinking time? No, I know. I'm aware it was absurd. Give me a little credit. I know how crazy I am.

Billy: I was in the control booth, listening to Eddie's overdubs, trying to get him to slow his stuff down a little when Daisy whips open the door and says she needs to talk to me.

Daisy: He tries to pretend he has no idea why I want to talk to him.

Billy: So I say okay and I step out into the kitchen with her. She hands me a napkin and the back of a bill or something. And she's scrawled all over it in black smudges.

Daisy: Eyeliner pencil smears easily.

Billy: I said, "What is this?"

She said, "This is our new song."

I looked at it again and I couldn't figure out what I was looking at.

She says, "It starts on the paper and then goes over to the napkin."

Daisy: He reads it one time and then he says, "We're not recording this."

And I say, "Why not?"

We are talking by a window and it's open and Billy leans over and he shuts the window. Just like, slams it shut. And then he says, "Because."

Billy: When you write a song that may or may not be about someone, you can be pretty sure they aren't going to ask. Because no one wants to sound like a jerk who thinks everything is about them.

Daisy: I said, "Give me one good reason why we shouldn't record this song."

He started talking and I interrupted him.

I said, "I'll give you five good reasons we should."

Billy: She put up her fist and then started counting her fingers off.

"One, you know it's good. Two, you were just saying the other day we need something hard, something less romantic. This is that. Three, we need at least one more song. Did you want to write another one together? Because I'll tell you right now, I sure don't feel like writing together. Four, it's written to the melody of that blues shuffle you've been working on so it's already on its way to a finished song. And lastly, five. I relooked at the track list. This album is about tension. If you want it to have movement, thematically, you need something to break. So here you go. It's all broken now."

Daisy: I had rehearsed my speech on the way over.

Billy: It was hard to make a case against it but I still tried.

Daisy: I said, "There's no reason not to record this song. Unless, there's something else bothering you?"

Billy: I said, "There's nothing bothering me, but I just say no."

Daisy: "You aren't the boss of the band, Billy."

Billy: I said, "We write together, and I'm not writing that with you." Daisy grabbed the papers and stomped out of the room and I thought that was that.

Daisy: I pulled everybody in the lounge. Everybody that was there.

Karen: Daisy literally dragged me by the sleeve.

Warren: I'm standing at the back door with a joint in my hand and I feel Daisy's hand on my shoulder and she's pulling me back into the studio.

Eddie: Pete was in the booth with Teddy. I'd been in the john. When I came out, Pete had come out, too. To see what was going on.

Graham: Pete and I were sitting in the lounge, working on something when suddenly, everyone's standing in front of us.

Daisy: I said, "I'm going to sing you all a song."

Billy: I found them all in the lounge. I was thinking, *What the fuck is going on?*

Daisy: I said, "And then we're going to vote on whether it should get recorded and put on the album."

Billy: I was so angry it was like I surpassed hot and went cold. Just frozen there, stunned. I could feel the blood drain out of me, like someone pulled the stop on a tub.

Daisy: I just went for it. Nothing accompanying me, just singing the song the way I heard it in my head. "When you look in the mirror/

take stock of your soul/and when you hear my voice, remember/you ruined me whole."

Karen: Her voice was guttural. Part of it was that she was clearly drunk or buzzed or something. And her voice was scratchy. But the combination of the two. It was an angry song. And she was angry singing it.

Eddie: It was rock 'n' roll! It was rage, man. She thrashed. When I tell people what it's like to make a rock album, I tell them about that day. I tell them about standing there in front of the hottest chick you've ever seen in your life, while she's singing her guts out, and everybody's feeling like she's about to lose her goddamn mind. In the best way possible.

Warren: You know when she had me? When I knew that song was fucking great? When she said, "When you think of me, I hope it ruins rock 'n' roll."

Billy: When she finished, everyone was dead quiet. And I thought, *Okay, good. They don't like it.*

Daisy: I said, "Who thinks the song should be on the album, raise your hand?" And Karen's hand went straight up.

Karen: I wanted to play on that song. I wanted to rock out onstage with a song like that.

Eddie: It's a scorned-woman song but it was a great one. I put my hand straight up. And Pete did, too. I think he liked that it really felt like dangerous stuff, you know? So much of what we were doing on that album sounded so soft.

Warren: I said, "Put me down as a yes," and then I put my joint back to my lips and went back to the parking lot.

Graham: We wouldn't have been voting if Billy liked the song, right? My instinct was to back him up. But it was also a great song.

Daisy: Everybody has their hands up but Graham and Billy. And then Graham put his up, too.

I looked at Billy in the back. I said, "Six against one." He nodded at me, at everybody, and he walked away.

Eddie: We recorded it without him.

Rod: It was time to think about how we were going to market this album. So I set the band up with a photographer friend of mine, Freddie Mendoza. Real talented guy. I played him a couple of the early tracks from the album just to give him a sense of what we were going for. He said, "I see it in the desert mountains."

Karen: For some reason I remember Billy saying he wanted to shoot the cover with us on a boat.

Billy: I'd thought we should do a shot of the sunrise. We'd already decided the album should be called *Aurora,* I think.

Daisy: Billy had decided the album should be called *Aurora* and nobody could really argue with him. But it was not lost on me. That this album I worked my ass off on was named after Camila.

Warren: I thought we should shoot the cover on my boat. I thought that would be cool.

Freddie Mendoza *(photographer)*: I was told to get a picture of the whole band with Billy and Daisy as the focus. Really no different than any other band photo shoot, right? You have to be keenly aware of who you're featuring and how to make it seem natural.

Rod: Freddie wanted a desert vibe. Billy said it was fine. So that was that.

Graham: We all had to be at this spot in the Santa Monica Mountains at the crack of dawn.

Warren: Pete was something like an hour late.

Billy: I looked at us all, as we were standing around waiting for the photographer to set up the shot, and I sort of stepped outside of myself a bit. I tried to see us as others would see us.

I mean, Graham was always a good-looking guy. Bigger than me, stronger than me. He'd grown a little rounder over the years we'd been living high on the hog but it looked good on him. And Eddie and Pete were gangly guys but they dressed well. And Warren had that mean 'stache that was cool back then. Karen was gorgeous in an understated way. And then there was Daisy.

Karen: We're all gathering up there and we all pretty much just have on jeans and a T-shirt. That's what Rod said, "Just wear what you'd normally wear." And then Daisy comes in and she's wearing cutoffs and a white tank top with no bra on. And she's got her big hoop earrings, the bangles up her arms. Her shirt was thin, and white, and you could see her nipples clear as day. And she knew that. And suddenly it was crystal clear to me: *This cover is gonna be about Daisy's chest.*

Daisy: I'm not apologizing for shit having to do with that album cover. I dress how I want to dress. I wear what I feel comfortable in. How other people feel about it is not my problem. I said that to Rod. I said that to Billy before. I had a lot of talks about it with Karen. *[Laughs]* She and I have agreed to disagree.

Karen: If we want to be taken seriously as musicians, why are we using our bodies?

Daisy: If I want to walk around topless, that's my business. Let me tell you, when you're my age, you're gonna be glad you took a picture of them then, too.

Graham: Billy and Daisy hadn't really spoken, that I could see, since "Regret Me."

Billy: There was nothing to say.

Daisy: He owed me an apology.

Freddie Mendoza: Billy had this denim-on-denim look, right? And then Daisy had on a shirt that was barely a shirt. And I knew that was the photo. His denim and her tank top.

I put the band along the road, against the guard-rail that stood between the pavement and the steep drop-off of the canyon. There was a huge, looming mountain, a hundred feet behind them. And the sun was coming up.

Between the seven of them standing there, all in their various poses, I could tell we were getting something great. I mean, it was just so much Americana in one photo, right? You got the road, and the dust and dirt. You've got this band on a cliff—half of them scruffy, half of them beautiful. You've got the desert and forest of the Santa Monica Mountains, with just a little bit of trees cropping up in the pale tan ground. And you've got the sun, shining down on all of it.

Then you've got Billy and Daisy, right?

They had each veered to opposite ends of the group. But I kept trying to get everyone to mix it up. And at one point, I watched as Daisy leaned forward. She was looking at Billy. I just kept shooting. I always try not to call any attention to anything. I try to hang back and let people do what they are going to do. So I just kept snapping as Daisy was looking at Billy. And everyone else is looking at me, at the camera. And then, for a split second, bam, Billy turns and looks at Daisy just as she's looking at him. And they locked eyes. And I caught it.

I thought, *That's good enough to be an album cover.* As soon as I think I have something good, I immediately feel freer, right? I feel ready to try stuff and move people around and I feel like I can push people a bit further because if they get mad at me and walk off, it's not a problem, right? So I said, "That's great, guys. Now let's go to the top of the mountain."

Billy: We had already been out there in the hot sun taking photos for an hour or two by that point. I was ready to go.

Graham: I said, "We're driving up. Not walking." And the photographer and I went back and forth a few times and finally it was decided that I was right.

Freddie Mendoza: We ended up in the perfect spot.

Billy and Daisy got out of the car and they stood there on top of this mountain. With just a clear blue sky behind them, right? And the rest of the band lined up, and they started standing in between Billy and Daisy and I said, "Let's do Billy, Daisy, Graham . . ." So I finally got Billy and Daisy next to each other and their body language was like they didn't want a single atom of their bodies in contact. I tried to make conversation to loosen them up. I said, "How did Daisy come to join the band?" Because I didn't know the story and I figured it would be easy to talk about.

Billy and Daisy both started talking at the same time and then they looked at each other again. I took a few shots and then I zoomed in on Billy and Daisy's torsos, their chests, as they were talking to each other. They were angled in, and there was so much . . . the negative space between them felt . . . alive somehow. Electric. There was so much *purpose* behind the not touching, right?

I could tell as I was looking through the viewfinder. I knew it was a great shot.

Daisy: When we were up there on top of the mountain, the guy put Billy and me next to each other and asked us some dumb question and immediately—Billy and I have barely said five words to each other in days—the first thing out of Billy's mouth is some dig at me.

Billy: It's some nerve, coming into my band and taking over my album and being at the center of my album cover and then interrupting me when I'm trying to answer the guy's question.

Karen: We were standing there, posing, the rest of us, and you could tell the camera wasn't even aimed at us. The guy wasn't even pretending to take our photo. Do you know how stupid you feel posing for a picture nobody's taking?

Warren: I accidentally sat on a rock that got loose and started tumbling down the hill. Almost knocked Eddie down with it. He had to jump out of the way.

Eddie: It was a long day. I was getting so sick of those fucking people.

Graham: I was standing on the top of a mountain, with the woman I loved, shooting a cover for an album we all knew was going to be a massive hit. I swear, I think about that day sometimes when I'm feeling low. I think about it to remind myself you never know what kind of crazy good shit is around the corner. But it's hard not to remember, when I think about that day, that lots of crazy bad shit is often around the corner, too.

Freddie Mendoza: When I started developing the images I knew the one of the band against the guardrail with Billy and Daisy looking at each other . . . I knew that one was great, right? But then I pulled out the best one from the shots of Billy and Daisy's torsos, and I just went, "Fuck yeah." It's the kind of great photograph that—the moment you see it—you can't help but have an emotional reaction.

He was in denim, you could see her chest. You knew who they were, even without seeing their faces. You could fill in the gaps yourself. With the clear blue sky between them, which was framed in a more or less straight line on Billy's side and then on Daisy's side it was curvy, because it ebbed and flowed with her body . . . it was masculine and feminine at the same time.

And then when you really looked, you could see there was something in her pocket. I didn't know what it was for sure. It looked like a vial—I was assuming for pills or powder. And it just brought it all together. It was America. It was tits. It was sex. It was drugs. It was summer. It was angst. It was rock 'n' roll.

So there it was, Billy and Daisy, their torsos on the front. And then the whole band with Billy and Daisy looking at each other on the back. A great fucking album cover. If I do say so myself.

Daisy: It was coke, in my pocket. What else would it be? Of course it was dope.

Billy: You know when you just can't stop clocking where somebody is? Even when you tell yourself you don't care? I just . . . I felt like I was always trying not to look at her. *[Laughs]* I swear that guy just caught the only two times I was looking at her. He caught me on the front cover and the back cover.

Graham: When Teddy showed us the full mock-up of the album sleeve, with Billy and Daisy on the front and then them looking at each other on the back . . . None of us should have been surprised. But it does sting a little, to know you're not the main attraction. I mean, I'd been living in my brother's shadow from basically the day I was born. I was starting to wonder how much longer I had to do that.

EDDIE: Billy and Daisy always believed they were the most interesting people in the world. And that whole album cover confirmed it for them.

BILLY: It's a great cover.

DAISY: It's iconic.

Karen: Recording was really starting to wind down. We were back in the studio putting finishing touches on stuff.

Eddie: I think it was sometime after we finished the overdubs on "This Could Get Ugly" and I was at the studio listening to some of the tracks with everybody. Well, not Warren and Pete or Billy. They weren't there. And then Teddy left at some point. And then Rod. And I think even Artie left. And then I was gonna call it a night so I went out to my car to go home and I realized I forgot my keys so I came back real quick. And I heard two people screwing! And I thought, *Who the hell is getting off in the bathroom?*

And then I heard Graham's voice. And I saw, through the crack in the door, Karen's hair. And I just ran right out of there. Got in my car. Drove home. But when I got home, I realized I was still smiling. I was happy for them. They made a lot of sense together. I thought, *I bet they get married*. And I never thought that about anybody.

Warren: I think I finished my last tracks somewhere in December. I remember thinking I was ready for this album to be done so we could get back on the road. I wanted the crowds and cheering and the groupies and the drugs. Also, something they don't tell you when you buy a houseboat . . . it's very easy to get cabin fever. That's really meant to be more of a *weekend* thing.

Karen: As we all got done with our parts on the album, we started taking off. Taking a much-needed break. When Graham and I had laid down everything we were supposed to, we rented a place in Carmel for a few weeks. Just the two of us, a cabin, the beach, the trees. Well, and shrooms.

Graham: I think Eddie and Pete went back to the East Coast for their mom's birthday or something.

Eddie: I needed to let loose. After our parents' anniversary party, Pete and Jenny stayed with our parents and I spent about two weeks in New York.

Daisy: There wasn't anything left for me to do. I'd recorded my vocals. The album cover was done. Our tour dates weren't set yet. I said, "Screw it, I'm going to Phuket." I needed a trip to clear my head.

Billy: I took a little bit of time off but then I went back in the studio with Teddy and we went through that album second by second, track by track, and we remixed and remixed and remixed until it was perfect. Teddy, Artie, and I were in the control room for what felt like twenty hours a day for three weeks or something.

Occasionally, I'd get in there and rerecord some of the instruments when we felt like a riff wasn't exactly right or we wanted to add tack piano or a Dobro or some brushes on the drums. Simple stuff.

Artie Snyder: It was one album when everyone left and when everyone came back it was . . . it was a different album. It was much more nuanced, layered, innovative. Teddy and Billy went in and filled in all the air. They added cowbells and shakers and claves and scrapers. I think at one point, we even recorded the sound of Billy's fist hitting the side of the arm of a chair because we liked the hollow sound it made.

Teddy and Billy had a real vision. They had a keen sense for how the songs needed to build and Teddy had a real focus on momentum.

You take a song like "Regret Me," which, when they started with it, was just the one vocal and a pretty simple shuffle and Teddy pretty much forced Billy to get in there and do a whole second vocal layer. Billy didn't want to at first, but by the end of it, he'd put a big stamp on that song. He rewrote and recorded the main riff, he and Teddy pulled Warren's drums back until the prechorus. I mean, they made it a new song.

On "Aurora," Billy slowed it down, thinned out Karen's keys, and turned Graham way up. It became much cleaner.

Teddy and Billy—and it got to be me, too—we had a shorthand. We were having fun with it. I think that really shows. I think it shows on the final cut. The final mix of that album is dynamite material.

Billy: When we had the songs how we wanted them, Teddy and I gave a lot of thought to the song order. People like it when you make them sad, I think. But people hate it when you *leave* them sad. Great albums have to be roller coasters that end on top. You gotta leave people with a little bit of hope. So we thought for a real long time about the track list. We had to get that just right. We ordered it, thematically and instrumentally.

You start big and bold, "Chasing the Night."

Things start getting more intense with "This Could Get Ugly."

Then "Impossible Woman" is wild and dark. It has a haunting quality to it.

"Turn It Off" takes off running. It's an anthem.

"Please" is desperate, there's urgency and begging.

You turn to side B.

"Young Stars" is tortured but up-tempo, it's a little dangerous but you can dance to it.

And then you go right into "Regret Me," which is hard and fast and raw.

And then come down off it with "Midnights," which gets a little sweeter.

You lead into "A Hope Like You." Slow, and tender and wistful and spartan.

And then, you know, the sun comes up at the end. You leave on the high note. You go out with a bang. "Aurora." Sprawling and lush and percussive.

The whole album . . . it's a great ride. Start to finish.

Simone: I was in Manhattan when I got a postcard from Daisy from Thailand.

Daisy: For the first few days I was in Thailand, I just wanted to decompress. I had this idea that I would go somewhere alone and maybe reflect on myself. Obviously, that didn't happen. Two days in, I was going stir-crazy. I was almost about to book myself a flight home, five days early.

Simone: The postcard she sent just said, "Come to Phuket. Bring coke and lipstick."

Daisy: But then I met Nicky.

I was laying outside at the pool, looking out over the water. High off my ass. And this incredibly handsome, tall, elegant-looking man came out and he was smoking a cigarette and I said, "Can you put that out please?" Because I hated smelling smoke unless I was smoking.

He said, "You think just because you're gorgeous you get what you want?" And he had this fabulous Italian accent.

I said, "Yes."

And he said, "Okay, then. You are right." And he put out the cigarette. He said, "I'm Niccolo Argento." And I thought that was such a great name. I kept saying it over and over. *Niccolo Argento. Niccolo Argento.* He bought me a drink. And then I bought him one. And then we did a line or two off the side of the pool, *as you do,* and then I realized he had no idea who I was. Which was sort of a novelty, at that point. Because most people at least knew "Honeycomb." So I tell him about the band and he tells me about himself, that he travels from place to place, never staying anywhere for too long. He calls himself an "adventurer." He says he's in search of a "full life of experiences." Then, it comes out that he's a prince. He's an Italian prince.

The next thing I know, it's four in the morning and we're in my hotel room, listening to records at full volume, and the hotel staff are telling us to keep it down and Niccolo has LSD and he's telling me he loves me and I'm saying that I know it sounds crazy but I think I love him, too.

SIMONE: I wanted to see her and I had a few weeks off between gigs and I was a little worried about her, which at this point was just status quo. So I bought a plane ticket.

DAISY: Over the next few days, I told Nicky everything. I bared my soul to him. He loved the music I loved. And the art I loved. And the pills I loved. He made me feel like he was the only one that could ever understand me. I told him how lonely I was and how hard it had been to work on that album. And how I felt about Billy. I didn't hide anything from him. I opened up and just let it pour out. And he listened to it all.

At one point, I said, "You must think I'm crazy."

And he said, "My Daisy, everything about you makes perfect sense to me."

It seemed like there wasn't anything about me, any truth that I could tell him, that he wouldn't accept. Acceptance is a powerful drug. And I should know because I've done 'em all.

SIMONE: I flew into Thailand and I was exhausted and jet-lagged and I got on a rickety bus to get to the hotel. I checked in. I asked the concierge what room Lola La Cava was in and . . . she'd checked out. She was gone.

Daisy: Nicky and I were out at this disco in Patong. And he got this idea that we should pack up and go to Italy. He said, "I have to show you my country." I must have called somebody and booked two tickets to Florence at some point because these tickets just showed up at the door one morning.

So Nicky and I flew to Italy. And I swear I was halfway there before I remembered Simone was on her way to meet me.

Simone: I tracked her down by pretending to be her while talking to her credit card company.

Daisy: Nicky and I were in the Boboli Gardens in Florence when he said, "Let's get married." So then we flew to Rome and got married by some family friend of his who was a priest. We said I was Catholic. I lied to a Catholic priest. But I was wearing this gorgeous ivory off-the-shoulder cotton lace dress with huge bell sleeves.

I regret that marriage, but I do not regret that dress.

Simone: I finally found Daisy in this grand, massive hotel room overlooking Vatican City in Rome. In Rome! I had to fly halfway around the world and back to find her. And when I did, she was completely bombed, naked except for a pair of underwear. And she had chopped her hair off into this shaggy bob.

Daisy: That was a great haircut.

Simone: It was a really good haircut.

Daisy: I've always said, "The Italians know hair."

Simone: Daisy didn't even seem all that surprised to see me. Which just told me how messed up she was. And the first thing I noticed when I sat down was that she had a huge diamond ring on her hand.

And this guy comes out—thin body, thick curly hair—and he had no shirt on. And Daisy says, "Simone, this is my husband, Niccolo."

Daisy: Technically, marrying Niccolo made me a princess. That can't be left out of the equation. I did like the idea of belonging to a huge royal family. Of course, that's not what my life with Nicky was like at all. I should have known being with Nicky wouldn't turn out the way he made it seem. Here's a lesson for everybody, take it from me: Handsome men that tell you what you want to hear are almost always liars.

Simone: I tried to get her to come home but she wasn't budging. Because when I would tell her there were things she had to do—you have to get ready to tour for your album or you should stop doing so many drugs at one time or you should try to spend a little time sober—there was Nicky telling her she didn't have to do anything she didn't want to do. He was there, amplifying all of her bad instincts. All the time. He was like a bird chirping in her ear, validating every impulse.

Karen: When we all met back up in January, Daisy wasn't anywhere to be found.

Graham: We are sitting in Teddy's office over at Runner with Rich Palentino and we're all gonna give the final mix a listen. And we were all expecting to . . . Well, we all figured we knew exactly what we'd recorded, give or take.

Warren: I was hungover and there was no coffee in either of the coffeepots at Runner's offices. I said to the secretary at the front desk, "What do you mean there's no coffee?"

And she said, "The machine is broken."

I said to her, "Well, I'm sure as shit not gonna be alive in this meeting then."

She said, "You're too much." And then she seemed a little bit mad, like I couldn't get a read on her. And I was really hungover.

I said, "Wait, I haven't slept with you, have I?"

I had not.

Karen: The album starts playing, we're all sitting around the table . . .

Eddie: First song, out of the gate, "Chasing the Night," he changed my fucking lick. He changed my motherfucking lick.

Billy: I don't think I realized, until we were listening to it all together . . . I don't think I realized just how many things Teddy and I had changed.

Eddie: It just got worse from there. He changed the tuning on "Please." Completely changed it and rerecorded it. As if I wasn't going to notice he'd shifted to Nashville tuning. Like I'm not going to notice that the song has to be played on a different goddamn guitar. And everybody else, they saw it! They could see what he'd done. But no one was going to speak up, you know what I'm saying? Because Teddy and Runner were so happy with the record that they were talking about booking stadiums and pressing over a hundred masters and all this shit. They're saying they want to release "Turn It Off" as soon as possible and they think it can hit number one. So everybody had dollar signs in their eyes and nobody said much of anything to Billy. Or Teddy.

Karen: He'd pulled my keys off of two songs. And I was mad, of course I was mad. But what were we gonna do? You've got Rich Palentino so excited about the album, he's spitting when he talks.

Warren: I'd have respected it a lot more if Billy hadn't tried to pretend he wasn't producing the album with Teddy. I don't like underhanded shit. I don't like saying one thing and doing another.

But I was also the drummer in a successful rock band that everybody was saying was headed to the top of the charts. I've always had a good sense of perspective. If I do say so myself.

Rod: That's when the whispering started. Everybody stopped talking to each other and all started whispering to me.

Karen would say, "He took out my keys and he didn't even run it by me."

And I'd say, "You have to talk to him about it."

And she wouldn't.

And Pete would say that the record was too soft now. That he was embarrassed by it. And I'd say, "Talk to Billy about it."

I'd say to Billy, "You need to talk to your bandmates."

He'd say, "If they want to talk to me, they'll talk to me."

And everybody's wondering when Daisy's coming back, but I'm the only one willing to try to track her down.

Graham: It was a strange reminder that things were changing. That we weren't the same band we were a few years ago. A few years ago, if Billy was going to rerecord Eddie's tracks, he would have talked to me about it. He would have bounced the idea off of me. Instead, he was talking to Teddy. But that was true of a lot of things between Billy and me. I had Karen. He had Camila and his girls. And when he wanted to talk about ideas . . . well, at least throughout the recording of *Aurora* . . . he had Daisy. I'm not going to say I was feeling like Billy didn't need me anymore. That's dramatic. But maybe I was feeling like we weren't a team all the time anymore. That we'd outgrown that.

You know, I think a lot of how I defined myself was in relation to him. I always—my whole life until around that point—I always felt like Billy Dunne's little brother. And that was when it occurred to me that he probably never defined himself as Graham Dunne's older brother. Would never have thought to.

Billy: In hindsight, I can see why they were mad. But I don't regret any work I did on that album. The work speaks for itself.

Karen: It's so complicated. Was the album our best one because Billy was forced to let us in on the composing and arranging from the outset? I think so. Was it the best one because Billy ultimately took the reins back? Because Teddy knew when to make Billy listen to other ideas and when to let him run the show? Was it only the best because of Daisy? I have no idea. I spent a lot of time thinking about it and I have no idea.

But when you're a part of something as big as that album ended up being . . . you want to know if you were an integral part. You want to believe they couldn't have done it without you. Billy never did put much effort into making everyone feel integral.

Billy: All bands have trouble with this stuff. You know how hard it is to get this many people to agree on anything this subjective?

Artie Snyder: I heard little inklings of grief, later. That some of the band weren't happy with the changes. Or maybe the *way* the changes were handled. But I thought it was sort of odd, the way everyone was getting upset at Billy as if he was in charge. Teddy was in charge. If Billy redid Eddie's tracks, it's because Teddy thought Billy should redo the tracks. I never once saw Billy do anything Teddy wasn't backing.

I even made a joke once, when Teddy was out of the room. Billy had wanted to take out the Dobro on some song but Teddy wanted it in. When Teddy was gone, I said, "Should we just go ahead and take it out and see if he notices?"

Billy shook his head, really serious. He said, "Biggest hit we've had was a song I thought I hated. Teddy's the only one that saved it." He said, "If it comes down to his opinion or my opinion, we go with his opinion."

Simone: I finally got Daisy to agree to buy a plane ticket to be back in L.A. for the start of rehearsals.

Daisy: When I told Nicky that it was time for me to go back to L.A., he wasn't very supportive. The band had to do press and prerelease stuff. We had to get ready to head out on tour. And he knew that. I had told him all of that when we met. But he said, "Don't go. Stay here. The band doesn't mean anything." And that hurt. Because the band meant everything. This thing that felt like all of my worth . . . he treated it like it was nothing. I'm embarrassed to say he almost had me. I almost didn't leave for the airport.

Simone knocked on the door and Nicky said, "Don't answer it."

I said, "It's Simone. I have to answer it." She was standing there and she had this furious look on her face, and I'll never forget, she said, "Get. Your. Fucking. Suitcase. And. Get. In. The. Cab. Now." I'd never seen her like that. And something just sort of clicked in me.

You have to have one person in your life that you know would never do anything to steer you wrong. They may disagree with you. They could even break your heart, from time to time. But you have to have one person, at least, who you know will always tell you the truth.

You need one person who, when the shit hits the fan, grabs your stuff, throws it in a suitcase, and gets you away from the Italian prince.

Simone: I dragged her ass home.

Karen: Daisy comes back from this monthlong vacation and she's somehow ten pounds lighter than when she left, which, you know,

Daisy didn't have ten pounds to lose. And she's cut all of her hair off and she's got a diamond ring on, and she's a princess.

Billy: I was floored—I mean absolutely positively floored, my jaw about hit the floor—when she showed up married.

Daisy: What did he care? Honestly, what did he care? That's what I was thinking. He was married. I couldn't be married?

Warren: Let's not go crazy here. She married *the son* of a prince. When she got back I asked her how many people had to die before this guy was king and she said, "Well, technically, the Italians don't have a monarchy anymore." So . . . that doesn't sound like much of a prince to me.

Rod: We were slating the album for release that summer. As it got closer, we started sending the finished record out to critics and magazines. We had a lot of requests for interviews.

We wanted a big, splashy magazine cover to hit the stands right as the album came out. Obviously, we wanted *Rolling Stone*. And Daisy, specifically, wanted Jonah Berg again. So I made the call and he agreed to do it.

Jonah Berg: The plan was that I was going to hang out with them during rehearsals.

I did feel a certain connection with them, the band, because I knew that it had been my article that had pushed them into doing an album together. So if I thought the album sucked, that would have been a little embarrassing. But I was really blown away by it. Lyrically, there was a lot going on. Billy and Daisy were credited equally. And some of the most gripping songs were ones where they were credited together. So I was coming into the situation assuming that the story here was that Billy and Daisy had an intense collaborative chemistry.

Karen: The first few days of rehearsal, it was really subtle, but if you were paying attention, you'd notice that Billy and Daisy never actually spoke to each other.

Graham: As we were talking about the set for the show, we were all sitting around on the stage, but Billy and Daisy wouldn't address each other directly. I remember Billy suggested we not play "Honeycomb" anymore, even though it was a big hit for us. He suggested sticking to *Aurora*—and maybe one or two other songs.

Daisy looked at me and said, "What do you think, Graham? I think people will expect it. We don't want to disappoint them." I could not understand why she was directing it to me.

Before I could even answer, Billy looked at me and said, "But it's slow. We have to keep in mind we're playing bigger venues. We need stuff that plays to a crowd." I was about to ask Billy if that meant he didn't want to do "A Hope Like You" either, because that's also a slow one. But before I could, Billy said, "So that settles it then."

And Daisy said, "Well, what does everybody else think?"

And the whole time, they weren't even making eye contact. We were all standing around, watching them talk near each other.

Billy: The first day we rehearsed, I came in with a good attitude. I said to myself, *This is somebody I need to work with. Forget whatever chaos is going on. This is a professional relationship.* I tried to put my personal issues with her aside. And you know what? I was still mad about her calling for a vote on "Regret Me." Yeah, I was. But it was water under the bridge. It had to be. So I made sure that my tone was kind and I kept my nose to the grindstone.

Daisy: I was ready to put all of that crap between Billy and me in the past. I was married now. I was trying to keep my focus on Nicky. I was really trying to make it work.

Nicky had finally agreed to join me as we went into rehearsals. He flew in from Rome and moved into my place at the Marmont.

He even had dinner with my folks. I almost never had dinner with my folks. But I asked them if they wanted to meet him and they invited us out to Chez Jay. He was incredibly polite and sweet and really impressed them. He pulled out the whole "Yes, Mrs. Jones. No, Mr. Jones" thing and they liked that and then the minute we got to my car afterward, he said, "How can you stand those people?" And I smiled about as wide as humanly possible.

I liked being married. I liked the idea of us being a team, of being tied to this one person. I had somebody who asked how my day was, every day.

Simone: In theory, marriage made a lot of sense for Daisy. She needed stability back then. I mean, she has always been my best friend. Always will be. But she wanted someone to share her life with. Someone who loved her and cared about her and worshipped her. She wanted someone that, when she wasn't home by a certain time, would wonder where she was. So . . . I understood what she was trying for. I wanted that for her, too.

She just picked the wrong person for the wrong reasons.

Daisy: Obviously there were a lot of signs that I'd made a wrong turn. Niccolo was deeper in the dope than I was. I was the one telling him to slow it down. I was the one turning down heroin. I was the one noticing just how much we were putting on my credit cards. And he was very threatened by Billy. He was jealous of anyone that I had previously dated or had feelings for and anyone that he perceived as someone I might *possibly* sleep with. At the time, I chalked it up to newlywed problems.

They say the first year of marriage is the hardest and I really took that to heart back then. I wish someone had told me that love isn't torture. Because I thought love was this thing that was supposed to tear you in two and leave you heartbroken and make your heart race in the worst way. I thought love was bombs and tears and blood. I did not know that it was supposed to make you lighter, not heavier. I didn't know it was supposed to take only the kind of work that makes you softer. I thought love was war. I didn't know it was supposed to . . . I didn't know it was supposed to be peace. And you know what? Even if I did know that, I don't know that I would have been ready to welcome it or value it.

I wanted drugs and sex and angst. That's what I wanted. Back then I thought that the other type of love . . . I thought that was for other types of people. Honestly, I thought that type of love didn't exist for women like me. Love like that was for women like Camila. I distinctly remember thinking that.

SIMONE: Niccolo had a lot of good qualities. He did. He cared about her. He made her feel secure, in his own way. He used to make her laugh. They had inside jokes I never understood. Something about the game Monopoly. I don't know. But he genuinely made her laugh. And Daisy had such a great smile, and she'd been unhappy for a while.

But he was possessive. And you can't own anybody, let alone somebody like Daisy.

WARREN: I met Niccolo and I went, *Oh, okay, got it. This guy's a con artist.*

EDDIE: I kind of liked Niccolo. He was always real cool with me and Pete.

BILLY: Niccolo came down to the studio to hear us rehearse a lot. There was one day when Daisy and I . . . we were rehearsing the vocal harmonies and it wasn't jibing. We had a few moments of downtime and I said to her, "Maybe we need to shift this into a different key." That was more than I'd said to her in I don't know how long. But Daisy just said it was fine the way it was. I said, "If you can't hit the note exactly, we have to change something." She rolled her eyes at me. And I apologized. Because I didn't want to make a scene. I said, "Okay, I'm sorry." I figured it would work itself out.

But she just said, "I don't need your apologies, all right?"

I said, "I'm just trying to be nice."

She said, "I'm not interested in your *nice*." Then she shivered. And it was cold in the studio and she was wearing basically nothing. She looked cold to me.

And I said, "Daisy, I'm sorry. Let's just be on good terms, all right? Here, take my shirt." I had on a T-shirt and then a button-down over it. Or maybe I was wearing a jacket or something. Anyway, I took it off and I put it around her arms.

And she shrugged it off and she said, "I don't need your fucking jacket."

Daisy: Billy always knows best. He knows when you're not singing right. He knows how you should fix it. He knows what you should be wearing. I was so sick of being told by Billy how things were going to go.

Billy: I was sick and tired of being treated like *I* was her problem. She was *my* problem. And all I tried to do was give her my jacket.

Daisy: I didn't want his coat. What did I want his coat for?

Graham: Daisy was raising her voice a little bit. And the minute she did, Niccolo just came running in.

Karen: He was over by the couches we had in the corner, next to the cooler of beers. He always wore blazers over his T-shirts.

Warren: That fucker was drinking all the good beers.

Billy: He came running in toward me and grabbed me by my shirt. He said, "What's the problem here?" I knocked his hand away and I could tell, by the look on his face when I did it, that he was trouble.

Graham: I was watching it happen—this fight brewing—and I was thinking, *At what point do I step in here?*

I'm worried Billy's gonna clock him.

Karen: You wouldn't have thought, at first, that Niccolo was tough. Because he was so smarmy. And he wasn't muscular or anything. And he was supposedly some prince or what have you. But I watched him puff out his chest a bit and, look, Billy's a formidable guy. But you just got this sense that Niccolo was a little bit unhinged.

Warren: There's a code to two men fighting it out. You don't punch the nuts. You don't really kick. You never bite. Niccolo would have bitten. You could just see it.

Billy: Could I have taken him out? Maybe. But I don't think he wanted a fight any more than I did.

Daisy: I was not quite sure what to do. I think I just waited, watching it happen.

Billy: He said, "You stay away from her, okay? You work together and that's it. You don't talk to her, you don't touch her, you don't even look at her." I thought that was bullshit. I mean, sure, this guy can try to tell me what to do. But he shouldn't tell Daisy what to do. I turned and I looked at Daisy and I said, "Is this what you want?"

And she looked away for a moment and then she looked back at me and said, "Yes, that's what I want."

Daisy: Oh, the tangled messes I've created in my life.

Billy: I couldn't believe it. That she would . . . I had trusted her when all signs said that I shouldn't. And I was done doing that. Completely done doing that. She was exactly who I'd thought she was. And I felt like I'd been an idiot for thinking otherwise. I put my hands up and I said, "All right, man. You won't hear a peep from me."

Eddie: I couldn't believe it. Somebody had actually put Billy Dunne in his place.

Karen: It was that afternoon or maybe the next day that Jonah Berg came by for the first time. I was on pins and needles. I think we all were. Because Billy and Daisy wouldn't even look at each other. We rehearsed "Young Stars" all afternoon, and even when they were singing together, in harmony, they weren't looking at each other.

Jonah Berg: I show up and I'm expecting this warm atmosphere. I mean, this is a band that has just finished a great album. One where they are clearly all on the same page, working together seamlessly. Or so I thought. But I walk in, and they are in the middle of a song, and Daisy and Billy are about as far away from each other as two people can be, while still on the same stage. It was, visually, very jarring. You don't realize how often singers stand close to one another until you see two people facing forward, fifteen feet between the two of them, not even looking at each other.

Graham: I kept thinking, *Just get it together while this guy is here.*

Karen: In this instance, I'd say it was on Daisy to fix what had just happened. And she wasn't gonna do that.

Jonah Berg: But even with this tension in the room, the band sounded great. And the songs they were playing were great. That's one thing that The Six has always done, and they did it even better when they had Daisy on board. They made music that—it could be the first time you heard a song—but you were tapping your foot along with them. That's a testament to the work of Warren Rhodes and Pete Loving. Daisy Jones & The Six get a lot of credit for the intrigue of their lyrics—and certainly everyone's paying attention to Billy and Daisy, as well they should—but that was one hell of a rhythm section.

Billy: I asked Rod, at some point, if we could reschedule Jonah to another day.

Rod: It was too late to move Jonah. He was already there watching them rehearse.

Daisy: I didn't see why Billy had to make such a big deal out of it. We could easily have just made nice in front of Jonah Berg.

Jonah Berg: After a few songs, they take a break, they all come say hi to me at various points. I shared a cigarette with Warren outside and I figured he was my best chance at the truth. I said, "Level with me. Something's up here."

And he said, "Nothing's up." Just kind of shrugged his shoulders like he had no idea what I was talking about. And I trusted him. I believed that nothing out of the ordinary had happened, that this was just the way they worked together. Billy and Daisy just truly didn't get along. And probably never really had.

Billy: I think it was that night that Jonah wanted to take us all out for a beer but I had told Camila I'd be home to help her get the kids in the bath, so I asked Jonah if he could do the next night and it didn't seem to be a problem for him.

Eddie: We're all supposed to be putting this band first, and Billy blows off the first night we're supposed to be hanging out with *Rolling Stone* for the cover.

Daisy: I figured it was good news Billy was going home. I could take the first swing at the interview without worrying about him being around.

Jonah Berg: I appreciated that Daisy made herself available to me. So often, you go into a situation and you have certain band members that won't really talk to you. Daisy made it easy to get a story.

Rod: Daisy didn't want to go home. You know when you're with someone and it's clear they want to just keep hanging out, keep partying all night, keep working all night, keep doing whatever it is all night, because they don't want to go and face whatever they have waiting for them at home?

That was Daisy when she was married to Niccolo.

Jonah Berg: We all go out that night, everybody but Billy. First, we head out to this Bad Breakers show over on the Strip. And it seems really obvious to me that Karen and Graham must be sleeping together. And I say to them, I said, "Are you two an item?" And Graham says yes and Karen says no.

Graham: I didn't understand. I just didn't understand Karen.

Karen: Graham and I could never last, it was never . . . I just needed it to exist in a vacuum, where real life didn't matter, where the future didn't matter, where all that mattered was, you know, how we felt that day.

Jonah Berg: Warren seemed busy hitting on every woman he could find. And Eddie Loving was talking my ear off, talking about tuning or something. Pete was off with some girl he was seeing. So I decided to focus on Daisy. She was who I wanted to get the most from anyway.

Now, I will say this: A lot of people were getting high on whatever they could get their hands on back then. That wasn't anything new. And even as a journalist, there wasn't much you couldn't allude to in the pages of a magazine, certainly one like *Rolling Stone*. You could imply all sorts of stuff about what everybody was getting up to. But there were some people who didn't seem like they were snorting things for fun. There were some people out there who were getting high because they couldn't hold it together without it. And it was my personal opinion, that the drug habits of those people were sort of . . . off-limits. A lot of people in my position felt differently. A lot of them behaved differently, wrote differently.

I certainly got into a few situations over the years where I felt pressured—or was pressured, I should say—to out those people in the interest of selling magazines. So I tended to not even write down what I observed, or tell a single person what I saw, if I thought somebody I was interviewing had a serious drug problem. It was a very "see no evil" sort of thing. For me.

When I'm with Daisy that night, we are hanging out in the back of the crowd. And I look over and Daisy is rubbing her gums. And at first I thought it was coke but I realize she was snorting amphetamines. She did not seem like a recreational user, I guess is what I'm saying. And there seemed a significant difference in the Daisy I met on tour the year before and this Daisy now. She was more frenetic, less eloquent. Sadder, maybe. No, that's not it. Less joyful.

She said to me, "Do you want to go outside?" I nodded and we went into the parking lot and we sat on the hood of my car. And Daisy said, "All right, Jonah. Let's do this. Ask your questions."

And I said, "If you don't want to go on the record now, because you're . . . not in the right state of mind, you need to say so."

And she said, "No, let's talk."

I had given her an explicit out. And she turned it down. That's all I felt obligated to do. So I said, "What's going on between you and Billy?"

Then it all just started pouring out of her.

Daisy: I shouldn't have said what I said. And then Billy shouldn't have gone and done what he did.

Billy: I come into the rehearsal space the next day and everybody's there and they are all talking and messing around and Jonah says, "When should we set aside some time to talk?"

And I say, "Let me see when Daisy's free."

And he says, "Well, I want to get some time just the two of us, if you're good with that." That's when I started to get worried. Just the way he said it . . . I sort of had this feeling like, *What did she do?* I looked over at her and she was up at the mike, talking to somebody. And she had on tiny shorts again in this cold studio. And I just thought, *Put some fucking pants on*. That's what I was thinking. *You're cold. Stop dressing like it's gonna be hot in here. You know that it's cold in here every day.* But of course she was hot, she was sweating bullets from all the drugs in her body. I knew that.

Daisy: I think that if I had gone up to Jonah that day, after talking to him that night, and tried to take it all back, he might have let me. And I considered it. I really did.

Jonah Berg: I absolutely would not have agreed to let Daisy rescind her comments. People have asked it before. I've always said no. That's why I'm very clear at the beginning, when I start recording. I make sure people understand what they are doing when they talk to me.

I gave Daisy plenty of outs. She moved forward. At that point, the question of integrity shifts from being my problem to her problem.

Billy: So we rehearse for the morning and Daisy and I just can't get the harmony right in the last verse of the song but I don't want to get into a fight with her in front of Jonah. I also don't want to be performing this poorly in front of him either. The last thing I want is an article that says that we don't have what it takes live. So when we break, I ask Graham to talk to her and he agrees. And Daisy and I, for at least the rest of that session, just sort of communicated through Graham.

Graham: I mean, how was I supposed to keep track of their bullshit? Who's not talking to who when and for what goddamn reason? I've got my own problems. I've got my own heart cracking, man. I'm in love with a woman that I am starting to think doesn't love me and I'm not telling a single soul about it and you don't see me asking for intermediaries to save me from my own brand of crap, do you?

Billy: After we call it a day, I go out with Jonah and I'm sitting there, banging the 57 on a bottle of ketchup, when he says, "Daisy says you spent your first tour cheating on your wife and dealing with alcoholism and drug addiction, possibly a heroin addiction. She says you're in recovery now but that you missed the birth of your first daughter because you were in rehab."

Warren: I don't consider myself to be very high on the list of good people. But you don't tell other people's stories.

Daisy: I did so many stupid things back then. Basically for all of the seventies. I did a lot of things that hurt people or hurt myself. But that one has always stuck out to me as one I particularly regret. Not just because of Billy. Although, I did feel badly that I shared something he told me in confidence. But I regret it more because I could have hurt his family.

And I just . . . *[pauses]* I would never want to do that. Truly.

Billy: You know, one of the things you learn in recovery is that self-control is the only control we have. That all you can do is make sure your own actions are sound because you can't control the actions of others. That's why I didn't do what I wanted to do, which was take the bottle of ketchup and throw it at the window. And I did not reach across the table and wring Jonah Berg's neck. And I did not get in the car, find Daisy, and start screaming at her. I did not do any of those things.

I stared right at him, and I could feel my breath growing really hot. I could feel my chest expanding up and down. I felt like a lion, like I was capable of destroying him. But I closed my eyes and I stared at the back of my own eyelids and I said, "Please do not print that."

Jonah Berg: That confirmed for me that it was true. But I said, "If you can give me something else to write about, then I won't." I mean, I told you. I don't like printing secrets when they're sad. I got into journalism to tell rock 'n' roll stories. Not to tell depressing ones. Give me rock stars sleeping with groupies, give me the crazy shit you did on PCP. Great. But I've never liked publishing depressing shit. People's families falling apart and all that. I said, "Give me something rock 'n' roll." That felt like a win-win.

And Billy said, "How about this? I can't fucking stand Daisy Jones."

Billy: I will tell you exactly what I said. It's right there in the article. I said, "She's a selfish brat who's been given everything she wants her entire life and thinks it's because she deserves it."

Jonah Berg: When he said, "Talent like Daisy's is wasted on people like Daisy," I went, *Oh, wow. Okay. Here is a great article.* It was a way more interesting story to tell, in my opinion. What's gonna sell more copies? Billy Dunne used to be an alcoholic and now he's reformed? Or the two lead singers in this hip new band loathe each other?

It was no contest. The world was filled with Billy Dunnes. So many men in this world missed their daughters' births or stepped out on their wives or whatever else he did. Sorry to say it but that's the world we live in. But not many people are so creatively in sync with someone they despise. That was fascinating.

My editor loved the idea. He couldn't have been more amped about it.

I told the photographer what I wanted for the cover and he said it would be easy enough to splice together from the photos he had taken. So I went back to New York and I wrote that article in forty-eight hours. I never write articles that fast. But it was just so easy. And those articles are always the best ones—the kind you swear wrote themselves.

Graham: The entire point of having Jonah Berg out with us was so that he could write an article about what a smart move it was to have Daisy join the band. And, instead, he writes about Billy and Daisy hating each other.

Eddie: It felt like those two assholes let their own personal crap taint the band and the music and all the hard work we'd all put into it.

Rod: It all landed so *perfectly.* The band just couldn't see it. They couldn't see how great it was.

We released "Turn It Off" as the first single. We booked the band on *Midnight Special.* We had them doing radio spots all over the country leading up to the album dropping. And then, the same week *Aurora* hits the shelves, so does the *Rolling Stone* cover.

Billy's profile shot on one side, Daisy's on the other, their noses almost touching.

And it says, "Daisy Jones & The Six: Are Billy Dunne and Daisy Jones Rock 'n' Roll's Biggest Foes?"

Warren: I saw that and I just had to start laughing. Jonah Berg always thinks he's one step ahead when he's two steps behind.

Karen: If there was any chance that Billy and Daisy were going to put the pettiness behind them and work together, really work together, over the course of the tour, I think that magazine interview ended it. I don't think there was much coming back from it.

Rod: Is there any headline that is going to make you want to see Daisy Jones & The Six perform live more than that?

Billy: I didn't care if Daisy was mad at me. I didn't care one bit.

Daisy: We both did things we shouldn't have. When someone says your talent is wasted on you and he says it to a reporter knowing full well it's going to make it into print, you aren't really inclined to mend fences.

Billy: You can't claim the high ground when you go around throwing other people and their families under the bus.

Rod: There's no diamond record without that *Rolling Stone* article. That article was the first step in their music transcending the limits of music. It was the first step toward *Aurora* not only being an album, but an *event*. It was the last kick it needed to blast off.

Karen: "Turn It Off" debuted at number 8 on the *Billboard* charts.

Rod: *Aurora* came out June 13, 1978. And we didn't hit with a splash. We hit with a cannonball.

Nick Harris *(rock critic)*: This was an album people had been waiting for. They wanted to know what would happen when you put Billy Dunne and Daisy Jones together for an entire album.

And then they drop *Aurora*.

Camila: The day the record hit the shelves, we took the girls down to Tower Records. We let Julia buy her own copy. I was a little wary of it, to be honest. It wasn't exactly child-friendly. But it was her dad's album. She was allowed to have her own copy of it. When we left the store, Billy said, "Who's your favorite member of the band?"

And I said, "Oh, Billy . . ."

And Julia pipes up and goes, "Daisy Jones!"

Jim Blades: I was playing the Cow Palace the day *Aurora* came out, I think. And I had a roadie go down to the record store and get it so I could listen to it. I remember sitting there, before we were about to go on, listening to "This Could Get Ugly," smoking a cigarette thinking, *Why didn't I think to get her to join* my *band?*

The writing was on the wall. They were gonna eclipse all of us.

With that cover, too. That cover was perfect California summer rock 'n' roll.

Elaine Chang *(biographer, author of* Daisy Jones: Wild Flower*)*: If you were a teenager in the late seventies, that cover was everything.

The way Daisy Jones carried herself, the way she was in full control of her own sexuality, the way she showed her chest through her shirt but it felt like it was on her own terms . . . it was a seminal moment in the lives of so many teenage girls. Boys, too, I understand. But I'm much more interested in what it meant for girls.

When you're talking about images in which a woman is naked, subtext is everything. And the subtext of that photo—the way her chest is neither aimed at Billy nor at the viewer, the way her stance is confident but not suggestive—the subtext isn't that Daisy is trying to please you or the man she's with. The subtext *isn't* "My body is for you." Which is what so many nude photos are, what so many images of naked women are used for. The subtext—for her body, in that image—it's *self-possession.* The subtext is "I do what I want."

That album cover is why I, as a young girl, fell in love with Daisy Jones. She just seemed so fearless.

Freddie Mendoza: It's funny. When I shot the album cover, I thought it was just a gig. Now, all these years later, it's all anybody asks about. That's what happens when you do something legendary, right? Ah, well.

Greg McGuinness (*former concierge, the Continental Hyatt house*): Once "Turn It Off" came out, everybody in town was talking about that record.

Artie Snyder: The week it came out—the very week it came out—I got three job offers. People were buying that album, listening to it, loving it, and they wanted to know who mixed it.

Simone: Daisy just blew up. She went from being well known to being an absolute sensation. She was it.

Jonah Berg: *Aurora* was a perfect album. It was exactly what we all wanted it to be, but better than we anticipated. It was an exciting band putting out a confident, bold, *listenable* album from start to finish.

Nick Harris: *Aurora* was romantic and brooding and heartbreaking and volatile all at once. In the age of arena rock, Daisy Jones & The Six managed to create something that felt intimate even though it could still play to a stadium. They had the impenetrable drums and the searing solos—they had songs that felt relentless in the best way possible. But the album also felt up close and personal. Billy and Daisy felt like they were right next to you, singing just to each other.

And it was deeply layered. That was the biggest thing *Aurora* had going for it. It sounds like a good-time album when you first listen to it. It's an album you can play at a party. It's an album you get high to. It's an album you can play as you're speeding down the highway.

But then you listen to the lyrics and you realize this is an album you can cry to. And it's an album you can get laid to.

For every moment of your life, in 1978, *Aurora* could play in the background.

And from the moment it was released, it was a juggernaut.

Daisy: It's an album about needing someone and having them love someone else.

Billy: It's an album about the push and pull of stability and instability. It's about the struggle that I live almost every day to not do something stupid. Is it about love? Yeah, of course it is. But that's because it's easy to disguise almost anything as a love song.

Jonah Berg: Billy and Daisy was our biggest-selling issue of the seventies.

Rod: *Rolling Stone* did a lot to get people to buy the record. But the real money was in how many people bought tickets to the show because of that article.

Nick Harris: You heard the album and you read about Billy and Daisy in *Rolling Stone* and you wanted to see it for yourself.

You *had* to see it for yourself.

AURORA WORLD TOUR

1978–1979

With "Turn It Off" summitting the charts and spending four weeks in the top spot, and Aurora *selling over 200,000 units every week, Daisy Jones & The Six was the act to see the summer of '78. The* Aurora *Tour was selling out stadiums and booking holdover shows in major cities across the country.*

Rod: It was time to get the show on the road. I mean that literally.

Karen: There was a weird feeling on the buses. And by buses I mean the blue bus and the white bus. They both said "Daisy Jones & The Six" across them, but one had Billy's denim shirt in the background and the other was Daisy's tank top. We had two buses because we had so many people. But also because Billy and Daisy never wanted to have to even look at each other.

Rod: The blue bus was Billy's bus, unofficially. Billy and Graham and Karen and myself, some of the crew, were normally on there.

Warren: I took the white bus with Daisy and Niccolo and Eddie and Pete. Jenny was with Pete sometimes. The white bus was a much better time. Also, yeah, I'll be on the bus with the tits painted on the window, thanks.

Billy: I had a full sober tour under my belt. I felt all right going back on the road.

Camila: I sent Billy out on tour like I did almost everything with him back then . . . with hope. That's all I could do, was just hope.

Opal Cunningham *(tour accountant)*: Every day that I went into the office, I knew three things. One, the band would spend more money than they had the day before. Two, no one would listen to my advice about how to curb spending. Three, anything of import—be it as big as baby grand pianos for the suites or as small as Sharpies for the autographs—you had to make sure Billy and Daisy both had the exact same thing. That rider was twice as long as it needed to be because one of them would get mad if the other had something they didn't.

I'd call Rod and I'd say, "There is no way they need two Ping-Pong tables."

Rod: I always said, "Just clear it. Runner will pay." I should have just made a recording of myself saying that. But I understood. Opal's job was to make sure we weren't wasting money. And we were wasting a lot of money. But we had the biggest album in the country at that moment. We could ask for whatever we wanted and it was in Runner's best interest to give it to us.

Eddie: First day out on the road, we stop at some gas station. Pete and I get out and go inside to get a soda or something. "Turn It Off" was playing on the radio. That wasn't that uncommon. Something like that had happened to us a lot in the past few years. But Pete makes a joke. He says to the guy, "Can you change the station? I hate this song." The guy changes the station and "Turn It Off" is on the next station, too. I said, "Hey, man, how about you just *turn it off*?" He thought that was funny.

Graham: It was the first time I saw how—what's the word I'm looking for?—how *invested*, I guess, people got in the band. Billy and I went to get a burger at a rest stop when we were somewhere in the desert. Arizona or New Mexico or something and this couple comes up to us. They say to Billy, "Are you Billy Dunne?"

Billy says, "Yeah, I am."

And they say, "We love your album." And Billy's handling it great, being really gracious. He always was. He was great with fans. He made it seem like every person who complimented him was the first person to do it. So Billy starts having a more one-on-one conversation with the guy and the woman pulls me aside and says, "I just have to know. Billy and Daisy? Are they together?"

And I pulled my head back and I said, "No."

And she nodded like she understood what I was trying to say. Like she knew they were sleeping together but accepted that I couldn't tell her that.

Warren: Real early on the tour, up in San Francisco, we check into this hotel the night before a show, and I walk right out of the white bus, Pete and Eddie coming out behind me. Graham and Karen come out of the blue bus. We walk right out onto the street and into the hotel, no problem.

Then Billy walks out of the blue bus and within, I don't know, thirty seconds, you hear girls start screaming. And then Daisy walks out of the white bus and this sound that you think can't get any louder, this shrieking sound that damn near burst my eardrums, it gets even louder somehow, even more shrill. I turn around and Rod and Niccolo are trying to push 'em all back so Billy and Daisy can get into the hotel.

Eddie: I once saw Billy decline to give a group of fans his autograph by saying, "I just play music, man. I'm no more important than anybody else." Watching that arrogant son of a bitch pretend to be humble was enough to make me want to scream. Pete kept telling me, "None of this matters. Don't get all confused thinking it matters." I didn't get what he meant until it was all too late, I think.

Daisy: When people asked for my autograph, I used to write, "Stay Solid, Daisy J." But when it was a young girl—which wasn't often but it did happen from time to time—I used to write, "Dream big, little bird. Love, Daisy."

Rod: People were excited about this band. They wanted to hear the album live. And Billy and Daisy could really deliver the goods. Not only were they dynamite but they were . . . hard to read. Enigmatic. They sang beautifully together, but they rarely got on the same mike. Sometimes they would look at each other and when they did, you couldn't figure out what they were thinking.

This one time in Tennessee, Daisy was singing "Regret Me" and Billy was doing backup and she turned toward him, at the end, at the very end, and sang right to him. She was looking right at him and singing at the top of her lungs. Her face went a little red. And he sang, looking right back at her. He didn't break her gaze. Then the song was over and they went on. Even I couldn't have told you what exactly had just happened.

Karen: In general, if you paid attention, you saw a lot of dirty looks between them. Especially during "Regret Me." Especially during that.

Rod: If you went to a Daisy Jones & The Six show thinking they hated each other, you could find some damning evidence for that. And if you went thinking something was up with them, that the hatred maybe masked something else, you could find evidence for that, too.

Billy: You can't write songs with somebody, write songs *about* somebody, know that some of the songs you're singing are ones they wrote about you . . . and not feel something . . . not be drawn to them.

Were there times I looked across the stage at Daisy and found myself unable to look away? I mean . . . yeah. Certainly, if you look at press photos from that tour, concert photos and what have you . . .

you'll see a lot of pictures of Daisy and I looking into each other's eyes. I told myself we were putting it on but it's hard to decipher, really. What was performance and what wasn't? What were we doing to sell records and what did we really mean? Honestly, maybe I knew at one time but I don't know anymore.

Daisy: Nicky was often jealous of what happened onstage.

"Young Stars" was about two people who were drawn to each other but forced to deny it. "Turn It Off" was about trying to fall out of love with someone you can't help but love. "This Could Get Ugly" was about knowing that you know someone even better than their partner does. These were dicey songs to be singing with someone. These were songs that made you feel something—made me feel what I felt when I wrote them. Nicky knew that. That was a very big part of our relationship. Making sure Nicky felt okay. That he was happy, making sure he was having a good time.

Warren: Night after night, it was packed shows, with a screaming crowd. With people singing along to every word. And then it always ended with Billy going back to his hotel room and the rest of us staying out partying until we found somebody to screw.

Except Daisy and Niccolo. They stayed out later than everybody. Everybody went to bed knowing Daisy and Niccolo thought the night was still young.

Daisy: The drugs aren't so cute anymore when you wake up with dried blood under your nose so often that cleaning it off is part of your morning routine, like brushing your teeth. And you always have new bruises and you don't know why. When there's a knot in the back of your hair because you have forgotten to brush it for weeks.

Eddie: Her hands were blue. We were backstage getting ready to go on in Tulsa and I looked at her and I said, "Your hands look kind of blue."

And she looked at them and said, "Oh, yeah." That was it. Just *oh, yeah.*

Karen: Daisy slowly became a person none of us felt much like dealing with. And for the most part, we really didn't have to. She wasn't particularly needy or anything. The only issues were when she let things get so out of control, it was everyone's problem. Like when she almost burned down the Chelsea.

Daisy: Nicky fell asleep having a smoke and the pillow caught fire at the Omni Parker House in Boston. I woke up because of the heat next to my face. Singed my hair. I had to put out the flames with the extinguisher I found in the closet. Nicky was completely unfazed by the whole thing.

Simone: I called her when I heard about the fire. I called her in Boston, I called her in Portland. I kept calling. She didn't return my calls.

Billy: I told Rod to get her help.

Rod: I offered to take her and Nicky to rehab and she said I was being silly.

Graham: She'd slur a word here or there, she took a fall down the stage steps at some point. I think maybe in Oklahoma. But Daisy knew how to make everything look like fun and games.

Daisy: We were in Atlanta. And Nicky and I had partied all night and somebody had mescaline. Nicky thought it was a great idea to do mescaline. Everybody else had gone to bed and so it was just Nicky and me, high on a lot of stuff at once. The mescaline had just kicked in.

We broke the lock on the door leading up to the roof at the hotel we were staying at. The fans that had staked outside the lobby of the hotel had all gone home. That's how late it was. He and I stood there, looking at the empty space where earlier in the day they had all been standing. It seemed romantic, the two of us up there. Everything quiet. Nicky took my hand and led me to the very edge of the roof.

I made a joke, I said, "What are you up to? You want us to jump?"

And Nicky said, "Could be fun."

I . . . Let me put it this way: When you find yourself high on the roof of a hotel with a husband who doesn't outright say that the two of you *shouldn't* jump off, you start to realize you have a lot of problems. That wasn't my rock bottom. But it was the first time I looked around and thought, *Oh, wow, I'm falling.*

Opal Cunningham: A large part of the growing budget was accounting for what damages they would leave behind. It was always Daisy's room that cost the most. We were paying hand over fist for broken lamps, broken mirrors, burnt linens. A lot of busted locks. Hotels expect a certain amount of wear and tear, especially when a band is coming through. But this was enough that they were demanding more than just keeping the security deposit.

Warren: I think it was around the southern leg of the tour that you could tell Daisy was . . . I don't know. Losing it. She was forgetting some of the words to the songs.

Rod: Before the show in Memphis, everyone's getting ready to go out onstage and no one could find Daisy. I was searching all over for her. Asking everyone about her. I finally found her in one of the bathrooms in the lobby. She'd passed out in one of the stalls. Her butt was on the floor, one of her arms over her head. For a second—a split second—I thought she was dead. I shook her and she woke up.

I said, "You're supposed to go onstage."

She said, "Okay."

I said, "You need to get sober."

And she said, "Oh, Rod." And she stood up, walked to the mirror, checked her makeup, and then walked backstage to meet the rest of the band like everything was right as rain. And I thought, *I don't want to be in charge of this woman anymore.*

EDDIE: New Orleans. Fall of 'seventy-eight. Pete finds me at sound check and says, "Jenny wants to get married."

I say, "All right, so marry her."

Pete says, "Yeah, I think I will."

DAISY: If you're fucked up all the time, you piece things together slower than you should. But I started to realize that Nicky never paid for anything, that he didn't have any of his own money. And he kept buying us more blow. I'd say, "I'm good. I've had enough." But he always wanted more. Wanted me to have more.

We were on the bus one morning, maybe December or so. We were laying down in the back, while everyone else was up front. I think we were stopped somewhere around Kansas because when I looked out the window all I saw were plains. No hills, not much civilization, even. I woke up and Nicky was there with a toot, right there. I just had this fleeting thought, *What if I didn't?* So I said, "No, thanks."

And Nicky laughed and said, "No, c'mon." And he put it right in my face and I snorted it.

And as I turned my head, to look down the aisle, I saw that Billy had stepped onto the bus for some reason, was talking to Warren or something. But . . . he saw the whole thing. And I caught his eye for a moment and I just got so sad.

BILLY: I made it a point to stay off the white bus. Nothing good for me happened on the white bus.

GRAHAM: We all went home for Christmas and New Year's.

BILLY: I was so happy to go home to my girls.

CAMILA: There was so much more to my life, so much more to my marriage, than the fact that my husband was in a band. I'm not saying that The Six wasn't a major factor, of course it was. But we were a family. Billy was expected to leave his work at the door when he came home. And he did that.

When I think back to the late seventies, I do think a lot about the band and the songs and . . . everything that we were going through with that. But I mostly think about Julia learning to swim. And Susana's first word sounding like "Mimia," and how we couldn't tell if she meant "Mama" or "Julia" or "Maria." Or Maria always trying to pull Billy's hair. And how he used to play a game with the girls called Who Gets the Last Pancake? As he was making pancakes, and the girls were eating them, he'd suddenly yell, "Who gets the last pancake?" And whichever girl put her hand up first got to eat it. But somehow, no matter what happened, he'd make them split the pancake.

That's the kind of thing I remember more than anything.

BILLY: Camila and I had just closed on our new house in Malibu, in the hills. Bigger than any house I ever thought I'd live in. With this long driveway and trees shading every part except the deck. The deck was totally unobstructed. You could see all the way out to the ocean. Camila used to call it "the house 'Honeycomb' built."

The two weeks that I was home for the holidays, we spent most of it moving in and getting settled. The first night we brought the girls, I said to Julia, "Which room do you want?" She was the oldest, so she got first pick. Her eyes went wide and she went off running down the hall, looking at each one. And then, she sat down on the floor in the middle of the hallway and she *deliberated*. And then she said, "I want the one in the middle."

I said, "Are you sure?"

She said, "I'm sure." She was just like her mom. Once she knew what she wanted, she knew.

Rod: That Christmas was the first time in a long time—a long, long time—that I didn't have to do any work. That I could just enjoy myself. That I didn't have to save some rock star from some crisis or make sure their rider was fulfilled or whatever I was doing.

I rented a cabin with this guy Chris. He and I moved in the same circles and I'd been seeing him whenever I was in town. We spent the holidays together in Big Bear. We made dinners together and went in the hot tub and played cards. For Christmas, I gave him a sweater and he gave me a day planner. And I thought, *I want to be normal*.

Daisy: Nicky and I flew to Rome for Christmas.

Eddie: Over the holiday, Pete asked Jenny to marry him and she said yes. I was real happy for him, you know? I gave him a big hug. He said, "I have to figure out when I'm going to tell everybody. I don't know how they are gonna take it."

I said, "What are you talking about? Nobody cares if you're married."

He said, "No, I'm leaving."

I said, "Leaving?"

He said, "At the end of the tour, I'm quitting the band."

We were at our parents' house in the den. I said, "What are you talking about? Quitting the band?"

He said, "I told you I didn't want to do this forever."

I said, "You never said that."

He said, "I've said that a thousand times to you. I told you this stuff doesn't matter."

I said, "You're talking about giving all of this up for Jenny? Really?"

He said, "Not really *for* Jenny. For me. So I can get on with my life."

I said, "What does that mean?"

He said, "I never wanted to be in a soft rock band. C'mon. You know that. I got on the train, I rode it for a little while. But my stop's coming up."

Daisy: Nicky and I got into a fight in the hotel room in Italy. He accused me of sleeping with Billy back in Kansas. I had no idea what he was even talking about. I didn't even talk to Billy in Kansas. But he said he'd known for weeks and he was sick of watching me try to hide it. Things got intense, really quickly. I threw a few bottles at him. He smashed his hand through the window. I remember looking down and seeing gray tears falling down my face. They were stained with my mascara and eyeliner. I don't remember exactly how it happened but one of my hoops got ripped out of my ear. Cut clear through. I was bleeding and crying and the room was trashed. And the next thing I know Nicky is holding me and we're promising to never leave each other's side and never fight like that again and I remember thinking, *If this is what love is like, maybe I don't want it.*

Rod: We had booked Daisy's flight to get in a full day early for the show in Seattle. I had her come in early because I was nervous she'd miss her flight and I needed to make sure we had a margin of error.

Daisy: The morning we were supposed to fly to Seattle, I woke up and Nicky was sitting over me. I realized I was soaking wet, sleeping in the base of the shower. I was groggy and confused but by that point I always woke up groggy and confused. I said, "What happened?"

He said, "I thought maybe you overdosed. On the Seconals or something. I couldn't remember what else we took." You know what happens when people overdose on Seconals? They die.

I said, "So you put me in the shower?"

He said, "I tried to wake you up. I didn't know what else to do. You wouldn't wake up. I was so scared."

I looked at him and my heart just sank. Because, while I have no idea whether or not I overdosed or what exactly happened that night, I could tell he had been truly terrified.

And all he did was put me in the shower.

My husband believed I might die. And he didn't so much as even call the concierge.

A switch flipped in me. It was like one of those breaker switches . . . Like on a circuit box. You know how they take a lot of pressure to flip? But then once they catch, they switch over with force? I switched over. I knew, right then and there, that I needed to get away from this person. That I had to take care of myself. Because if I didn't . . .

He wasn't gonna kill me but he would let me die.

I said, "Okay, thank you for watching me." I said, "You must be tired. Why don't you take a nap?" And then, when he was asleep, I packed all my things. I took both plane tickets and I went to the airport. When I got there, I found a pay phone. I called the hotel. I said, "I need to leave a message for Niccolo Argento in room 907."

The lady said okay. Actually, she probably said, "Bene."

I said, "Write, 'Lola La Cava wants a divorce.'"

Warren: When we all got back after hiatus, that show in Seattle . . . Daisy seemed, I don't know, lucid.

I said, "Where's Niccolo?"

And Daisy said, "That period of my life is over." That was it. End of discussion. I thought that was badass.

Simone: She called me and said she'd left Niccolo in Italy and I started clapping.

Karen: She started making sense when you were talking to her. She started showing up clearheaded to sound checks.

Daisy: I would not, unfortunately, use the word *sober*. But you know what? I showed up to places on time. I did start doing that.

Billy: I don't think I had realized just how much of her was gone until it was back.

Daisy: I had gotten back to being aware of myself onstage, those first months away from Nicky. Of being aware of my relationship with the audience. I started making a point to be in bed by a certain time and awake by a certain time. I had rules about when to do what drugs. Only coke at night, only six dexies at a time, or whatever number I'd come up with. Only champagne and brandy.

When I was onstage, I was singing with intention. Which I hadn't done in a long time. I cared about the show. I cared about making it good. I cared about . . .

I cared about who I was singing with.

Rod: Daisy high is fun and carefree and a good time. If she's having fun, you're having fun. But if you want to rip people's hearts out of their chests, bring Daisy back down to earth and have her sing her own songs. There's nothing like it.

Daisy: I was drunk at the Grammys. But it barely mattered.

Billy: Before the award for Record of the Year was announced, sometime earlier in the night, Rod told me that Teddy didn't want to speak. It's sort of a producer's award, but Teddy preferred to be the guy behind the guy, so Rod asked if I wanted to be the one to do it and I said, "It doesn't matter. We aren't gonna win."

He said, "So it's okay if I give it to Daisy?"

I said, "You're giving her a big fat bowl of nothing but sure."

Look, you can't be right all the time.

Karen: When we won Record of the Year for "Turn It Off," we were all standing up there, the seven of us and Teddy. Pete wore a goddamn bolo tie. Hideous. I was so embarrassed for him. I thought, for certain, that Billy would be the one to give the acceptance speech. But Daisy went up to the mike instead. I thought, *I hope she says something coherent.* And then she did.

Billy: She said, "Thank you to everybody who listened to this song and understood this song and sang it along with us. We made it for you. For all of you out there hung up on somebody or something."

Camila: "For everyone hung up on somebody or something."

Daisy: I didn't mean anything by it except to give a voice to people feeling desperate. I was feeling desperate about a lot of things. I was feeling desperate and also, somehow, more myself.

It's funny. At first, I think you start getting high to dull your emotions, to escape from them. But after a while you realize that the drugs are what are making your life untenable, they are actually what are heightening every emotion you have. It's making your heartbreak harder, your good times higher. So coming down really does start to feel like rediscovering sanity.

And when you rediscover your sanity, it's only a matter of time before you start to get an inkling of why you wanted to escape it in the first place.

Billy: When we walked off the stage, with that award, I caught her eye. And she smiled at me. And I thought, *She's turning it around.*

Elaine Chang: Daisy accepting the Grammy for Record of the Year, where her hair is disheveled and she's wearing the bangles up to her elbows and she's got on this thin cream silk slip dress and she seems entirely in control of that band and confident in her talent . . . that night alone might be why she's considered one of the sexiest rock singers of all time.

Shortly after that, they recorded the famous video of the band performing "Impossible Woman" at Madison Square Garden—where she's singing deep from her gut and fearless about even the highest notes, where Billy Dunne can't seem to keep his eyes off her.

All of this was during those months just after she had left Niccolo Argento. That's when she was fully self-actualized, fully in command of herself. All the magazines were talking about her, everybody knew who she was. All of rock 'n' roll wanted to be her.

Spring of 'seventy-nine is the Daisy Jones we all talk about when we talk about Daisy Jones. You would have thought she was on top of the world.

Karen: There's something I haven't mentioned.

Graham: Did Karen tell you about it? It's not my place to say anything if she hasn't told you already. But . . . I guess if she did, then it's okay.

Karen: We were in Seattle, I think, when I realized what was going on.

Eddie: I never brought it up with Graham and Karen, that I knew they were sleeping together. But I did think it was odd they kept it so quiet. People would have been happy for them. Maybe it was just a one-time thing between them. Sometimes, my memory is so hazy I wonder if I imagined it. But I don't think I did. I don't think I would make up something like that.

Karen: I was taking a shower in the hotel and Graham had the adjoining room and he came in. And then he got in the shower with me. I pulled him into me, put my arms around him. That's part of what I liked about Graham so much, was how big he was, how strong he was. He was hairy and bulky and I liked all of that. I liked how gentle he was, too. But this time, as he pressed his chest into mine, my boobs felt swollen. They felt sore. And I knew. I just knew.

I'd heard women talk about being able to sense when they were pregnant. But I thought it was some Flower Power shit. But it's true. At least for me. I was twenty-nine. I knew my body. And I knew I was pregnant. This dread just seeped into me. It was like it started at my head and filled my whole body. I remember being so thankful when

Graham heard Warren knocking on his door because he rushed out of the shower.

I was so relieved to be alone. To not have to pretend to be human, in that moment. Because I felt . . . gone. I felt like my soul had left my body and I was just a shell. I stayed in the shower for I don't even know how long. I just stayed in there, under the showerhead, staring off into space until I could muster the energy to step out.

Graham: You know how sometimes you can tell that something is off with somebody? But you can't put your finger on it? And you ask what's wrong and they seem to have no idea what you're talking about? You feel crazy. You feel like you're going crazy. This feeling in your gut that the person you love isn't okay. But they look okay. They look okay.

Karen: I took a pregnancy test in Portland. I'd kept it a secret from everybody. But then . . . that meant I was alone in my hotel room. Seeing the line turn pink or whatever color it was. I stared at it for a long time. And then I called Camila. I said, "I'm pregnant." I said, "I don't know what to do."

Camila: I said, "Do you want a family?"

And she said, "No." When she said "no . . ." it sounded like this croak. In her throat.

Karen: It was silent on the phone. And then Camila said, "Oh, honey, I'm so sorry."

Graham: When we got to Vegas, I finally said, "C'mon, you have to talk to me."

Karen: I just blurted it out. Told him. I said, "I'm pregnant."

Graham: I didn't know what to say.

Karen: He didn't talk for a long time. Just paced around the room. I said, "I don't want to do this. Go through with it."

Graham: I figured she was just wrestling with it a bit. I said to her, "Let's just give this some time. We still have time, right?"

Karen: I told him I wasn't going to change my mind.

Graham: I said the wrong thing. I knew it was the wrong thing. I said, "We can get a different keyboardist, if that's what you're worried about."

Karen: I don't really blame Graham, honestly. He was just thinking like most people. I said, "Do you understand how hard I worked to get here? I'm not giving this up."

Graham: I didn't want to say it but I thought it seemed selfish. Choosing anything over our baby.

Karen: He kept calling it "our baby." *Our baby our baby our baby*.

Graham: I told her that she should just take some time. That's all I said.

Karen: It was *our baby* but it was *my responsibility.*

Graham: People change their minds about this stuff all the time. You think you don't want something and then you realize you do.

Karen: He said that I didn't know what I was saying and that if I didn't go forward with the pregnancy I'd regret it for the rest of my life. He just didn't understand.

I wasn't scared of regretting *not* having a child. But I was scared of regretting *having* a child.

I was scared of bringing an unwanted life into this world. I was scared of living my life, feeling like I'd anchored myself to the wrong dock. I was scared of being pushed to do something I knew I did not want. Graham didn't want to hear it.

Graham: Things got heated and I stormed out. We had to have the conversation when we felt calm. You can't scream about something like that.

Karen: My mind wasn't going to change. I've been judged for it every time I've said it but I'll keep saying it: I never wanted to be a mother. I never wanted children.

Graham: I just kept thinking, *She'll change her mind.* I thought, *We will get married and have a baby and figure it all out.* She was going to realize how much she wanted to be a mother, how much family meant to her.

Daisy: After the Grammys, Billy and I started talking again. Well, sort of. We had just won for a song we wrote together, a song we sung together, and that resonated with me.

Billy: She leveled out. She loosened up. With Niccolo gone, it was . . . easier to have a conversation with her.

Daisy: We were on an overnight flight to New York to do *Saturday Night Live.* Rich had given us the Runner jet. I think almost everybody had fallen asleep. Billy was on the other side of the plane from me. But our chairs were sort of facing each other. I had on a tiny dress and I was cold and I took a blanket and wrapped it around myself and I saw Billy see me. And he laughed.

Billy: Some people will never stop being themselves. And you think it drives you crazy but it is the very thing you will think about when they are gone. When you don't have them in your life anymore.

Daisy: I looked at him and I laughed, too. And it was, for a moment, at least, like we could be friends again.

Rod: By the time they did *Saturday Night Live,* "Young Stars" had become a hit, too. It was number 7 on the charts, I think. Somewhere in the Top Ten. We were selling so many albums they couldn't print them fast enough. Runner had teed up "This Could Get Ugly" as the next hit.

Daisy: For *SNL,* the decision was that we would do "Turn It Off" as the first song, and then we would do "This Could Get Ugly" for the second.

Karen: I bet Warren that Daisy wouldn't be wearing a bra and I won two hundred bucks.

Warren: We're all deciding what we were gonna wear and I bet Karen fifty bucks that Billy wore a denim shirt and Daisy didn't wear a bra. I won fifty bucks.

Karen: During dress, Daisy and Billy were actually speaking to each other. You could tell there had been a shift, somewhere.

Graham: We did the dress rehearsal for "Turn It Off" and it went really well. So did "This Could Get Ugly."

Billy: When the show started, I planned on doing it just like we'd rehearsed.

Daisy: Lisa Crowne announced us, you know, "Ladies and gentlemen, Daisy Jones & The Six," and the crowd went crazy. I'd been in huge stadiums with crowds cheering but it felt different. This small group of people just in front of us, making that much noise. It was this jolt of energy.

Nick Harris: By the time Daisy Jones & The Six performed "Turn It Off" on *Saturday Night Live,* they were performing a song almost everyone in the country knew. It was the Record of the Year.

Daisy was wearing faded black jeans and a satin pink tank top. Of course, she's got the bracelets on. She's barefoot. Her hair is this brilliant red. She was dancing around the stage, singing her heart out, and tapping the tambourine. She looked like she was having a great time. And Billy Dunne is in his classic denim and denim. He's up close on the mike, watching her, having a great time himself. They looked like they belonged up there together.

The band is hitting every beat with a crispness and a freshness that you don't expect when a song has been played as many times as you know they've played this song.

And Warren Rhodes is a showstopper for anybody interested in learning what it means to hold an entire band together with the drums. He was electric behind those things. If you could take your eye off Daisy and Billy long enough, it would go right to him slamming down on the floor toms.

And then as the song progresses, and the lyrics get a bit more pointed, Billy and Daisy both seem transfixed with one another. They move to the same mike and they sing facing one another. This emotive, hot-blooded song about wishing you could get over someone . . . they seem like they are singing to each other.

Billy: There was so much going on during that performance. I had to be aware of my timing and the words and where I was looking and where the camera was. And then . . . I don't know . . . Suddenly Daisy was there next to me and I forgot about everything but just looking at her and singing this song that we wrote together.

Daisy: The song ended, and I sort of snapped out of it, and Billy and I looked at the audience and then he took my hand and we bowed. That was the first time my body had so much as grazed his in a very long time. It was the sort of thing where, even after he let go, my hand still hummed.

Graham: Daisy and Billy had something no one else had. And when they played it up, when they actually engaged with each other . . . It's what made us. That was one of those moments where you think their talent is absolutely worth all the bullshit.

Warren: Between songs, Billy told me he had an idea for "A Hope Like You." I liked the idea. I told him as long as everybody else was okay with it, then I was, too.

Eddie: "This Could Get Ugly" went great at dress. And at the last minute, Billy wants to do "A Hope Like You." A slow ballad. And he wants to play the keys instead of Karen. So it's just him and Daisy onstage.

Billy: I wanted to really surprise everyone. I wanted to do something unexpected. I thought it could be . . . something to really remember.

Daisy: I thought it sounded really, really cool.

Graham: It all happened so fast. One minute we're all supposed to go out there to play "This Could Get Ugly" and the next, Billy and Daisy are going out there alone to play a different song.

Karen: I'm the keyboard player. If someone is out there with Daisy, it seemed like it should have been me. But I understand what he was selling when he went out there. I got it. Doesn't mean I liked it.

Rod: It was a brilliant move. The two of them out there alone. It made for great TV.

Warren: They were facing each other, Billy at the piano, Daisy standing opposite him with the mike. The rest of us watched from the sidelines.

Daisy: Billy started playing and I caught his eye, for just a moment, before I started singing. And . . . *[pauses]* It just seemed so obvious, so painfully embarrassingly obvious. Without Nicky there to distract me, without keeping myself so drugged up I wasn't even mentally present, it just seemed so obvious that I loved him.

That I was in love with him.

And getting high and going to Thailand and marrying a prince wasn't going to make me stop. And him being married to somebody else . . . That wasn't going to stop it either. I think I finally resigned myself to it in that moment. Just how sad it all was.

And then I started singing.

Karen: You know when you can hear that there is a lump in somebody's throat? That's what she sounded like. And it . . . it killed everybody in the room. Her looking at him like that. Singing to him like that. Singing, "It doesn't matter how hard I try/can't earn some things no matter why." I mean, c'mon.

Billy: I loved my wife. I was faithful to my wife from the very minute I straightened up. I tried desperately to never feel anything else for any other woman. But . . . *[breathes deeply]* Everything that made Daisy burn, made me burn. Everything I loved about the world, Daisy loved about the world. Everything I struggled with, Daisy struggled with. We were two halves. We were the same. In that way that you're only the same with a few other people. In that way that you don't even feel like you have to say your own thoughts because you know the other person is already thinking them. How could I be around Daisy Jones and not be mesmerized by her? Not fall in love with her?

I couldn't.

I just couldn't.

But Camila meant more. That's just the very deepest truth. My family meant more to me. Camila meant more to me. Maybe, for a little while there, Camila wasn't the person I was the most drawn to. Or . . .

. . .

. . .

. . .

Maybe Camila wasn't the person I was the most in love with. At that time. I don't know. You can't . . . Maybe she wasn't. But she was always the person I loved the most. She was always the person I would choose.

It is Camila, for me. Always.

Passion is . . . it's fire. And fire is great, man. But we're made of water. Water is how we keep living. Water is what we need to survive. My family was my water. I picked water. I'll pick water every time. And I wanted Daisy to find her water. Because I couldn't be it.

Graham: Watching Billy play the piano and look at Daisy, I thought, *I hope Camila doesn't see this.*

Billy: You try playing a song like that with a woman like Daisy knowing your wife will see it. You try doing that. And then tell me you're not about to lose your goddamn mind.

Rod: It was electric, that performance. The two of them, together, performing *to* each other. It felt like they were ripping their hearts out on national TV. Those moments don't happen all the time. If you were up late that Saturday night watching them, you felt like you'd witnessed something big.

Karen: When the song was over, the small audience there erupted and Billy and Daisy took their final bow. And the rest of us came out and joined them. And, you know, I did kind of have this feeling, then, that we were big and we were only going to get bigger. It was the first time that I thought, *Are we going to be the biggest band in the world?*

Warren: We went to the after-party with the whole cast and everybody. Lisa Crowne was the host and I thought, you know, *Just play it cool with her and maybe she'll be into you.* And so that's what I did. And then she was.

Graham: When I looked over, sometime in the early morning, and Warren had his arm around Lisa Crowne, I thought, *Shit, we must be really fucking famous.* I mean, we'd have to be for Warren to have a chance with Lisa Crowne.

Eddie: Pete and I partied with the *SNL* band to the point where I couldn't feel my own nose and Pete puked into a tuba.

Warren: By the time I left with Lisa, I didn't see Daisy anywhere.

Graham: At some point, we all lost track of Daisy.

Billy: I was polite, and I went to the bar with everybody. But I couldn't stay long. *SNL* parties are not where you want to be when you're sober.

When I got back to my hotel, I got a call from [Camila] and we talked for a little while and there was a lot that we weren't saying. She had watched the show and I think she was wrestling with how to feel about all of it. We talked around it a long time. And then she said she wanted to go to sleep and I said, "Okay," and then I said, "I love you. You are my 'Aurora.'" And she said she loved me too and hung up the phone.

Camila: No matter who you choose to go down the road with, you're gonna get hurt. That's just the nature of caring about someone. No matter who you love, they will break your heart along the way. Billy Dunne has broken my heart a number of times. And I know I've broken his. But yes, that night watching them on *SNL* . . . that was one of the times that my heart cracked.

But I just kept choosing trust and hope. I believed he was worthy of it.

Daisy: I was sitting in a booth next to Rod at the *SNL* party and a bunch of girls went into the bathroom to do a line and I was so bored.

I was so incredibly bored of my life. Of the speed and coke and the cycle. It was like watching a movie for the hundredth time. You already know when the bad guy's gonna show up, you already know what the hero will do. It was so boring, the thought of it, that I wanted to die. I wanted real life, for once. Anything real. So I got up and I got in a cab and I went back to the hotel and I went to Billy's room.

Billy: There was a knock at my door. Just as I was falling asleep. And at first I just let the person knock. I figured it was Graham and it could wait until the morning.

Daisy: I just kept knocking. I knew he was in there.

Billy: Finally, I get out of bed and I'm in just my skivvies. And I answer and I say, "What do you want?" And then I look and it's Daisy.

Daisy: I just needed to say what I needed to say. I had to say it. It was then or it was never and it couldn't be never. I couldn't live like that.

Billy: I was genuinely in shock. I could not believe it.

Daisy: I said, "I want to get clean."

Billy immediately pulled me into his room. And he sat me down and he said, "Are you sure?"

I said, "Yes."

And he said, "Let's get you into rehab now."

He picked up the phone and he started dialing and I got up and I hung up the phone and I said, "Just . . . right now just sit with me. And help me . . . understand what I'm doing."

Billy: I didn't know how to help somebody else. But I wanted to. I wanted to help somebody the way Teddy had helped me. I owed so much to him, felt so grateful to him. For getting me into rehab when he did. And I wanted to do that for someone. I wanted to do it for her. I wanted her to be safe and healthy. I wanted that for her . . . I . . . yeah, I wanted that for her very badly.

Daisy: Billy and I talked about rehab and what that would mean and he told me a little bit about what it would be like. It seemed so daunting. I was starting to wonder if I didn't really mean it. If I wasn't actually ready to go through with it. But I kept trying to believe in myself, that I could. At one point, Billy asked if I was sober. *Was I sober right then?*

I'd had a drink or two at the party, I'd had dexies earlier in the day. I couldn't have told you what sober meant, exactly. Had everything worn off? Did I even remember what it was like to be entirely straight?

Billy opened the minibar to get a soda and there were all these nips in there of tequila and vodka and I looked at them. And Billy looked at them. And then he just took them and walked to the window and threw them out the window. You could hear a few of them break on the roof of the floor below. I said, "What are you doing?"

Billy just said, "That's rock 'n' roll."

Billy: At some point, we got to talking about the album.

Daisy: I asked him something that had been plaguing me for the past couple months. "Are you worried we'll never be able to write another album as good as this?"

Billy: I said, "I worry about it every fucking day."

Daisy: All my life I'd wanted people to recognize my talent as a songwriter and *Aurora* had brought it, the recognition. And I'd immediately started to feel like an impostor.

Billy: The higher that album went, the more nervous I felt thinking about how to make another one. I'd be scribbling down songs in my notebook on the bus and I'd just end up crossing it all out and throwing it away because it wasn't . . . I couldn't tell if it was any good anymore. I didn't know if I was just exposing myself as a fraud.

Daisy: He was the only one that could understand that level of pressure.

Billy: When morning came, I brought up rehab again.

Daisy: The thought I kept hearing in my head was *Go for a little while just for a break. You don't have to stop forever.* That was my plan. To go to rehab without planning to quit forever. It made perfect sense to me. I'll tell you: If a friend lied to me the way I lie to myself, I'd say, "You're a shitty friend."

Billy: I picked up the phone to call information to get the number for the rehab center I went to. But when I picked up the receiver, there was no dial tone. And someone on the other end was saying, "Hello?"

I said, "Hello?"

It was the concierge. He said, "I have an Artie Snyder on the phone for you."

I told him to put it through but I was thinking, *Why is my sound engineer calling me at the ass crack of dawn?* I said, "Artie, what on earth . . . ?"

Daisy: Teddy had a heart attack.

Warren: A lot of people live through heart attacks. So when I found out, I thought . . . I didn't immediately realize that meant he was dead.

Billy: Gone.

Graham: Teddy Price isn't the kind of guy you think is going to die of a heart attack. Well, I mean, he ate like shit and drank a lot and didn't take great care of himself but . . . He just seemed too . . . powerful, maybe. Like if a heart attack came to town he was going to tell it to screw off and it would.

Billy: It just knocked the wind right out of me. And my first thought when I got off the phone, the very first thought in my head was *Why did I throw the booze out the window?*

Rod: I got them all home to L.A. for the funeral.

Warren: We'd all been devastated to lose Teddy. But, man, watching Yasmine, his girlfriend, break down in these awful tears at his grave . . . I just kept thinking that so little in life mattered. But how Yasmine felt about Teddy . . . that mattered.

Graham: Teddy was a lot of things to a lot of people. I'll never forget being at the memorial and seeing Billy holding Yasmine's hand, trying to make her feel all right. Because I knew he wasn't all right.

Every man needs a man to look up to. For better or worse, I had Billy. Billy had Teddy. And Teddy was gone.

Billy: Things had sort of spun out of control for me. I could barely make sense of anything. I couldn't process it. Teddy being gone. Teddy being . . . dead. I think I died inside, for a little while. I know that sounds kind of extreme. But that's what it felt like. It felt like my heart sort of turned to stone. Or . . . you know how people get cryogenically frozen? Like, they just put themselves on ice in the hopes that they can come back one day? That's what happened to my soul. On ice.

I couldn't handle reality. Not sober. Not without a drink or a . . . I just checked out. I checked out of my life. I had no other way of coping but to die inside. Because if I tried to stay alive, to *live* during that period of time, it might actually have killed me.

Daisy: When Teddy died, that was it. I'd decided there was no sense in getting sober. I rationalized it. You know, *If the universe wanted me* *to get clean, it wouldn't have killed Teddy.* You can justify anything. If you're narcissistic enough to believe that the universe conspires for and against you—which we all are, deep down—then you can convince yourself you're getting signs about anything and everything.

Warren: I'd spent about three weeks on my boat. Smoking cigars, getting drunk, barely changing my clothes. Lisa and I had been talking a bit, since the show on *SNL*. She came out to see me. She said, "You live on a boat?"

I said, "Yeah."

She said, "You're an adult. Get a real house." She had a point.

Eddie: I'd thought the best thing for all of us was to get back out on the road. We lost a cousin of mine in a car accident about ten or eleven years before, and my dad had said, "Work through pain." That's been my way ever since. I thought it might make Pete stay in the band. But, if anything, it made him more ready to leave.

Billy: One time, Camila asked me to scrub the toilet and I went in there and I started scrubbing the bowl and I just kept scrubbing it. And then she came in and she said, "What are you doing?"

I said, "I'm cleaning the toilet."

She said, "You've been cleaning the toilet for forty-five minutes."

I said, "Oh."

Camila: I said to him, "You need to get back on the road, Billy. We'll all go with you. But you need to get back out there. Sitting at home thinking is killing you."

Rod: At some point, you have to get back on the bus.

Graham: You think that tragedy means that the world is over but you realize the world is never over. It's just never over. Nothing will end it.

And I kept focusing on the fact that, with Karen and I, you know, *life is just beginning.*

Karen: I was very thankful to Rod that he got us back out on the road. That he didn't let us capsize.

Billy: I did what Camila said. I got back out there. The first show, we were in Indianapolis. I flew out with the band. Camila and the girls were going to join me at the next stop.

Indianapolis was . . . it was tough. I showed up at the hotel, checked in, saw Graham, saw Karen, and then at sound check there was Daisy. She was wearing overalls. She looked strung out. You could see it. Her sunken eyes and her skinny arms. I had a hard time looking at her.

I'd failed her. She had asked me to help her get sober. And once Teddy died, I abandoned her.

Daisy: That first night back, I think we were in Ohio, I was so embarrassed to even let Billy see me. Because I had come to him and said that I wanted to get sober. And then I hadn't done it. I'd fallen even further than before.

Karen: I told Graham I'd decided to have an abortion. And he said I was crazy. And I told him I wasn't. And he asked me not to do it.

I said, "Are you going to quit this band to raise this baby?" And he didn't respond. And that was it.

Graham: I thought we were still discussing it.

Karen: He knew. He knew what I was going to do. He just feels more comfortable pretending he didn't. He has that luxury.

Billy: Camila and the girls came to join us in Dayton. I picked them up from the airport and as I was waiting for them, I could see a guy ordering a tequila on the rocks at the bar. I could hear the ice in the glass. I could see it sitting in the tequila. It was announced that their plane was stuck on the runway and I was sitting there, staring at the gate.

As I was telling myself that I wasn't going to order a drink, I walked over to the bar and I sat down on a stool. The guy behind the counter said, "What can I get you?" And I stared at him. And he said it again. And then I hear, "Daddy!" and I looked and there was my family.

Camila said, "What's going on?"

I stood up and I smiled at her and, in that moment, I had it under control. I said, "Nothing. I'm good."

She gave me a glance and I said, "I promise." And I picked up my girls in a big bear hug and I felt okay. I felt all right.

CAMILA: To be honest, that's when I questioned my own faith. Finding him sitting at a bar. Flags went up.

I started to wonder if maybe Billy was capable of doing something that I would be incapable of forgiving.

KAREN: Camila was with us from then on. For as long as that tour lasted. She'd fly back and forth, sometimes she had all the girls with her. But she almost always had Julia there. Julia was about five, by that point, I want to say.

DAISY: Every night was starting to feel like torture. It had been one thing to sing with Billy when I was with someone else, when I didn't know how I felt, when I had lies I could hide behind. Denial is like an old blanket. I loved to get on under that thing and curl up and sleep. But, leaving Nicky, singing that song with Billy on live TV, telling him I wanted to get clean . . . I'd ripped the blanket off of myself. And there was no putting it back on. And it was killing me. The vulnerability, the rawness. It was killing me to get up there on that stage. To sing with him.

When we did "Young Stars," I was praying Billy would look at me and acknowledge what we were saying to each other. And when we did "Please," I was begging him to pay attention to me. I was having a hard time singing "Regret Me" with any real anger because I wasn't angry, most of the time. Not anymore. I was sad. I was so goddamn sad.

And everybody wanted to see "A Hope Like You" the way we had done it on *SNL* and the two of us kept trying to deliver that. It just kept slicing me in two every night.

To sit next to him and smell his aftershave. And see his big hands with his swollen knuckles playing the piano in front of me and to be singing, from the very bottom of my heart, that I ached for him to love me back.

I spent the hours of the day we weren't onstage trying to repair my wounds and it was like I was pulling them back open every night.

Simone: I was getting a lot of phone calls from Daisy at all hours of the day. I'd say, "Let me come get you." And she'd refuse. I thought about trying to force her into rehab. But you can't do that. You can't control another person. It doesn't matter how much you love them. You can't love someone back to health and you can't hate someone back to health and no matter how *right* you are about something, it doesn't mean they will change their mind.

I used to rehearse speeches and interventions and consider flying to where she was and dragging her off that stage—as if, if I could just get the words right, I could convince her to get sober. You drive yourself crazy, trying to put words in some magical order that will unlock their sanity. And when it doesn't work, you think, *I didn't try hard enough. I didn't talk to her clearly enough.*

But at some point, you have to recognize that you have no control over anybody and you have to step back and be ready to catch them when they fall and that's all you can do. It feels like throwing yourself to sea. Or, maybe not that. Maybe it's more like throwing someone you love out to sea and then praying they float on their own, knowing they might well drown and you'll have to watch.

DAISY: I'd chased this life with all of my heart. I wanted so badly to express myself and be heard and bring solace to other people with my own words. But it became a hell I'd created myself, a cage I'd built and locked myself in. I came to hate that I'd put my heart and my pain into my music because it meant that I couldn't ever leave it behind. And I had to keep singing it to him, night after night after night, and I could no longer hide how I felt or what being next to him was doing to me.

It made for a great show. But it was my *life*.

BILLY: Every night, after the show was over and the girls were in bed, Camila and I would sit out on the balcony of whatever hotel we were in and we'd just talk. She'd talk about how the girls were stressing her out. She'd talk about how she really needed me to stay sober. I'd tell her how hard I was trying. I'd tell her how scared I was of just about everything the future held. Runner had started asking about a new album. The weight was on me.

At one point she said, "Do you honestly think you can't write another good album without Teddy?"

And I said, "I've never written an album without Teddy, period."

WARREN: We were on the bus heading into Chicago and Eddie seemed upset about something. I said, "Talk if you want to talk." I don't like it when people try to force you to ask them what's going on.

He said, "I haven't told anybody this but . . ." Pete was gonna leave the band.

EDDIE: Pete was not listening to reason. Warren said I should talk to Billy, get Billy to talk some sense into him. As if Pete was going to listen to Billy if he wasn't going to listen to me. I was his brother.

WARREN: Graham overheard us talking.

EDDIE: So Graham gets involved and he's already getting on everybody's nerves lately because he's so tightly wound about God-knows-what. Anyway, he says we should talk to Billy. And I, again, mention that Pete isn't going to listen to Billy if he wasn't going to listen to me, you know what I'm saying? But Graham doesn't hear me and, instead, when we pull up to this diner outside Chicago, Billy comes to find me. He says, "What's going on? What do we need to talk about?"

I was just looking for the john, minding my own business. I said, "It's nothing, man. Don't worry about it."

Billy says, "It's my band. I deserve to know what's going on in my own band."

That really pissed me off. I said, "It's everybody's band."

Billy said, "You know what I meant."

And I said, "Yeah, we all know what you mean."

Karen: We were outside of Chicago. Staying the night in a hotel. Camila had called ahead to this clinic. She walked me in, sat next to me. I was bouncing my knee and she put her hand on my leg and stopped the bouncing. I said, "Am I making a mistake?"

And she said, "Do you think you are?"

And I said, "I don't know."

And she said, "I think you do know."

And I thought about what she meant.

And then I said, "I know I'm not making a mistake."

And she said, "There you go."

And I said, "I think I'm pretending to be conflicted so that everybody feels better."

She said, "I don't need to feel better. You don't need to pretend anything for me." So I stopped.

When they called my name, she squeezed my hand and she didn't let go. I didn't ask her to come into the room with me and I didn't think she was going to, but she just kept walking with me—she never left my side. I remember thinking, *Oh, I guess she's gonna be here for this.* I got on the table. The doctor explained what was going to happen. And then he left for a moment. And there was a nurse in the corner. And I looked at Camila and she looked like she was going to cry. And I said, "Are you sad?"

And she said, "A part of me wishes you wanted kids, because my kids make me so happy. But . . . I think in order to be happy like I'm happy, you need different things. And I want you to have whatever those things are." And I started crying, then. Because somebody understood.

Afterward, she brought me back to the hotel and she told everyone I wasn't feeling well and I laid in bed by myself. And . . . it was a bad day. It was an awful day. Knowing you did the right thing doesn't mean you're happy about it. But when I called in room service, and I laid there in my hotel room, I knew that I was childless and that Camila was out with her children. And that . . . that seemed right. That little bit of order amidst the chaos.

Camila: It's not my place to say what happened that day. All I will say is that you show up for your friends on their hardest days. And you hold their hand through the roughest parts. Life is about who is holding your hand and, I think, whose hand you commit to holding.

Graham: I didn't know what had happened.

Karen: As we were all leaving the hotel, heading out to Chicago, I saw Graham get in the elevator alone, and I thought about taking the stairs. But I didn't. I got in the elevator with him. Just the two of us. And as the elevator started going down, he said, "Are you okay? Camila said you weren't feeling well."

And I said, "I'm not pregnant anymore."

He turned to me with this look on his face like, *I never thought you'd do this to me.* The elevator doors opened and we both just stood there. Not saying a word. They closed. And we took the elevator all the way to the top. And then all the way back down. Right before we got to the lobby again, Graham hit the button for the second floor. And he got off.

GRAHAM: I walked up and down the hallway of that hotel, over and over and over and over. At the end of the hallway there was a window, and I put my head on it. My forehead. And I looked down at all of the people below me. I was only a few floors up from them. I watched them walking from place to place, and I felt jealous of every single one of them. That they weren't me right then. I wanted to switch places with every man down there.

When I pulled my forehead off the glass, there was a huge greasy smudge where I'd touched it. I tried to wipe it away but it just made the window cloudy. I remember looking through this cloudy window, trying to rub it to make it better and nothing would help. I just kept rubbing and rubbing and rubbing. Until Rod found me somehow.

He said, "Graham, what are you doing? We gotta be in Chicago this afternoon. Bus is gonna leave without you, man."

And somehow, I put one foot in front of the other and walked with him down to the bus.

CHICAGO STADIUM

July 12, 1979

Rod: It started like any other show, really. We had it down to a fine art. The lights went up, the band went out there. Graham played the opening of "This Could Get Ugly" and the crowd started screaming.

Billy: Camila was on the side of the stage. She let Julia stay up late. The twins were back at the hotel with the babysitter. I remember looking out onto the side, behind the curtains, and seeing Camila there, holding Julia on her hip. Camila's hair was down to her waist, practically, by that point. And it was normally brown but the summer had made it lighten up a bit, it looked more gold. The two of them—Camila and Julia—had earplugs in their ears. These bright orange things poking out of either side of their heads. I smiled at them and Camila smiled back at me. Such a gorgeous smile. Her incisors were flat. Isn't that funny? Everyone's incisors are pointed. But hers were kind of flat. And it made her smile perfect. It was a straight line. Her smile always put me at ease.

And that night, in Chicago, when she smiled at me from the side of the stage . . . for that brief moment, I thought, *Everything is going to be okay.*

Daisy: It killed me. To look at him look at her. I can't think of any two things that make you quite as self-absorbed as addiction and heart-break. I had a selfish heart. I didn't care about anyone or anything but my own pain. My own need. My own aching. I'd have made anyone hurt if it could have taken some of mine away. It's just how sick I was.

Billy: We played everything. The way we normally did. We did "Young Stars" and "Chasing the Night" and "Turn It Off." But it didn't feel right. It felt . . . it felt like the wheels were coming off.

Warren: Karen and Graham seemed like maybe they were mad at each other. Pete seemed checked out. Eddie had been complaining about Billy—but what else was new?

Daisy: Someone in the front had a sign that said, "Honeycomb."

Billy: People requested "Honeycomb" a lot on that tour. And I usually ignored it. I just didn't want to sing it. But I knew that Daisy liked that song, I knew she had been proud of that song. And . . . I don't know what came over me but I said into the mike, "Do you guys want to hear 'Honeycomb'?"

Graham: I was sleepwalking through that show. I was there but I wasn't there.

Karen: I just wanted to get through it and go back to my hotel. I just wanted some quiet. I didn't want . . . I didn't want to be up on that stage watching Graham watch me, feeling his judgment.

Warren: When Billy said "Honeycomb," the whole place sounded like thunder.

Eddie: We're all just here to perform the way Billy wants us to, right? We don't need to be told we might play a song we haven't played in a year.

Daisy: What do you say to a roaring crowd? Do you say no? Of course not.

Billy: Daisy said, "All right, let's do it." I got up to her mike and the moment I did it, I regretted it. I could tell she didn't want me that close. But I couldn't leave. I had to make it look like everything was okay.

Daisy: He smelled like pine and musk. His hair was about half an inch too long, you could see it hanging behind his ears. His eyes were clear, and green as ever.

People say it's hard to be away from the people you love but it was so hard to be right next to him.

Billy: It's sometimes difficult to say what I knew and when I knew it. It's . . . it's all a mess in my memory. It's hard to parse out, I guess. What happened when or why I did what I did. Hindsight bias. But I do remember distinctly that Daisy was wearing a white dress. She had her hair pulled back in a ponytail. She had big hoop earrings on. Her bracelets. And I looked at her, just before we started singing, and I think—I really do think this—I think I thought she was the most beautiful woman I'd ever seen in my life. In that way that you appreciate things more acutely . . . I mean . . . you appreciate people more acutely when they are fleeting, right? And I think I knew she was fleeting. I think I knew she was leaving. I don't know how I knew. But I feel like I knew. I probably didn't know. It just feels like it.

So I guess what I'm saying is, when we started singing "Honeycomb," I either knew I was losing her or I didn't. And I either knew I'd loved her or I didn't. And I either appreciated her, for all she was in that moment . . . or maybe I didn't.

Daisy: I started singing and I looked at him. And he looked at me. And, you know what? For three minutes, I think I forgot we were performing for twenty thousand people. I forgot his family was standing there. I forgot we were singers in a band. I just existed. For three minutes. Singing to the man I loved.

Billy: The right song, at the right time, with the right person . . .

Daisy: And then right before the end of the song, I looked over to the side of the stage to see Camila standing there.

Billy: And I just . . . *[pauses]* God, I was so frayed at the edges.

Daisy: And I knew he wasn't mine.

He was hers.

And then I . . . I just did it. I sang the song as Billy originally wrote it. No questions.

"The life we want will wait for us/we will live to see the lights coming off the bay/and you will hold me, you will hold me, you will hold me/until that day." It was the hardest line I've ever had to get through.

Billy: When I heard her, singing the lines as I originally wrote them, singing about this future that Camila and I would have . . . There had been so much doubt in my heart. So much doubt in myself that I could keep going down the good road I was on. And I . . . *[breathes deeply]* Those lyrics. That small gesture. For one moment, Daisy didn't remind me that I might fail. She sang the song like she knew I'd succeed. Daisy did that. *Daisy.* I didn't know how much I needed it until she gave it to me. And it should have just made me feel better but it hurt, too.

Because if I was the man I wanted to be—if I could give Camila the life I'd promised her—well, I mean . . . there was loss in that, too.

Daisy: I fell in love with the wrong guy who was exactly the right guy. And I had made decisions time and time again that made it worse and never made it better. And I'd finally pushed myself right over the edge.

Billy: When we got off the stage, I turned to Daisy and I didn't have any words. She smiled at me but it was one of those smiles that isn't a smile at all. And then she walked away. And my heart sank.

It just became so perfectly clear to me that I had been holding on tightly to the *possibility*. The possibility of Daisy.

And suddenly, I was having a very hard time with the idea of letting that go. Of saying, "Never."

Daisy: I saw Billy Dunne as he was coming off the stage and I didn't trust myself to say a single word to him. I couldn't be around him. So I waved goodbye and I left.

Karen: After we got offstage, I accidentally bumped into Graham and I said, "Sorry," and he said, "You've got about a million things to be sorry for."

Graham: I was angry.

Karen: He seemed to think that his pain was the only pain that mattered.

Graham: I started screaming at her. I know that I called her names.

Karen: He didn't have to go through what I'd gone through. And I knew he was hurting. But what right did he have? To yell at me?

Warren: I got backstage and Karen and Graham were screaming at each other.

Eddie: I grabbed Karen's hand before she could hit Graham.

Rod: I brought Karen back into one of the rooms backstage. Somebody grabbed Graham. Kept them apart.

Graham: I tried to find Billy. To talk to him. I needed somebody to talk to. When I found him in the lobby at the hotel after the show, I said, "Man, I need your help." And he cut me off. He said he didn't have time.

Billy: Camila and Julia had gone upstairs and I'd hung back. I was standing in the hotel lobby. I wasn't sure what I was going to do. There was so much going on in my head. And then, before I knew it I was . . . *[sighs]* I was on my way to the hotel bar. I was walking, one foot in front of the other, to the bar to get a tequila. That's what I was doing. That's what I was doing. I was walking to the bar to get a drink when Graham came in to find me.

Graham: He blew me off. I said, "It's important. For once, please. I gotta talk to you."

Billy: I couldn't do anything but focus on what I was doing. A voice was calling to me and telling me to go get a tequila. And that's what I was going to do. I couldn't help anyone else. I couldn't do anything for anybody.

Graham: I'm standing there in the lobby and I know I look like I'm struggling. I'm on the verge of tears. I don't cry. I don't think I've cried more than twice in my life. Once when my mom died in 'ninety-four and the other . . . The point is I needed my brother. I needed my brother.

Billy: He grabbed my shirt and he said, "With all the shit I've done for you our entire lives, you don't have five fucking minutes to talk to me?" I took his hand and I pulled it off of me and I told him to go away. And he did.

Graham: You shouldn't spend that much time with your brother. You just shouldn't. You shouldn't sleep with your bandmates and you shouldn't work with your brother and there was a lot of shit that if I had it to do over, I would do differently.

Karen: I went back to the hotel and I slammed my door shut and I sat on the bed and I cried.

Warren: Eddie, Pete, Rod, and I smoked a spliff after the show. Everybody else was nowhere to be found.

Karen: Then I went to Graham's room and I knocked on the door.

Graham: I understood why we couldn't have a baby. I did. But I felt so alone. In what I'd lost. I was the only one who felt like we'd lost something. I was the only one grieving. And I was mad at her about that.

Karen: He answered the door and I stood there and I thought, *Why did I come here?* There was nothing I could say to him to fix anything.

Graham: Why couldn't she see the future I saw?

Karen: I said, "You don't understand me. You expect me to be someone I'm not."

And Graham said, "You never loved me the way I loved you."

And both of those things were true.

Graham: What could we do? How do you come back from that?

Karen: I leaned into him and I pushed my body against his. He wouldn't hug me at first. He wouldn't put his arms around me. But then he did.

Graham: She felt warm in my arms. But for some reason I remember her hands being cold. I don't know how long we stayed like that.

Karen: Sometimes I wonder, if I was Graham, maybe I would have wanted a baby, too. If I knew someone else would raise it, someone else would let go of their own dreams, someone else would sacrifice and keep everything together while I went and did what I wanted and came back on weekends . . . maybe then I might want a baby, too.

Although, I don't know. I'm still not sure that I would.

I guess what I'm saying is that I wasn't mad at Graham. For not understanding me. And, ultimately, I don't think he was all that mad at me, for what I wanted.

Graham: We hurt each other very badly. And that is my biggest regret. That is my very biggest regret. Because I loved her with all of my fucking soul. To this day, there is a piece of me that still loves her. And there is a piece of me that will never forgive her.

Karen: Even now, talking about him feels like poking a bruise.

Graham: I knew when I went to bed that night, I couldn't be in a band with her.

Karen: There was no way we could be around each other, day to day, anymore. Maybe stronger people could have. We couldn't.

Billy: I sat down at the bar and I ordered a tequila neat. And it arrived. And I sat there and I picked it up and swirled it around and I sniffed it. And then two women came up to me, and asked me to sign autographs for them. Said they'd never seen anything like Daisy and me. I signed two cocktail napkins and pretty soon after, they left.

Daisy: It was the middle of the night when I got back to the hotel. I don't remember what I'd been doing. I just remember that I was avoiding Billy. I think I probably walked around the city or something. I was still plastered when I got back to the lobby. And I turned right, to head for the bar. I remember thinking I didn't even want to be conscious.

But I must not have realized where I was going or what I was doing because I ended up walking straight into the elevator. I thought, *All right, guess I'll take my reds and go to bed.* But when I got to my room, I couldn't get my key in the door. I kept trying but I couldn't get it to fit. I think I was making a lot of noise.

And then I thought I heard a child's voice.

Billy: I grabbed the glass—the tequila, I mean—I grabbed it again and I stared at it. And I thought about what it would taste like. Clean smoke. I was lost in it when the guy next to me went, "Hey, you're Billy Dunne, aren't you?" And I put it down.

Daisy: I was stuck out there, in the hallway. Unable to get into my room. And I slumped down on the ground and I started crying.

Billy: I said, "Yes, I am."

And the man said, "My girl's got a real thing for you."

I said, "Sorry about that."

And he said, "What are you doing down here in a bar by yourself? You seem like a guy who could be with any woman in the world."

I said, "Sometimes you have to be alone."

Daisy: I looked down the hall and I realized it was . . . well . . . out into the hallway comes Camila and she's holding Julia . . .

Author: Wait a minute.

Author's Note: While I have made a concerted effort to remove myself from the narrative, I have included here a verbatim transcript of one conversation I had with Daisy Jones because I am, in fact, the only one that can corroborate this essential piece of Daisy's story.

Daisy: Yeah.

Author: You were wearing a white dress.

Daisy: Yeah.

Author: And you were sitting in the hallway. You couldn't open your own door.

Daisy: Yeah.

Author: And my mom . . .

Daisy: Yeah, your mom opened the door for me.

Author: I remember this. I was with her. I had woken up and had a bad dream.

Daisy: You were about five or so, I think. So . . . you've got a good memory.

Author: I mean, I completely forgot about it but now that you're saying it, I do remember being there with you. But my mom never mentioned anything. I wonder why she didn't talk about this with me.

Daisy: I always got the impression that if the story were to be told, Camila would consider it mine to tell.

Author: Oh, okay. All right, well, then what happened?

Daisy: Your mom . . . well, Camila . . . or . . . should I keep saying everyone's names? You said earlier that I had to always say her name.

Author: Yeah, go ahead. Call me Julia. Call my mom Camila. Just as we've been doing.

This marks the end of the transcript.

Daisy: Camila came into the hallway and she was holding Julia. And she said, "Do you need help?" I didn't understand why she was being so nice.

I said yes and she took my key and she let me into my room. And she walked in with me. She put Julia down on the bed. She told me to sit down and she brought me a glass of water. I said, "You can go. I'll be okay."

And she said, "No, you won't."

I remember feeling really relieved. That she could see through me. That she wasn't going to leave. She sat down next to me. And she didn't mince words. She knew exactly what was happening. Exactly what she wanted to say. I was . . . unnerved. I felt so out of control and Camila was so in control.

She said, "Daisy, he loves you. You know that he loves you. I know that he loves you. But he's not going to leave me."

Billy: I said to the guy, "You know, sometimes you need to clear your mind a bit."

He said, "What kind of problems can a guy like you have?"

He asked me how much money I had and I just told him. I just told him my net worth right there.

He said, "You'll pardon me if I don't feel too bad for you."

I nodded my head. I understood. I picked the drink back up and I put it to my lips.

Daisy: Camila said, "What I need you to know is that I'm not going to give up on him. I'm not going to let him leave me. I will see him through this. The way I've seen him through the rest. We are bigger than this. We are bigger than you."

Julia got under the covers of one side of the bed and I looked at her.

Camila said to me, "I wish Billy didn't love anyone else. But do you know what I decided a long time ago? I decided I don't need perfect love and I don't need a perfect husband and I don't need perfect kids and a perfect life and all that. I want *mine*. I want *my* love, my husband, my kids, my life.

"I'm not perfect. I'll never be perfect. I don't expect anything to be perfect. But things don't have to be perfect to be strong. So if you're waiting around, hoping that something's going to crack, I just . . . I have to tell you that it's not gonna be me. And I can't let it be Billy. Which means it's gonna be you."

Billy: I took a taste of it. Not even a sip, but a taste. It took everything I had not to gulp it down, not to throw it into the back of my throat. It tasted like comfort and freedom. That's how it gets you—what it feels like is the opposite of what it is. But my whole body went slack, from the relief of it being on the tip of my tongue.

Daisy: Camila got up and poured me another glass of water and she got me a tissue. Which is when I realized I was sobbing. She said, "Daisy, I don't know you very well, but I know you have a great heart and you're a good person. I know my daughter wants to grow up and be you one day. So I don't want you to get hurt. I want good things for you. I want you to be happy. I really mean that. You probably think I don't but I do." She said she just wanted to make one thing really clear. "I can't just sit here and watch you and Billy torture each other. I don't want that for the man I love. I don't want that for the father of my children. And I don't want it for you."

I said, "I don't want it for me either."

Billy: The man next to me, the one with the girlfriend, he was watching me. He had a full beer in his glass and he was sipping it, like you can sip something you're indifferent to.

I glanced at him and then . . . I did it.

I drank it.

Maybe half of a finger or so. And then I held on to the glass. Like someone was going to try to steal it from me.

He said, "Maybe I was wrong. Maybe it is possible for a guy like you to be messed up about something." I told myself to put down the glass. *Just put it down.*

Daisy: Camila said, "Daisy, you need to leave this band."

Julia was fast asleep by this point. Camila said, "If I'm wrong, and you're already in the process of moving on, and you're willing to let him move on, then don't listen to me. You have no responsibility to me. But if I'm right, you'd be doing us all a favor if you left and got yourself clean and found a life away from him. You'd be doing it for yourself. And yes, you'd be doing him a service. But also, you'd be helping me take care of my children."

Billy: I couldn't put it down. My hand held on to the glass. And I thought, *I wish this man would take it out of my hands before I finish it. Just take it out of my hands and throw it across the room.*

Daisy: I was quiet for a while, trying to process what Camila was saying. And then she said, "I think it's time for you to go. But whatever you decide to do, Daisy, just know I'm rooting for you. I want you to get clean, take care of yourself. That's what I'm rooting for."

I finally said, "Why do you care about what happens to me?"

She said, "I think almost everybody on this planet cares about you."

I shook my head and I said, "They like me, they don't care about me."

She said, "No, you got that wrong." She was quiet for a moment. Then she said, "Do you want to know something I've never told Billy?

'A Hope Like You' is my favorite song. Not my favorite Six song but my favorite song, period. It reminds me of the first boy I ever loved. His name was Greg and I knew from the moment I met him that he was never going to love me as much as I loved him and I wanted him anyway. And just like I knew he would, he broke my heart in a million pieces. And when I first heard the lyrics to that song, you put me right back there. Right back in the middle of my first love. With all the heartbreak and the hope and the tenderness. You made it feel new and real, all over again. You did that. You wrote a beautiful song about wanting something you know you'll never have and wanting to have it anyway. I care about you because when I see you, I see an incredible writer—who suffers from the very thing that the man I love suffers from. The two of you think you're lost souls, but you're what everybody is looking for."

I let it all sink in. I really listened to her. And then I said, "That song isn't . . . it's not about Billy. If that's what you were thinking. It's about wanting to have a family, kids. And knowing you'd be awful at it. Feeling like you're too much of a fuckup to deserve anything like that. But wanting it anyway. And I look at you and everything that you are and I know it's everything I can never be."

Camila looked at me for a moment and then she said something that changed my life. She said, "Don't count yourself out this early, Daisy. You're all sorts of things you don't even know yet." That really stuck with me. That who I was wasn't entirely already determined. That there was still hope for me. That a woman like Camila Dunne thought I was . . .

Camila Dunne thought I was worth saving.

BILLY: The man looked at my hand and it seemed like he was looking at my wedding ring and he said, "Are you married?" I nodded. He laughed and said his girlfriend would be crushed. Then he said, "You got kids?" That caught my attention, caught me off guard. I nodded again. He said, "Got any pictures?" And I thought of the photos, in my wallet, of Julia and Susana and Maria.

And I put the glass down.

It wasn't easy. I fought for every inch, as my hand moved closer to the bar it felt like it was moving through wet cement. But I did it. I put the glass down.

Daisy: Sometime in the early morning, Camila picked Julia up out of my bed, and she grabbed my hand. I grabbed her hand back. She said, "Good night, Daisy."

And I said, "Good night." Julia was slumped into Camila's chest, fast asleep. And she readjusted herself a little bit and pushed her head into Camila's neck, like it was the safest, softest place she'd ever been.

Billy: I pulled out my wallet and I showed the man the photos I had of my daughters. And as I did, he took my glass from in front of me and put it on the bar on the other side of him.

He said, "Gorgeous girls."

I said, "Thank you."

And he said, "Makes you want to live to fight another day, doesn't it?"

And I said, "Yes. It does."

He looked at me and I stared at the glass and . . . I felt strong enough. To walk away from it. And I didn't know how much longer I'd feel that strong. So I put down a twenty and I said, "Thank you."

He said, "Don't mention it." And then he picked up my twenty and handed it back to me and said, "Just let me buy it, all right? So I can know I did something for somebody once."

I took the money back and he shook my hand.

And I left.

Daisy: I opened the door for her and she slipped out into the bright hallway with Julia. She said, "No offense, but I hope I never see you again." And, to be honest, it stung. But I understood what she meant. When she got to her door, Camila looked back at me and it was the first time I realized she was nervous. Her fingers were shaking as she put her key in the door.

And then she slipped into her room. And she was gone.

Billy: I went back up to my hotel room and I shut the door behind me and slumped against it. Camila and the girls were asleep and I just watched them. And then I broke down crying, right there on the floor. And I thought to myself, *That's it. I'm done. It's gonna come down to rock 'n' roll or my life and I'm not choosing rock 'n' roll.*

Daisy: I was on the next flight out.

Rod: The next morning, I see Daisy's gone and she's left a note saying she's left the band and would never come back.

Warren: I woke up in the morning and Daisy had left. Graham and Karen didn't want to be in the same room with each other. Then Billy comes onto the white bus and announces he's taking a break from touring. So Rod has to cancel the rest of the tour.

Rod: I can't fulfill a tour without Billy or Daisy.

Warren: Eddie got mad—flew off the handle.

Eddie: There's only so long you can live your life while it's being dictated to you by somebody else, you understand? And I don't care how much money is in it for me, I'm not somebody's lackey. I'm not some indentured servant. I'm a *person*. And I deserve a say in my own career.

Warren: Pete said he was leaving regardless of what happened.

Graham: It all just started crumbling down.

Rod: Daisy was MIA. Billy wanted to shut the whole thing down himself. Pete was out. Eddie refused to work with Billy. Graham and Karen wouldn't speak to each other. I went to Graham and I said, "Talk some sense into Billy."

And Graham told me he wouldn't "say shit to Billy."

And I thought, *If the bottom falls out here, what am I going to do?* I thought about signing other bands and doing this all over and taking another set of screwed-up people and trying to make their careers and I just . . . I don't know.

Warren: I appeared to be the only person who didn't have his panties in a twist about something.

But we'd had a good ride. And if it was over . . . I guess, there wasn't much I could do about that, was there? So, so be it.

Billy: I never knew why Daisy left, exactly. What it was about that night, that show, that made her leave. But the way I saw it: I didn't know how to write a good album without Teddy. And I didn't know how to write a hit album without Daisy. And I couldn't do it with either of them. And I wasn't willing to let any of it cost me a fraction of what it had already cost me.

I turned to everybody on the bus and I said, "It's over. The whole thing. It's over."

And not one person in the band—not Graham, not Karen, not Eddie or Pete, not even Warren or Rod—tried to convince me otherwise.

Karen: When Daisy left, it was like the Ferris wheel stopped turning and we all got off.

Daisy: I left the band because Camila Dunne asked me to. And it was the very best thing I've ever done. It is how I saved myself. Because your mother saved me *from* myself.

I may not have known your mother very well.

But I promise you, I loved her very much.

And I was so very sorry to hear she passed away.

Author's Note: My mother, Camila Dunne, died before the completion of this book.

I spoke with her a number of times during the course of my research, but I could not hear her point of view of the events that took place in Chicago on July 12 and 13 due to the fact that I learned the full scope of them only after her passing.

She died on December 1, 2012, at the age of sixty-three from heart failure, a complication of lupus. It brings me great comfort to be able to report that she died surrounded by our family, my father, Billy Dunne, at her side.

THEN AND NOW

1979–Present

Nick Harris: Daisy Jones & The Six have never played together, never been seen together, since their show at Chicago Stadium.

Daisy: When I left Chicago, I made my way straight to Simone and I told her everything and she got me into rehab.

I've been sober since July 17, 1979. And when I left the facility, I changed my life. All of the things I've achieved since then have been because of that decision. When I left the music business, when I published my books, when I started meditating, when I started traveling the world, when I adopted my sons, and opened the Wild Flower Initiative, and changed my life for the better in ways that I could never even fathom in 1979—it was all possible because I got clean.

Warren: I married Lisa Crowne. We have two kids, Brandon and Rachel. Lisa made me sell the houseboat. Now I live in Tarzana, California, in a huge house surrounded by strip malls, my kids are in college, and no one asks me to sign their tits anymore. I mean, occasionally Lisa does. Just to be nice. And I take her up on it. Because there are about a million different guys who would have loved to sign Lisa's tits at some point in their lives. And I try to never lose sight of that.

Pete Loving *(bassist, The Six)*: I don't have much to say about any of this. I don't have any ill will toward anyone or anything. I have great memories of everybody. But that part of my life is long gone. I own my own artificial turf installation company now. Jenny and I live in Arizona. My kids are grown. It's a good life.

That's really all I have to contribute. I'm nearing seventy but I'm still looking forward, okay? I'm not looking back. You're welcome to put this in your book but that's going to have to be it for me.

Rod: I bought a place in Denver. For a little while, Chris lived with me. We had some good years together. And then he left. And I met Frank. My life is small and manageable. I sell real estate. I have what I think of as the best of both worlds. An easy life but with some wild stories about the good old days.

Graham: When the band split, Karen and I . . . we were over. Our friendship was gone. We might run into each other once in a while but that's about it.

It's the ones who never loved you enough that come to you when you can't sleep. You always wonder what the future might have held and you'll never know. Maybe you almost don't want to know. Don't tell your aunt Jeanie that I'm talking like this. I don't want her to get the wrong idea. I love her. I love your cousins.

And I'm damn glad your dad and I don't work together anymore but we have fun playing around now and again. He still tries to tell me how to play my own guitar. *[Laughs]* But that's just Billy. He taught both my kids piano, built the tree house in the backyard.

I guess I'm saying I feel lucky we had the band and we survived the band. Him and me.

Anyway, if you're doing one of those where-are-they-now things, make sure you tell everybody that I have my own hot sauce. Dunne Burnt My Tongue Off.

Eddie: I'm a record producer now. Probably what I should have been all along. I have a recording studio over in Van Nuys. I do all right. Ended up on top.

Simone: Disco died in 1979 and I tried to keep going after that but I just could not catch on on the radio the way I had in the clubs. So I invested my money, I got married, I had Trina, I got divorced.

And now Trina's ten times more famous than I ever was, making money hand over fist, making music videos that are so crass Daisy and I would never have even thought about doing something as crazy as that. She sampled "The Love Drug" on her new one. "Ecstasy." Boy, nothing is innuendo anymore. They all just come out and say it. But she's a boss. I will give her that. She's killing the game.

Damn right, my baby's killing the game.

Karen: After I left The Six, I took gigs playing in one touring band or another for twenty years. Retired in the late nineties. I did what I wanted with my life and I don't regret any of it in the slightest.

My whole life, I have been a person who loves to sleep in a bed alone. And Graham is a guy who likes to wake up next to somebody. If he had had it his way, I'd've conformed to what everybody else did, to what everybody else wanted for their lives. But it wasn't what I wanted.

Maybe if I was of the younger generation, marriage would have been more attractive to me. I see the way a lot of younger marriages are these days, truly egalitarian, nobody serving anybody else. But that wasn't the mold I saw. That wasn't a mold most of us even had back then. What I wanted didn't fit in with having a husband. I wanted to be a rock star. And then I wanted to live alone. In a house in the mountains. And that's what I've done.

But if you get to be my age and you can't look back at your life and wonder about some of your choices . . . well, you have no imagination.

Billy: I packed it all in, signed a publishing deal with Runner Records and I've been writing songs for pop singers since 'eighty-one. It's a good life. It's been quiet and stable even though I spent the eighties and nineties in a noisy house with three screaming girls and a great woman.

Somebody said the other day that I gave up my career for my family. And I suppose I did, though I think that makes it sound like it was more noble than it was. It was just a man hitting his limit. Not sure how much nobility there really is in that. It's more that I knew that if I was going to hit that bar Camila had set for me, I had to walk away from that band.

Do you understand why I loved your mother the way I did?

She was an incredible woman. She was the greatest thing that ever happened to me. Give me all the platinum albums you want, all the drugs and all the Cuervo and all the fun times and the successes and the fame and all of it, I would hand them all back to you, just as the cost of my memories with her. She was an absolutely incredible, incredible woman. And I didn't deserve her.

I'm not sure the world deserved her. I mean, don't get me wrong. She was very pushy and around the mid-nineties she developed a really terrible taste in music, which, for a musician, is awfully hard to look past. And she made the world's worst chili and she thought it was great and she'd make it all the time. *[Laughs]* I'm not saying anything you don't know. But she had serious faults, too. She was stubborn to the point where she stopped talking to your grandma for a few years. But that stubbornness also really paid off a lot of the time. She was stubborn about me. And I'm the man I am because of it.

When she was diagnosed with lupus, I think we were all set back. And I wouldn't wish that disease on anybody. But I was determined to take it as an opportunity to give back to your mother. I could take over when she was too tired, when her body ached too much. I could be home to raise you girls so it didn't fall on her to do everything. I could be her partner and be by her side through it all.

We bought the house in North Carolina . . . I guess it's about twenty years ago now. After you and your sisters were all off at college. We scoured the coastline, looking for exactly the house she had seen in her dreams. We didn't find it so we built it. There's no honeycomb there. It's not exactly the one in the song. It's just a two-story ranch with acres of land and a bay she liked to go crabbing in. But it was the home she'd always wanted. I feel so lucky to have been the man to do that for her.

I know you know how hard it was to lose her. We're all still reeling from it.

I admit I'm feeling lonelier than lonely these days, with you and your sisters spread out all over the country and your mom gone. It's been over five years now. She wasn't supposed to go that early. Taking a woman like that, at sixty-three, seems cruel even for a vengeful God. But it's the hand she was dealt—the hand we've all been dealt. So I'm playing it.

You know, I didn't talk to you very much about all of this when you were growing up. Never wanted to bog you down with my own issues, my own stories. Your life isn't about me, honey, my life is about you.

But I will say that I'm thankful to you for asking these questions and giving me something to do.

I hope this sheds some light on all of it for you, sweetheart. I really do. About your mom and me and the band. Sometimes I'm surprised people still care. I'm surprised they still play us on the radio. Sometimes I listen. The other day, they were playing "Turn It Off" on the classic rock station. I sat in the car in the driveway and listened.

[Laughs] We were pretty good.

Daisy: We were great. We were really great.

ONE LAST THING BEFORE I GO

November 5, 2012

From: Camila Dunne
To: Julia Dunne Rodriguez, Susana Dunne, Maria Dunne
Date: November 5, 2012 11:41 P.M.
Subject: Your Dad

Hi Girls,

I need your help.

After I'm gone, give your dad some time. And then please tell him to call Daisy Jones. Her number is in my date book in the second drawer of my nightstand.

Tell your father I said at the very least, the two of them owe me a song.

Love,

Mom

CHASING THE NIGHT

Trouble starts when I come around
Everything's painted red when I'm in town
Light me up and watch me burn it down
If you're anointing a devil, I'll take my crown

Foot on the gas, add fuel to the fire
I'm already high and going higher
Charging faster, ready to ignite
Headed for disaster, chasing the night

You turn wrong when you turn right
White light at first sight
Oh, you're chasing the night
But it's a nightmare chasing you

Life's coming to me in flashes
Wearing my bruises like badges
Don't know when I learned to play with matches
Must want it all to end in ashes

Foot on the gas, add fuel to the fire
I'm already high and going higher
Charging faster, ready to ignite
Headed for disaster, chasing the night

You turn wrong when you turn right
White light at first sight
Oh, you're chasing the night
But it's a nightmare chasing you

Foot on the gas, add fuel to the fire
I'm already high and going higher
Foot on the gas, add fuel to the fire
Look me in the eye and flick the lighter

Oh, you're chasing the night
But it's a nightmare, honey, chasing you

THIS COULD GET UGLY

The ugly you got in you
Well, I got it, too
You act like you ain't got a clue
But you do
Oh, we could be lovely
If this could get ugly

Write a list of things you'll regret
I'd be on top smoking a cigarette
Oh, we could be lovely
If this could get ugly

The things you run from, baby, I run to
And I know it scares you through and through
No one knows you like I do
Try to tell me that ain't true
Oh, we could be lovely
If this could get ugly

C'mon now, honey
Let yourself think about it
Can you really live without it?

Oh, we could be lovely
If this could get ugly

IMPOSSIBLE WOMAN

Impossible woman
Let her hold you
Let her ease your soul

Sand through fingers
Wild horse, but she's just a colt

Dancing barefoot in the snow
Cold can't touch her, high or low
She's blues dressed up like rock 'n' roll
Untouchable, she'll never fold

She'll have you running
In the wrong direction
Have you coming
For the wrong obsessions
Oh, she's gunning
For your redemption
Have you headed
Back to confession

Sand through fingers
Wild horse, but she's just a colt

Dancing barefoot in the snow
Cold can't touch her, high or low
She's blues dressed up like rock 'n' roll
Untouchable, she'll never fold

Walk away from the impossible
You'll never touch her
Never ease your soul

You're one more impossible man
Running from her
Clutching what you stole

TURN IT OFF

Baby, I keep trying to turn away
I keep trying to see you a different way
Baby, I keep trying
Oh, I keep trying

I gotta give up and turn this around
There's no way up when you're this far down
And, baby, I keep trying
Oh, I keep trying

I keep trying to turn this off
But, baby, you keep turning me on

I keep trying to change how I feel
Keep trying to tell myself that this isn't real
Baby, I keep trying
Oh, I keep trying

Can't take off when there's no runway ahead
And I can't get caught up in this all over again
Baby, I keep trying
Oh, I keep trying

I keep trying to turn it off
But, baby, you keep turning me on

I'm on my knees, my arms wide
I'm finding ways to stay alive
Lord knows I'm pleading, pleading
To keep this heart still beating, beating

I keep trying to turn it off
But, baby, you keep turning me on

Baby, I'm dying
But, baby, I'm trying
I can't keep selling
What you're not buying

So I keep trying to turn it off
And, baby, you keep turning me on

I'm on my knees, my arms wide
I'm finding ways to stay alive
Lord knows I'm pleading, pleading
To keep this heart still beating, beating

I keep trying to turn it off
But, baby, you keep turning me on

PLEASE

Please me
Please release me
Touch me and taste me
Trust me and take me

Say the things left unsaid
It's not all in my head
Tell me the truth, tell me you think about me
Or, baby, you can forget about me

Please me
Please release me
Relieve me and believe me
Maybe you can redeem me

Say the things left unsaid
It's not all in my head
Tell me the truth, tell me you think about me
Or, baby, you can forget about me

I know that you want me
Know that you wanna hold me
Know that you wanna show me
Know that you wanna know me

Well do something and do it quick
Not much more I can stand of this

Say the things left unsaid
Don't act like it's all in my head
Tell me the truth, tell me if you think about me
Or, baby, can you forget about me?

Please, please, don't forget about me
Please, please, don't forget about me

YOUNG STARS

A curse, a cross
Costing me all costs
Knotting me up in all of your knots

An ache, a prayer
Worn from wear
Daring what you do not dare

I believe you can break me
But I'm saved for the one who saved me
We only look like young stars
Because you can't see old scars

Tender in the places you touch
I'd offer you everything but I don't have much

Tell you the truth just to watch you blush
You can't handle the hit so I hold the punch

I believe you can break me
But I'm saved for the one who saved me
We only look like young stars
Because you can't see old scars

You won't give me a reason to wait
And I'm starting to feel a little proud
I'm searching for somebody lost
When you've already been found

You're waiting for the right mistake
But I'm not coming around
You're waiting for a quiet day
But the world is just too loud

I believe you can break me
But I'm saved for the one who saved me
We only look like young stars
Because you can't see old scars

REGRET ME

When you look in the mirror
Take stock of your soul
And when you hear my voice, remember
You ruined me whole

Don't you dare sleep easy
And leave the sleepless nights to me
Let the world weigh you down

And, baby, when you think of me
I hope it ruins rock 'n' roll
Regret me
Regretfully

When you look at her
Take stock of what you took from me
And when you see a ghost in the distance
Know I'm hanging over everything

Don't you dare sleep easy
And leave the sleepless nights to me
Let the world weigh you down

And, baby, when you think of me
I hope it ruins rock 'n' roll
Regret me
Regretfully
Regret me
Regretfully

Don't you dare rest easy
And leave the rest of it to me
I want you to feel heavy

Regret me
Regret setting me free
Regret me

I won't go easily
Regret it
Regret saying no
Regret it
Regret letting me go

One day, you'll regret it
I'll make sure of it before I go

MIDNIGHTS

Don't remember many midnights
Forgotten some of my best insights
Can't recall some of the highest heights
But I've memorized you

Don't remember many daybreaks
How many sunrises have come as I lay awake
Don't dwell on my worst mistakes
But I always think of you

You're the thing that's crystal clear
The only thing that I hold dear
I live and die by if you're near
All other memories disappear
Without you
Without you

Don't remember how I was then
Can't keep straight where I was when

What is my name, where have I been
Where did I start, where does it end

You're the thing that's crystal clear
The only thing that I hold dear
I live and die by if you're near
All other memories disappear
Without you
Without you

Don't remember who I used to be
Can't recall who has hurt me
Forget the pain so suddenly
Once I'm with you

You're the thing that's crystal clear
The only thing that I hold dear

I live and die by if you're near
All other memories disappear
Without you
Without you

A HOPE LIKE YOU

I'm easy talk and cheap goodbyes
Second-rate in a first-class disguise
My heart sleeps soundly, don't wake it
A hope like you could break it

I'm lost deep in crimes and vice
Can't get to the table to grab the dice
My heart is weak, I can't take it
A hope like you could break it

It doesn't matter how hard I try
Can't earn some things no matter why
My heart knows we'd never make it
A hope like you could break it

People say love changes you
As if change and love are easy to do
My heart is calling and I can't shake it
But a hope like you could break it

Some things end before they start
The moment they form, they fall apart
My heart wants so badly just to say it
But a hope like you could break it

Told myself this story a thousand times
Can't seem to break the wants free from my mind
So much of my world goes unnamed
Some people can't be tamed

But maybe I should stake my claim
Maybe I should claim my stake
I've heard some hopes are worth the break

Yeah, maybe I should stake my claim
Maybe I should claim my stake
On the chance the hope is worth the break

AURORA

When the seas are breaking
And the sails are shaking
When the captain's praying
Here comes Aurora

Aurora, Aurora

When the lightning is cracking
And thunder is clapping
When the mothers are gasping
Here comes Aurora

Aurora, Aurora

When the wind is racing
And the storm is chasing
When even the preachers are pacing
Here comes Aurora

Aurora, Aurora

When I was drowning
Three sheets and counting
The skies cleared
And you appeared
And I said, "Here is my Aurora"

Aurora, Aurora

ACKNOWLEDGMENTS

This book would not exist without the enthusiasm of my agent, Theresa Park. Theresa, your excitement about this concept is what made this book a reality for me. I'm honored to have you steering my career, and I'm stunned at the results. Thank you for encouraging me to take risks and shoot for the moon.

To Emily Sweet, Andrea Mai, Abigail Koons, Alexandra Greene, Blair Wilson, Peter Knapp, Vanessa Martinez, Emily Clagett: Not only do you all handle your jobs with integrity and unmatched skill, but you are like the cast of *Friends* in that I can never decide which of you is my favorite. My favorite is all of you. I am truly humbled at how much you all have my back.

Sylvie Rabineau, thank you for loving Stevie Nicks the way I do and for handling the chaos that was Daisy Jones with grace and joy.

Brad Mendelsohn, thank you for being the person with all of the answers. I wish you knew how many times "Maybe we should ask Brad" is said in my house. You are my Jerry Maguire—and I'm talking the real end-of-the-movie, tears-in-my-eyes, pointing-at-you-with-all-of-my-heart kind of Jerry Maguire.

To my new friends at Ballantine, I am so honored and excited to be a part of this team. To my editor, Jennifer Hershey: from our first conversation I could tell that you would push me to be a better writer, and you have proven me right. I hope you understand the profound gratitude I have for how much more nuanced and honest this book is because of you. You approach every step with thoughtfulness and openness—and the results have been extraordinary. Nowhere else is that more apparent than in the art. So I must extend a huge thank-you to Paolo Pepe for such a fantastic approach to the art of this book. And Erin Kane, thank you for keeping it all straight. To Kara Welsh, your passion for this story has made all the difference. I immediately felt at home at Ballantine thanks to you. To Kim Hovey, Susan Corcoran, Kristin Fassler, Jennifer Garza, Quinne Rogers, Allyson Lord, and the rest of the marketing and publicity teams, I have been so happy to put this book in the hands of people with this much talent, drive, and enthusiasm.

I was able to write this book because of the people who have helped me throughout my career. Sarah Cantin, Greer Hendricks, and the great people at Atria Books, as well as the readers and bloggers who supported my other work. Thank you.

Crystal Patriarche, I don't know how you do it but you just keep doing it. Thank you and the whole BookSparks team.

More so than any other book I've written before, *Daisy Jones & The Six* required a village. For one, I needed my brother, Jake, to help me learn how to have good taste in music. So thank you, Bear, for fixing me.

And I needed someone to take care of my daughter. As fortunate as I am to do what I love, it requires the work of others to give me time to do it. I must acknowledge the efforts of our nanny, Rina, for taking such wonderful care of our baby girl while my husband and I are working. And I want to extend a huge, never-ending thank-you to my in-laws for watching Lilah on such a regular basis and often on short notice. I know that when she is with you all, she is having the time of her life. Maria, thank you. Warren, we are so lucky to have you. Rose, you make it all possible, time and again. Thank you from the bottom of my heart.

To Alex: It was hard to know where to acknowledge you because you have your hand in every aspect of this story. You came up with the idea with me, taught me about music theory, listened to *Rumours* with me, fought about Lindsey Buckingham and Christine McVie with me, gave up a job to be home more, became the primary parent, and read the book approximately nine million times. And most of all, you make it easy to write about devotion. When I write about love, I write about you. We're ten years into this party and I'm still mad for you.

And lastly, the *pièce de résistance* of my world, Lilah Reid. You have changed me in ways that I am truly grateful for, my tiny captain—and this book and the heart and soul within it is a testament to how I feel about being your mother. There are so very many ways to be in this world and sometimes I think I'm writing just so I can show you some of them. No matter what, I'm going to make sure you keep that feisty, opinionated, curious, offers-everyone-her-Cheerios heart you have going on right now because you are one in a million.

ABOUT THE AUTHOR

TAYLOR JENKINS REID is the author of *The Seven Husbands of Evelyn Hugo, One True Loves, Maybe in Another Life, After I Do,* and *Forever, Interrupted.* She lives in Los Angeles with her husband, their daughter, and their dog.

taylorjenkinsreid.com
Facebook.com/taylorjenkinsreidbooks
Twitter: @tjenkinsreid
Instagram: @tjenkinsreid

ABOUT THE TYPE

This book was set in Fairfield, the first typeface from the hand of the distinguished American artist and engraver Rudolph Ruzicka (1883–1978). Ruzicka was born in Bohemia (in the present-day Czech Republic) and came to America in 1894. He set up his own shop, devoted to wood engraving and printing, in New York in 1913 after a varied career working as a wood engraver, in photoengraving and banknote printing plants, and as an art director and freelance artist. He designed and illustrated many books, and was the creator of a considerable list of individual prints—wood engravings, line engravings on copper, and aquatints.